# EVIL DEAD CENTER

ALSO BY CAROLE LAFAVOR

*Along the Journey River*

# EVIL DEAD CENTER

*A Mystery*

CAROLE LAFAVOR

Foreword by LISA TATONETTI

Afterword by THERESA LAFAVOR

University of Minnesota Press
Minneapolis
London

Published by the University of Minnesota Press
111 Third Avenue South, Suite 290
Minneapolis, MN 55401-2520
http://www.upress.umn.edu

The University of Minnesota is an equal-opportunity educator and employer.

Library of Congress Cataloging-in-Publication Data
Names: LaFavor, Carole, author. | Tatonetti, Lisa, writer of foreword. | Lafavor, Theresa, writer of afterword.
Title: Evil dead center : a mystery / Carole laFavor ; foreword by Lisa Tatonetti ; afterword by Theresa Lafavor.
Description: Minneapolis : University of Minnesota Press, [2017]
Identifiers: LCCN 2017052712| ISBN 978-1-5179-0356-5 (pb)
Subjects: LCSH: Ojibwa Indians–Fiction. | Indian reservations–Minnesota–Fiction. | Lesbians–Fiction. | Mystery fiction. | BISAC: FICTION / Mystery & Detective / General. | FICTION / Lesbian.
Classification: LCC PS3562.A274 E9 2017 | DDC 813/.54–dc23
LC record available at https://lccn.loc.gov/2017052712

*To Theresa, my* odanissimi

*A daughter who's brought challenge, frustration, light, joy, laughter, and love to my life for seventeen years*

*Get ready, world—here she comes!*

# FOREWORD

*Lisa Tatonetti*

Carole laFavor (1948–2011), a Two-Spirit Ojibwa, was a nurse, author, and activist who directly engaged the intersectional nature of sexuality, gender, Indigeneity, and HIV/AIDS at a time when few people were acknowledging these connections. Her life and her writing deserve careful attention because of their rich contributions to the field of health advocacy as well as to the literary tradition of Minnesota, to Native American and Indigenous literary studies, and to queer Indigenous literature.

In every sense of the word, laFavor was a pathbreaker. She was a member of the first out lesbian softball team in Minnesota, the Wilder Ones, and was an American Indian Movement member who took part in sending medical supplies to Wounded Knee during the 1973 standoff between Indigenous activists and the U.S. government. She testified at the 1983 Pornography Civil Rights Hearings in Minnesota, where she spoke about her own personal experience of assault as well as the pattern of violence against Indigenous women.[1] At key moments, laFavor stepped up and spoke out when critical issues faced by Native peoples were not being addressed.

Carole laFavor's social justice work is perhaps most significant in her HIV/AIDS activism during the late 1980s and 1990s. The only Indigenous person appointed to the first Presidential Advisory Council on HIV/AIDS (PACHA), which was formed by U.S. President Bill Clinton in 1995, laFavor worked toward what we now would term health sovereignty by using her 1986 diagnosis as a springboard to social and political engagement on behalf of HIV-positive Indigenous peoples.

An important and now little known aspect of laFavor's activism is her work to help the Centers for Disease Control and Prevention (CDC) educate the public about the then-growing epidemic: she was featured in "Understanding AIDS," the first public informational pamphlet the U.S. Secretary of Health and CDC produced for widespread public distribution. In May and June 1988, the CDC attempted the unprecedented task of contacting every U.S. citizen by mail. As a result, laFavor's picture and first name—accompanied by the text "Obviously women can get AIDS. I'm here to witness to that. AIDS is not a 'we,' 'they' disease, it's an 'us' disease"—was included in a mailer sent to more than 107 million households and reprinted in national publications with vast reading audiences, such as *TIME* and *People*. That same year, the CDC also featured laFavor in televised public service announcements (PSAs) that were essential to late 1980s HIV/AIDS education. While the CDC intentionally elided laFavor's race and sexual orientation in its campaign to raise mainstream awareness and gain broad funding support for the rapidly spreading disease, laFavor foregrounded her identity as well as her diagnosis in her interviews, videos, and innumerable public speaking engagements for tribal nations, colleges, community centers, and health organizations across the United States and Canada.

As this history demonstrates, laFavor was never content to simply point out problems; instead she was committed to enacting productive change. She helped found Positively Native, a national organization for Native Americans with HIV/AIDS and subsequently edited the periodical of the same name. During this pivotal historical time she also was a founding member of the Minnesota American Indian AIDS Task Force (now the Indigenous Peoples Task Force), a landmark organization that began as a volunteer-led effort in 1987. Sharon M. Day (Bois Forte Band of Ojibwe) headed the creation of the task force and became the organization's executive director in 1990. Day and laFavor's commitment to serving Indigenous peoples and, importantly, to making the needs and presence of queer Native peoples visible shaped the educational response and essential materials the organization produced. As Day notes, "So much of the work then . . . really ignored women and . . . still does to a great extent today.

But our first two clients were Native lesbians and I believe we, the task force, put out the first lesbian brochure in the country." She continues, "We created some posters by Native artists that were targeted to gay and bisexual men. And when we did training, we decided that we weren't going to sort of soft shoe around the whole issue of sexuality. . . . And so what we did was [to start with] the conversation around sexuality."[2]

The Minnesota American Indian AIDS Task Force and laFavor, in particular, gained international exposure with *Her Giveaway: A Spiritual Journey with AIDS* (1987), directed by noted Sisseton Wahpeton Dakota filmmaker Mona Smith.[3] Smith's film, which is part public service announcement and part biography, focuses on laFavor's experiences as an Indigenous woman living with HIV/AIDS. *Her Giveaway*, the first film on Native American people and HIV, quickly became one of the most widely used resources in the country. Smith explains, "Within two months after it was released, it was in Sweden and Brazil and other places around the world. So it found a market because of the AIDS epidemic and because Carole's story was one that people of all kinds could connect with."[4]

The feminist and activist interventions laFavor made through the American Indian Movement and the Minnesota American Indian AIDS Task Force were paralleled by her contributions to the literary world. Thus the publication of *Along the Journey River* in 1996 represented, on one hand, a unique intervention into mainstream detective fiction, while on another, an important contribution to the growing body of queer Indigenous literature. As the first detective novel by an out Indigenous lesbian, *Along the Journey River* takes the settler project of the private investigator, which most often highlights urban locales and the entangled laws of the U.S. nation-state, and repurposes it with an eye toward reservation spaces and Indigenous justice. In doing so, laFavor joined an increasing number of LGBTQ/Two-Spirit Native writers who were reclaiming historical traditions and recognizing queerness as part of the very fabric of Indigeneity.

Before highlighting laFavor's notable place among out Indigenous writers of the 1980s and 1990s, I turn first to the term "Two-Spirit," which she uses in both *Along the Journey River* and her second novel, *Evil Dead Center* (1997). Just like the author, the protagonist Renee LaRoche employs the term as a way to gesture toward the complex gender traditions that existed in most Indigenous nations before invasion and colonization. The violence visited on alternatively gendered Native peoples by conquistadors, Christian missionaries, and settlers—who murdered, beat, derided, and isolated nonheteronormative Indigenous peoples—drove these gender traditions underground. For hundreds of years such Indigenous gender traditions were suppressed but not erased by ongoing settler colonial practices; not until the 1970s and 1980s were these multiple gender practices publicly invoked by Indigenous peoples who identified as bisexual, gay, and/or lesbian. The rise of the Red Power movement in the late 1960s and early 1970s included the formation of groups like the Gay American Indians (GAI), which was started by Barbara Cameron (Lakota) and Randy Burns (Northern Paiute) in 1975. These groups recalled and purposefully reclaimed the complexity of Native genders and sexualities. By the late 1980s, Indigenous activists and Native anthropologists began using "Two-Spirit"; in 1990, these activists, scholars, and their non-Native allies formally brought the term to anthropologists as a replacement for *berdache,* a word with marked negative connotations that anthropologists had long used to refer to multiply gendered Native peoples. Like her HIV/AIDS activism, laFavor's use of "Two-Spirit" for herself and her protagonist speaks to her intention to reclaim queer desire and gender diversity as a space of productive understanding for Native peoples.

This recognition of the healing power of the erotic was taken up by queer Indigenous writers like Paula Gunn Allen (Laguna Pueblo), Beth Brant (Bay of Quinte Mohawk), Chrystos (Menominee), Janice Gould (Koyangk'auwi Maidu), Maurice Kenny (Mohawk descendant), and Vickie Sears (Cherokee). Through poetry and fiction that spanned an array of topics—from explicitly naming and reclaiming third-gender roles, to celebrating the gender bending of trickster narratives, to exploring the lives of contemporary queer Native people—these Native authors were among the first group of writers to overtly claim lesbian, gay, and/or Two-Spirit identities in public spaces and to directly address queer Indigeneity in their texts. Carole laFavor's novels followed and added to an important literary tradition that by this time included single-authored texts like Kenny's *Only as Far as Brooklyn* (1979), Brant's *Mohawk Trail* (1985) and *Food and Spirits* (1991), Chrystos's *Not Vanishing* (1989) and *Dream On* (1991),

Gould's *Beneath My Heart* (1990), and Sears's *Simple Songs* (1990), as well as edited collections like Brant's *A Gathering of Spirit: A Collection by North American Indian Women* (1988) and the Gay American Indians' *Living the Spirit: A Gay American Indian Anthology* (1988).[5]

In terms of situating laFavor's writing within the tradition of queer Indigenous literature, *Along the Journey River* was only the second novel with a queer Indigenous protagonist. Both novels are groundbreaking, but laFavor's Renee LaRoche offers readers a very different sense of queer Indigeneity than does Paula Gunn Allen's Ephanie Atencio from *The Woman Who Owned the Shadows* (1983). Ephanie, as is common for this period in Native American literature, presents readers with a character painfully caught between Native and non-Native traditions who never overtly names herself a lesbian; by contrast, in Renee, laFavor depicts a tribally grounded woman who fully embraces both her sexuality and her Indigeneity. *Along the Journey River* therefore represents a significant contribution to Native American literature on multiple levels.

Throughout *Along the Journey River* and *Evil Dead Center*, Renee embraces and draws strength from a Two-Spirit erotics that ties her to family and, through her detective work, helps her support her tribal community (the fictional Red Earth reservation) from instances of racism, abuse, and injustice. When we first meet Renee in *Along the Journey River*, we encounter a strong, centered Native woman who is secure in her Two-Spirit identity and accepted by both her immediate family and her larger reservation community. As the narrator notes, her grandmother's "attitude about her being a lesbian wrapped Renee with the love she needed" (page 11). That reciprocal relationship forms the basis of Renee's calling to undertake investigative work for her nation.

Carole laFavor depicts Renee's investigative skills as having a spiritual impetus. For example, Renee's grandmother places her detective work within the clan responsibilities of her people and, when sacred items are stolen from the tribe, those items call out to Renee in dreams. In *Along the Journey River* and *Evil Dead Center*, laFavor builds on the project of groups like the GAI by explicitly referring to the history of Anishinaabeg gender traditions while also envisioning Two-Spirit people's present-day potential to support the ongoing health and welfare of Indigenous communities: sexuality, spirituality, and nationhood are intimately entwined in laFavor's fiction.

Ultimately these new editions of Carole laFavor's novels under-score the significance of her writing to the Indigenous literary canon, remind us of the power of her activism for HIV-positive Native peo-ples, and return her important claims for the centrality of Two-Spirit peoples, bodies, and histories to the public eye.

## NOTES

1. See Catharine A. MacKinnon and Andrea Dworkin, editors, *In Harm's Way: The Pornography Civil Rights Hearings* (Cambridge, Mass.: Harvard University Press, 1998).

2. Sharon M. Day, personal interview with author, January 2016.

3. Skyman-Smith (producer) and Mona Smith (director), *Her Giveaway: A Spiritual Journey with AIDS* (New York: Women Make Movies, 1987).

4. Quoted in J. A. Machiorlatti, "Video As Community Ally and Dakota Sense of Place: An Interview with Mona Smith," in *Native Americans on Film,* ed. M. E. Marubbio and E. L. Buffalohead (Lexington: University Press of Kentucky, 2013), 324.

5. Maurice Kenny, *Only as Far as Brooklyn* (Boston: Good Gay Poets Press, 1979); Beth Brant, *Mohawk Trail* (New York: Firebrand Books, 1985) and *Food and Spirits* (New York: Firebrand Books, 1991); Chrystos, *Not Vanishing* (Vancouver: Press Gang Publishers, 1989) and *Dream On* (Vancouver: Press Gang Publishers, 1991); Janice Gould, *Beneath My Heart* (New York: Fire-brand Books, 1990); and Vickie Sears, *Simple Songs* (New York: Firebrand Books, 1990); Beth Brant, editor, *A Gathering of Spirit: A Collection by North American Indian Women* (New York: Firebrand Books, 1988); Gay American Indians and Will Roscoe, editors, *Living the Spirit: A Gay American Indian Anthology* (New York: St. Martin's Press, 1988). Discussed in the next para-graph is Paula Gunn Allen, *The Woman Who Owned the Shadows* (San Fran-cisco: Spinsters Ink, 1983).

# EVIL DEAD CENTER

# 1

The weather had apparently decided break time was over. Renee LaRoche sat huddled and shivering, as the warmer-than-usual early April succumbed to a late-season Alberta clipper. While her jeep's white canvas top snapped noisily in the wind, the Ojibwa woman cursed the fact she'd delayed fixing the tear, put there by a low-hanging branch coming off Gi sina Nibi Lake below her gram's place a month ago. She didn't usually come off the lake ice at that spot, but she'd been hurrying to get home. When the weather warmed, some of the urgency to fix the top passed. So now here she was, in below-freezing temperature, fiddling with the duct tape that was her temporary solution. Finished, Ren nudged the cocker spaniel next to her, sliding a newspaper out from under the little black dog. "Least you could do is have some sympathy, you ol' rez dog. I'm freezing my tootsies here."

Mukwa opened one eye. *Not a chance. You made your bed, now shiver in it.* And, with a look Renee could swear was a grin, the dog made a half-turn and snuggled back into the blanket her very own two-legged had laid on the seat for her.

Several large snowflakes danced down from the overcast sky. The temperature was definitely falling, but not enough yet to suck the moisture out of the big flakes. A sudden wind gust flattened a bevy of flakes against the jeep's windshield where they paused, displaying their lacy designs, then slid easily down the glass. "Look at that, Mukie. They would've stuck like glue on a city windshield," Renee chuckled, watching their effortless glide.

The incident two weeks before that brought Renee to this isolated spot on Mosquito Creek Road had warranted only fifteen seconds on the six o'clock news and a two-inch article on page four of the *Thunder Lake Gazette*. "Indian Woman Found Dead," a tiny, 14-point headline had whispered. The body of the article recorded:

> Dr. James Thorton, Chippewa County coroner, ruled the unidentified woman died of hypothermia. "All initial evidence points to an intoxicated Indian woman who stopped to take a rest, maybe another drink, passed out, and never woke up. Or, maybe she planned it that way. Didn't want to wake up," Doctor Thorton told the *Gazette*. Then he added, "She'd been dead for about five days before her body was found leaning against the big oak tree at the southeast edge of Isaiah Jaspers' farm."

The article continued:

> Taking advantage of the March thaw, Jaspers had been getting a jump on spring fence repair on his 320-acre farm abutting the Red Earth Reservation, along the northeastern boundary. Authorities are trying to identify the body…

"Two weeks, and they don't know any more than when the body was found," Renee grumbled, peeking at Mukwa, who was back asleep on her blanket.

The phone call about the dead woman had shocked Renee. "We meant a lot to each other once, eh?" Caroline Beltrain had begun. "I know I'm callin' from outta the blue, Renee, but I need your help." Even after eighteen years, Renee remembered the unmistakably hushed, raspy voice of her old friend, and hearing it rolled the years back to one of the last times she'd seen Cal.

On the run from BIA police and the FBI in the woods of the Minnesota Arrowhead, they had taken refuge at Delores Brings Her Back's homestead on Sugar Hill Island. When Rodney Jamisson slit Cal's throat in his frenzied attempt to flee the island, it was the first anyone in the Movement knew for sure he was a paid FBI informant. Caroline survived the attack, but would forever carry the telltale mark of a voice one vocal cord short. Jamisson disappeared behind the veil of the FBI, no doubt resurfacing in some other movement, with some other name. Renee and Cal split up shortly after, and Renee hadn't been in touch with her since. Eighteen years until late yesterday when, picking up the phone she heard, "Runner, I need your help. They're covering up the real cause of death on that unidentified woman."

Renee's initial inquiry into the incident revealed there'd been little effort spent on identifying the Native American woman. Said to be in her late thirties, she was buried two days after being discovered, in an unmarked county pauper's grave. *And here I am,* Renee LaRoche scowled, fiddling with the newspaper article and a copy of the official autopsy report in her lap, *freezin' my butt off. Beltrain always could get me to do anything.*

The autopsy report revealed little. "Unidentified Native American woman, 35-40 years old. Height: 5'6". Weight: 145 lbs," it began. Identifying two tattoos, one on each hand, the report described a crudely tattooed reservation-style *LOVE* across the left fingers near the knuckles, and a closed fist holding an eagle feather professionally tattooed on the back of her right wrist. It went on to briefly describe normal internal organs and that was it. "Evidently stuporous from ETOH intoxication, subject lost consciousness. Cause of death determined to be hypothermia," was the report's final declaration. Renee puzzled how the coroner could officially pronounce alcohol intoxication with no mention of a blood alcohol level. *He must have decided being Indian with a bottle next to her was enough to make it official.* There was a notation at the end of the report indicating four photographs had been taken of the body.

"*Gaie oma winawa ondass,* Mukie. Here they come," Renee said aloud, patting Mukwa's sleeping head. In the rearview mirror she watched Chief Hobart Bulieau pull up behind them and kill the motor on his Red Earth tribal squad car.

"*Boozho,* Ogima," Renee called, as she and Mukwa hopped from the jeep.

"Hey to you, too." The chief slid out of his car and patted his left knee, as though reminding it it had to move and bear some weight. "Bette Davis said aging ain't for sissies, and boy was she right," Hobey grimaced, handing Renee a manila envelope.

"From the coroner?"

"Four pictures. They're kinda gruesome, Renny, go easy."

Renee paused, looking up at the man who'd been like a father to her since she, her daughter Jenny, and the dog moved back to the rez four years ago. She valued the closeness they'd developed over the last year during their investigation of the theft of the tribe's ancient ceremonial items and the murder of the Red Earth tribal chairman. She had come to depend on it—making up for what she never had.

Turning the envelope over and over, Renee looked from Hobey to the tree where the body was found to the envelope. After a deep breath she lifted the flap and slowly slid the four photos out of the nine-by-twelve envelope. The top one, taken at the site, was of the victim leaning against the tree, facing west. At the angle it was shot the Native woman looked like she was sleeping, her chin resting on her chest, hands folded in her lap. The next three were more graphic. Even in cool weather, after five days a body begins to deteriorate. All of the woman's features were bloated and contorted into a waxy visage. The body, naked in the rest of the photos and laid out on the steel table at the morgue, appeared grotesque and out of shape. At the sight of the photos Ren's turkey sandwich, eaten an hour before, did a somersault. She swallowed hard several times trying to hang onto it. The last swallow met the turkey sandwich on its way up, and she just had time to lean over before her entire stomach contents spewed onto the side of the frozen dirt road.

"Easy, Renny, easy. First time I saw someone that'd been dead for more'n a few days, I did the same thing. If a body freezes and is left outside the skin starts turnin' a silky white color. It's called adiposeer, or somethin' like that, body fat's chemical reaction to moisture. Gives it that waxy look. Then, when it starts to thaw…" The chief shrugged, hoping that putting a scientific spin on the pictures might help Renee detach a little. He pulled a handkerchief out of his pocket and handed it to his friend.

It took several minutes, but Renee recovered. They were standing by the tree now where the farmer had found the woman's body. "Hobey, if she was in the Movement like Cal said, and came here to kill herself like the coroner believes, she would've brought her medicine bag, tobacco, maybe even worn ceremony clothes." Renee paused. "If they hadn't stuck her in the ground so damn fast, maybe they could've found more out."

"Heard they were busy that night. Had several autopsies goin'."

"All white I suppose?"

The chief shrugged.

"Goddamnit, Hobey. I thought with Peterson gone over there, things'd be different. Maybe the county medical elite'd treat us with more respect."

"*Kin bejigenabandang*, Renny. You're a dreamer." Chief Bulieau put an arm around her. "One of your many charms. Say, why do you suppose your friend Cal didn't give you a name on this woman?"

"That was weird, but I figure she'll call back. My guess is she's testin' me, seein' if she can still trust me. Been a long time since we crossed paths. And, if she hears I've been working with the tribal fuzz," Renee raised her arms in a who-can-say shrug, "there's no tellin' what suspicions'll be runnin' around in that head of hers."

"You take a big risk with your reputation hangin' around us, eh?"

"Yeah, but my friends jus' don't know you the way I do." Renee nudged the chief.

"How'll Beltrain know if she can still trust you?"

"I've been thinkin' about that. How 'bout if we put something in the *Bow and Arrow*. You know, maybe about tribal police reopening the case?"

The chief hesitated before saying, "And tell me LaRoche, why should I be wantin' to reopen—or open, depending on your point of view—this case?"

"I think if she says something's wrong, it is. Besides, look at these pictures. I bet we can rule out suicide," Renee pleaded.

Watching her intently, the chief declared, "I'll go with it for a while, just..." he added, frowning, "a while. Then we'll see."

"*Megwetch*, Hobey. 'Preciate it. I think an article in the rez paper'll get her to call again."

"Why's she bein' so secretive anyway?" Hobey knew who Caroline Beltrain was, but he hadn't heard anything about her for several years. The last he knew about the Ojibwa activist was a memo he'd seen saying the FBI was looking to question her about some political activity. What, he couldn't remember. He'd known the woman's father a little—the family was from a neighboring reservation and the older Beltrain had been in his unit in Korea.

"She's secretive all right," Renee agreed. "Comes from years in the Movement."

The day's events were beginning to weigh on Renee like a front of gloomy weather. After the murder last year she had planned to settle in and live out her days teaching the young ones on the reservation about culture and the art of beading and basketmaking. And with Sam away…what would she say about all this? About her getting involved in another mystery on the rez?

Taking the photographs out of the crook of the tree where she'd stuck them, she studied them again for several minutes. "Look at this one, Hobey." Renee held out photo number three, a view of the back side of the body. "Looks like bruising, here on her back."

"It's just the blood pooling," Hobey explained, taking the photo. "They call it blood lividity. Gravity pools the blood in the lowest spot when the body dies. Takes about thirty minutes."

The two were silent for a long time, staring at the photo. Renee spoke first. "Hobey, if she died like in the first picture, sitting by the tree, wouldn't the blood've pooled in her butt or thighs?"

The chief nodded in agreement. "This looks like she died on her back." Spacing his words and enunciating each syllable through clenched teeth, he said, "Flat on her back. Means she was either propped up like that after she died, or brought here after she was dead."

"If that's true, Hobey, it sure could've been murder, right? They prob'ly brought her here and set her up like this to make it look like she passed out and froze to death." Renee held up the first picture. "Cal's right. She was murdered."

"Hold up now, Renee. Don't go gettin' ahead of yourself. It's something to look into, that's for sure. My first question is, why wasn't that blood pooling noticed on autopsy?" He picked up photo number three again. "And what else did they miss? The real cause of death maybe? Even if she was poisoned, you know, somethin' not visible at first, they should've found somethin' in her stomach contents …somethin'." The chief shook his head. "Any signs of drugs in the autopsy report?"

"There was no toxicology analysis with the autopsy," Renee responded, looking up from the report. "Can't find where they even did one."

"I'll be goddamned," Chief Bulieau snapped, clapping his gloved hands together, "now I'm starting to get mad."

Renee smiled at his typical understatement. "Can we get another look at the body?" She released the words haltingly, unsure about the spiritual implications of digging a body up after it had been buried.

"Legally, that's a whole other story. It'll take some work 'cause technically it's not even our case. She wasn't on the rez side of Creek Road, remember? Possibly I can make a case for gettin' into it 'cause she's Indian," Hobey hesitated, taking in a long, slow breath. "Maybe threaten to make a stink about incompetence, or a cover-up..." His voice trailed off into the upturned collar of his winter police jacket.

"Want me to check with Gram about the spiritual stuff? You know, bringin' the body back up?"

The chief agreed, then said, "I was wonderin' about this, Renee. Look on her hand here." He pointed to a dark spot on the back of the woman's left hand in the first photo.

"Hard to tell, eh? Dirt maybe?"

"Maybe."

"Or maybe...it's somethin' else," Renee frowned, looking more closely at the picture.

"I'll get it blown up. Give us a better look." He took the photo. As they moved to leave he turned to Renee and asked, "Wanna pay a visit to Farmer Jaspers with me?"

Renee stooped to pick up her gloves where they'd fallen off the fence. "Look, Hobey. Two sets of deer tracks. I remember when Benny taught me how to track. I couldn't figure this one out. They looked too small for deer 'til Benny told me deer walk on their toes."

"You and Benny. I remember him chasin' you around the rez. Then later," Hobey gave her a nudge, "him tryin' to keep you outta trouble. Lucky you had an older brother. You needed one."

Renee let the comment slide. "The pointed end of the track shows which way they're walkin'," she said, more to herself than anyone. She touched the track reverently, then stood and let go a big sigh. The dead. An image of her brother Ben wavered before her eyes: a tall, slender Ojibwa, forever forty-one, dark brooding eyes that sparkled instantly whenever she came into his sight.

"I know you miss him, Renny."

"Twelve years, Hobey, he's been dead twelve years and I still miss him." Renee looked off across the field, thinking back to life before Ben, eleven years older than her, was stabbed to death beside a Minneapolis railroad track. "Ready to go?"

"Soon's I get these damn thistles off my pants," Hobey grumbled, picking at them with little success. "Sticky little suckers."

"Mr. Jaspers? I'm Chief Bulieau, this is Renee LaRoche. Tribal Police. We're following up on a few things concerning the Indian woman you found dead on your property. Mind if we ask you a couple questions?"

Hobey had preceded Renee up the Jaspers' side walk, past two old Red Wing crocks with their signature red wing on the side below a scrolled number five, indicating the gallon size of the container. Renee had to smile at the casual, functional use country people made of things that would go for some hefty cash in antique circles in the Twin Cities.

"Come on in." Isaiah Jaspers' booming voice echoed off the windows of the still winter-hearty back porch of his four-bedroom white clapboard house.

"Mind tellin' us how you came upon the body?" Hobey began after they were settled around the large, round oak kitchen table, warming their hands on thick stoneware coffee mugs.

"Was a shock, I'll tell ya. With the warm-up, I was makin' my way 'round the land lookin' for bad fence. I didn't get my snow fence up last fall on that stretch on Mosquito Creek Road. Took sick before I got to it, then it snowed early, ya know. You remember, the big one just before Halloween? Anyways, saw a car parked on the road, down a ways on the reservation side. Thought someone might be in trouble, and I guess I had my mind on that 'cause I damn near tripped over her."

Renee didn't know a lot about the Jaspers, but it didn't surprise her that Mr. Jaspers thought about someone needing help before he thought about drunken Indians being in the car, or someone parked there planning to rob him.

"There wasn't much snow left out in that open area there after the early thaw and there she was, deader'n dead," Jaspers continued. He looked at the two Red Earthers. Renee and the chief sat quietly. They had questions, but were sure that if they waited, Jaspers would fill the silence. Most white folks did. It was like they had an allergy to quiet. Jaspers went on to describe the shape the body was in and its position, leaning against the oak tree next to the fence, "like she'd jus' fell asleep there."

"So she was sitting up when you found her?"

"Yup, sure was."

"Did you ever see the people in the car?"

"Car?"

"The one on the rez side of the road," Renee reminded the old man.

"Oh...yeah."

"Issy, didn't they say they thought it might be her car?"

Mrs. Jaspers had been standing silently in the doorway. The high pitch to her voice startled the Red Earthers, who both made quick half-turns to stare at the plump woman. "Issy's a little forgetful these days," she added, throwing her husband a loving look.

"Did you say *her* car?" Renee smiled at the woman, hiding her growing irritation with how the sheriff's department had investigated this incident.

"Well, that's what they thought at the time. The sheriff's deputy, Rod Johanson, I mean. Don't know 'bout now. They towed it off right behind the coroner's wagon." Isaiah Jaspers glanced first at his wife, then at the two Ojibwa, giving a slight shrug of his shoulders.

Chief Bulieau and Renee thanked their elderly neighbors and walked out into the cold northwoods air. Despite the fact that March was usually the snowiest month in Minnesota, sometimes with as much as fifteen inches falling before the April rains took over, this winter'd been different, warming mid-March then sinking back into an extended bout of hunched-shoulder weather in early April. Renee zipped up the Columbia parka she'd retrieved from storage when the temperature took its plunge, then slid her hands into the leather-and-rabbit fur mittens Delores Brings Her Back had taught her how to make ten years before at a gathering on her island.

Bidding Chief Bulieau good-bye, Renee made her way back out to the main road and headed west on Mosquito Creek, past the boarded-up house of murdered tribal chairman Jed Morriseau. At Old Bridge Road she crossed over the Journey River on the reservation's only remaining wooden bridge. The ice had thinned enough to reveal the water flowing over the rocky river bottom. A few solid weeks of above-freezing weather and the Journey River would be so full with winter run-off, early white water rafters would flock to the area. For now, the water flow was gentle and reflective.

Once across the river, Renee pulled off onto the frozen shoulder and she and Mukwa walked back onto the bridge. It had been a little more than a year since Hobey found the body of Red Earth's tribal chairman, Jed Morriseau, on the river flats below. Renee had been running the trails high up along the Journey River cliff since she returned to the rez four years before and hated that the murder clouded her favorite meditation spot. Now every time she looked down onto the flats she thought of Jed and all the problems he had caused. The tribal ceremony returning the stolen bones of the ancestors back to the caves in the cliff had taken some of the negative energy away, but still, when she looked at the river flats below...

Mukwa's short yip turned Renee's head. "Ready to go home to our empty cabin? Okay. This place is kinda depressing." She frowned. "Can't wait for Sam and Jenny to get back." The cocker jumped straight up into Renee's arms, licking her face enthusiastically.

Renee rarely made the turn from Old Bridge onto Loon Road without it bringing a smile to her lips. Memories. She, her best friend Mollie, and Mollie's brother had been to Rice Lake in the Flandreau wagon for groceries, then picked up Granny Flandreau at Holy Rosary Church. Granny'd won $2.15 at bingo and treated the girls to a popsicle. After arguing over the flavor, Renny finally gave in. It was Mollie's granny's dime, so orange it was. Mollie's brother George and Granny sat on the wagon seat, just above the bony roan rump of the horse, while the two ten-year-old girls sat with their dusty brown legs and bare feet dangling off the back. It was right at this turn Mollie dropped the last bite of her orange popsicle down the back of her brother's muscle shirt. He jumped straight up and lost the reins, spooking the horse. If Granny hadn't caught the reins and calmed the horse, they'd have all hit the ditch. For punishment, the girls had to unhook the horse and take it to feed, punishment Granny knew the girls would gladly do. Renny loved it when the old horse ate out of her hand, her tongue scratchy, warm and wet, with the long white hairs growing out of her lips tickling Renny's cheek when she brushed over them.

"You know, Mukwa, you had to be tough to survive parents that drank too much and only came home to sober up and sleep. Some perks, though. When we ran out of powdered milk I ate my corn flakes with orange Kool-Aid. And, if you were lucky enough to have someone like Gram, you knew that no matter who you were it was okay—because you were Creator's work." Renee fell into silence again, and Mukwa opened one eye to check what she was up to. Satisfied that her two-legged was okay, she relaxed. Renee gave the dog's head a pat. "You're a good listener, Mukie."

*I try, I try. But you do go on sometimes.*

Gesturing out the window, Renee asked, "Wanna stop over at Gram and Auntie's?" Mukwa rolled over on her back, legs in the air and visions of warm fry bread dancing in her head. "I'll take that as a yes," Renee chuckled, rubbing the dog's soft belly. There wasn't anyone Renee respected more than her gram and auntie—Ojibwa elders were the living memory of the people. "To lose one was like white folks losing a library," is how she explained it to Jenny, her daughter, when she asked why it was so important they move back to the reservation. Being just a rooster's crow away from the elders, when Ren worried on something she often found herself pulling up next to their giant Eastern pine before she even realized she'd made a decision to go there. Renee was glad she'd returned to the reservation—coming back to herself, to who she really was.

"*Boozho.*" Ren followed the well-worn path on the white-and-black checkered linoleum through the kitchen.

"*Boozho, nin ikkwesens,*" came Lydia's reed of a voice. "*Anin,* my girl."

Renee collapsed onto the couch next to her auntie. "I'm bushed," she moaned.

"Gimme some a that brown sugar, my girl." Lydia leaned over to her great-niece. "Lonely, eh."

"Never could fool you, Auntie," the younger woman grinned, giving her aunt a kiss. "What's up?"

"Let's see." Lydia held up several new yards of yellow cotton material.

Ren smiled, imagining her auntie's shopping trip. Lydia was a combat shopper, back on the road home before word could get from one end of town to the other that she was there. Notice of her presence was well taken by drivers and pedestrians alike, though: Auntie's driving reputation preceded her.

"Where's Gram?"

"Bingo."

"Without you?"

"Went with Esther," Lydia replied, referring to Esther Little Wolf, Lydia's friend since childhood and the tribal chair elected after Jed Morriseau's murder.

"You feelin' all right, Auntie?" The last time Renee could remember her aunt turning down a chance to use her beaded dab-a-dot bingo marker was a year ago. She'd gone to the hospital instead and had her gallbladder out.

"Wanted to catch this re-run of *Northern Exposure*, and the old birds wouldn't wait," Lydia replied, sticking out her lower lip.

A quick check of her watch told Renee she had about five minutes to visit with her aunt before the show started. "Thought you'd lose interest in that show after it went off the air, Auntie."

"Now, you know I'm loyal as an ol' dog," Lydia crowed, giving Mukwa a pat. "Long's they keep showin' 'em, I'll keep watchin'."

Renee laughed, watching Lydia as the old woman enjoyed one of her favorite pastimes—amusing herself. Her great-aunt was about the funniest person Ren knew, and until the age of twelve, she'd thought the smartest, too. Information-keeper, because all Lydia's comments and answers were said with such conviction.

One day, five-year-old Renny stumbled breathless into Mollie's house. "Auntie keeps all the answers in the world tied up in an ol' shoe box. She told me herself, but she won't say where she keeps it." The two friends searched for the shoe box off and on for years, dreaming of finding it and never having to go back to school. They talked about how smart they'd be if they could just find that box. Eventually it was forgotten until, as an adult, Renee asked Gram, "How come you never told me Auntie didn't really have a shoe box with all the answers in the world in it?"

"Oh, she didn't?" Gram answered, a twinkle in her eye. And that was the end of that.

Some elders, like Gram, walked a quiet path, said little, and stayed in the shadows so as not to stand out. Auntie Lydia moved in the sunshine, dancing and singing through life as if she had an army of termites marching along in front of her, clearing the way. Once she told Renee, "Keep yourself polished and smooth. Tuck in your edges. Then nothin' they do can get to ya." And that's how Auntie lived: edges tucked in and flying through life like she was sitting on a brick of commodity lard. She took off at the jump, Renee thought, grinning over at her auntie, and the whole rez's been runnin' to catch up ever since. The pain and discrimination of Lydia's life lived in the set of her jaw and how the elder vacated her eyes when she talked to anyone but another Indian. The real Auntie was not seen by many.

"Do you remember my friend Caroline Beltrain?"

"Benet's *nojishe?* Over at Yellow Cliff?"

"That's the one. You knew her grandmother, eh? Would you trust her if she showed up after not seein' her for a long time and told you that the unidentified Indian woman they found dead out on Creek Road was really murdered?"

Lydia turned on the TV. Renee waited through a Budweiser and a Hefty bag commercial before Lydia said, "When Gitchi Manitou made the directions he made east, south, west, and north, above and below right away. Then he tried to think of someplace to put the seventh, the most important one. Finally he decided to put it in the last place us two-leggeds prob'ly'd ever look—our hearts."

Renee stared at the TV through *Northern Exposure*'s opening credits. "Trust my heart?" she finally said, as Lydia raised the sound on the TV.

"You'll know what to do, *nind ikkwesens*. Jus' remember, she's like the *obodashkwanishi*. In the blink of an eye they can disappear into their surroundings."

Renee nodded.

"We admire that dragonfly," Lydia added, brushing back her raven hair braided in one long twist down her back.

"*Megwetch*, Auntie...you're right. I do know what to do." They lapsed into silence then, watching the show together.

"Before you go, *nin ikkwesens*, I wanna give you somethin.'" Lydia crinkled a brown face creased with the story lines of her eighty-six years. Hitching up faded Levis, Auntie stood. She'd taken to wearing a pair of Gramps' old red suspenders to hold them up after losing weight following last year's surgery. She still had on her yellow rubber boots, the prize she'd retrieved from her last weekly trip to the "rich folks" dump outside of Thunder Lake, and they clumped on the wooden floor as she went into her bedroom. After rummaging for several minutes, the elder came out holding a copy of Red Earth's *Bow and Arrow,* turned to an article titled, "Squirrel Catches Murderer."

"And you'll be needin' this too if you're gonna be gettin' into things again." Auntie handed Renee a small yellow bundle. From the smell Renee could tell it was sage and cedar. "Remember, my girl, you belong to the Mukwa Odem, protectin's in Bear Clanner's blood. You jus' gotta be like a worm walkin' along the edge of a skinnin' knife and you'll be okay."

# 2

The second call in eighteen years from Caroline Beltrain came sooner than Renee expected. As usual, her old friend was brief and to the point.

"I'll be right there, Cal." Renee hung up and left the cabin so quickly, Mukwa barely got out the door with her.

Caroline Beltrain had come to be known as a chipper during the '70s. From her own experience, Renee knew using drugs turned you into someone even you didn't recognize, and that certainly had been the road her friend was on the last time she saw her. But now, sitting across from her in Mabel's Cafe, Renee could see things had changed. Although Cal looked a little rough around the edges, with that nasty scar across her neck, and scars on her left forearm and hand, she looked clean, no longer chipping heroin to avoid the feeling part of her life.

"Jus' tryin' to protect my throat, Runner," Cal rasped, noticing Renee staring at the scars on her left arm.

"Runner...haven't heard that since the last time I saw you. You're the only one who ever called me that."

"That's 'cause no one else spent time with you runnin' from the Feds. I miss those times, *washkobisid*. Haven't found anyone like you since."

"Sweetcakes—somethin' else I haven't heard for a long time." A smile danced across Renee's lips. "I'm glad you called, Beltrain."

They sat staring at each other. Just as Cal leaned toward her, Renee said, "It took me a long time to get over you, Cally. A long time. But three years ago I met someone. A soul mate. Her name's Samantha, and," Renee held up a hand, "before you ask, she's white. Don't say anything, jus' don't, okay? *Chimook* or whatever color, I love her. More every day." The Ojibwa smiled at the thought of her partner. Samantha had wrapped herself around Renee's spirit, smoothing the edges and lighting the center with a passionate flame. Sometimes, lying next to her in that moment before waking, Renee could feel their spirits releasing each other to their individual lives, as if they'd spent the night as one.

"You've got a true heart, Runner. I know that much. If you didn't exist, the world'd have to invent you. I wouldn't be here otherwise."

"So, you saw the article in the *Bow and Arrow* about the case?"

Cal's nod was barely perceptible.

"That why you called again?"

Another nod followed, so small it brought a smile to Renee's lips. The silence grew while Cal alternated between playing with her silverware and staring at Renee. Her spirit seemed to have retreated to the edge of life and perched there, watching.

The waitress, whose name tag introduced her as Martha—a solid, reassuring, trustworthy kind of name—offered the two a friendly smile before the standard, "Coffee?" The TV near the ceiling in the west corner of the cafe blasted the CBS morning news, updating the country on the latest superstar scandal, but the topic had lost its appeal. No one was paying attention anymore.

When their breakfast came, Ren checked her eggs. Seeing her onions on the plate in front of Cal, she switched. Cal caught her wrist as she set the plate down. "Can you tell me what the paper meant sayin' Bulieau's lookin' into clues found?" Cal rasped.

Renee wanted to ask Caroline Beltrain who the dead woman was, but it was Cal's call. She wouldn't ask. Instead she answered, "We know the body was moved to the spot where that farmer found her."

"How?"

"Autopsy pictures. By the way the blood pooled after death." The color drained from Caroline's face, and she dropped her fork on the table. "I'm sorry, Cally." Renee laid her hand over the other woman's. "She meant a lot to you, eh?"

Ren chased the remaining scrambled eggs around her plate. The quiet extended through the last bite of breakfast. Cal's food sat untouched in front of her. Out of the blue she said, "Rosa Mae Two Thunder." Renee looked up to her old friend, who was poking her fork at the now-cold breakfast. The last jab was full force into the biscuit, tearing it down the middle. "Rosa Mae Two Thunder," Cal whispered through clenched teeth, "was dedicated to the people, Runner. Funny thing is, she was the nonviolent one in the group. Remember Malcolm X's slogan in the '60s, 'by any means necessary'? Not the sister. She said we could accomplish everything we wanted without violence. Her father's a Cree healer. Lives on a reserve north of Winnipeg. She grew up around traditionals."

"Rosa Mae Two Thunder?"

Cal nodded. A hush fell over the table.

"I wondered about her spirituality," Renee began after the two sat for several minutes. She'd decided against questions about Cal's relationship with Rosa Mae Two Thunder.

"You wondered about her spirituality?"

"Okay," Renee nodded, "that sounds weird, I know." She could see the hesitation to trust still there in Cal's eyes. "I was wondering because the picture of her when they found her didn't show any spiritual stuff—except she was facing west—but no medicine bundle, tobacco ties, ceremonial clothes, giveaway stuff. Nothing."

Cal relaxed a little. "Yeah, she would've had those with her if she was planning to kill herself."

Renee let the stillness respond for her.

"So, workin' with the cops now, eh?"

"Off and on since I been back." Ren leaned forward and dropped her voice. "That was somethin'. Tribal chair murdered, they stole sacred stuff from the tribe. Auntie got me involved. Didn't expect to be doing any more sleuthing though."

"No?"

"Then you called. 'Course Gram and Auntie'd say it's the spirits. Us bein' Bear Clan and all." Renee offered a brief smile.

"You don't agree?" Caroline looked surprised.

"Oh, no. I do," Renee paused. "I do. It just isn't always easy to fit the old ways in with all the *chimook* ways. A foot in each world," she shrugged, "not easy."

Then Cal began to talk. "Met Rosa 'bout four years after you left, Renee." Cal's use of *Renee* meant she was deep in thought. "Maesy read about the land reclamation project here on the rez, came to help and learn how to do it so she could take the idea back to her reserve. Talk about divide and conquer, those damn Canucks make it an art form. They separate 'em. First Nations, Metis, and Inuit. Money doesn't cross between groups, the mixed bloods can't share money with the Inuit and like that. Plus, each group's got its own regs. They want 'em to all fight each other and not the suits in Ottawa. Nice scam, eh?"

Renee pulled the fork out of Cal's biscuit, the sight of it sticking up oddly disconcerting. Listening to Cal talk about Rosa Mae Two Thunder was starting to make her uncomfortable. Why? It couldn't be jealousy she was feeling, could it? She and Cal had been over for years; besides, she was crazy about Samantha. So why was the pit of her stomach churning? *Get over it, LaRoche, you big baby. Did you think she'd pine away for you forever?*

"Runner?"

"What?"

"You were frowning."

"Jus' thinkin' back, Cal. Movement memories."

Caroline didn't react, her pain over talking about the dead woman seeming to consume her now. "When they sent me out East to prison for trashin' the Rapid BIA office ten years ago, Maesy wrote at least twice a week. Came to see me six times the three years I was there, too. Prison's a weird place, Renee. Stone and iron—the buildings *and* the hearts. Runs on the most negative view of human nature there is. Upside-down society with upside-down values. Violence, or its threats, everywhere. Without someone on the outside to keep you sane you're done for. I thank Rosa for savin' me." Cal looked weary, her eyes holding a deep sadness. "After I got out we could never quite get back on track though, romantically. The sex was great—she was a fireball in bed. Kinda like you, Runner." For the first time this morning, Cal smiled. She busted out in an ear-to-ear grin that made Renee laugh out loud.

"Nice to see that smile I usta love so much, Cally."

"Yeah," she stopped, the smile fading. "But beyond the sex, we weren't in synch anymore. Finally we gave it up and went back to jus' bein' friends. Saw a lot of action together. The Navajo and Hopi deal, Wisconsin spearing wars, even spent a month with the Zapatistas and the Mosquito Indians in Chiapas. I was in South Dakota when they murdered her."

"I don't get it, Cal. Why didn't someone in the Movement call and ID her?" Renee knew she was taking a chance, moving too fast into a world she was no longer a part of. There were things she needed to know.

An imperceptible frown ran across Cal's forehead as she slid out of the booth and stood. Her glance down at Renee was unreadable, then she turned and strode out of Mabel's Truck Stop Cafe. Renee threw some money on the table and followed her.

Cal was leaning against Renee's jeep. "The FeeBees are looking for me. Want to question me about the bombing at the Prairie Peninsula power station."

"You're kidding, right?"

"Do I look like I'm kidding?" Cal scanned the parking lot.

"No, guess not. But you, a terrorist bomber? Hardly."

"Yeah, well, they don't agree. Guess I'm one of those venomous public enemies Hoover was always siccing FeeBees after, eh?"

"Hoover? Puhleese. I always wondered if they buried the guy in a pair of those lacy women's underwear he wore under his stuffy FBI suit." Renee took a deep breath. "Anyway, Cally, back to my question. Couldn't anyone else make that call?"

"Runner—"

"Come on, Beltrain, for chrissake, gimme a break here. Our friendship's older than dirt."

Cal strode to the end of the jeep, kicked a clump of snow from under the rear fender with her battered Red Wing boot, then walked back to Renee. "After that tiny little article in the paper, someone *did* call. Before that, no one knew she was back. They called the sheriff's office over in the Lake and told 'em who it was they'd found."

"When?"

"The day before they buried her as a Jane Doe."

"And?"

"And nothin', Runner. Goddamned nothing."

"What'd they say?"

"They asked who was callin', and then they said, 'Are you sober?'"

Renee could feel something familiar starting in her gut—some feelings were never very far from the surface. The cops could still roil her insides. "Goddamnit, Caroline, this is the '90s. Isn't anyone past that crap yet?"

Cal's burst of laughter was edged with bitterness. "I hope that sounds more naive than you really are, LaRoche."

Embarrassed, Renee was glad for the relative emptiness of the parking lot. "I know, I'm dreamin'," she shrugged, stuffing her gloved hands into her parka pockets.

"Yeah, always the dreamer. I remember, Runner, I remember. Drove me crazy then, too. Like I said, if you didn't exist, we'd have to invent you."

She turned and threw her arms around Renee. Cal's kiss took Renee by surprise, as did how familiar her lips felt. She leaned into the kiss a little before breaking it off. Cal took Ren's face in her hands, staring deep into her eyes. "Gotta go, Runner. I'll be in touch."

"Can I drop you somewhere?" Renee said to Cal's back. The woman's stride was unbroken as she rounded the corner. "Walk with the spirits, my friend," Renee whispered after her, touching her lips. Asking her about Rosa's car would have to wait.

"Yo, Hobey. What's up, my friend?" Renee settled into the jeep and hooked the cell phone under her chin.

"You sound pretty chipper for so early in the morning, LaRoche."

"Got some more info from our friend. Should I come in? You got time?"

"I was gonna go over to the coroner's and pick up Jane Doe's personal effects."

"Not Jane Doe anymore, but I'll tell ya later. I can go over there."

"You sure? Gotta go all the way into Thunder Lake."

"No problem. Don't have to teach a class 'til later today. Me and Mukwa'll enjoy the drive."

"Okay, I'll give 'em a call. Let 'em know you're comin' instead of me. Oh, by the way, got a call into BCA, and our friend Agent Lawton."

"FBI?"

"If this goes somewhere, we're gonna at least need to keep the Feds off our backs."

"I guess. Catch up with ya later, Chief." Renee hung up just as she made the turn off Hole In The Day Boulevard onto County 3.

The coroner who had taken over the duties in Chippewa County couldn't have been more different from the previous one. A transplant to the area from Denver, Dr. James Thorton was a tall man, eternally ruffled and unkempt, with an intense look that began at the furrows between his eyebrows and ice-blue eyes. His sharply angular nose and chin were separated by a large, friendly mouth. Graying brown hair clung like a spider web to the top of his head, looking like he'd failed to duck in a musty basement. Glasses hanging around his neck completed the image of a man passing into middle age.

Standing in the coroner's reception area, Renee remembered the last time she'd been here. She had graphic memories of the previous coroner, Dr. Gerald Peterson, who blew his brains out in his office rather than face charges of grave robbing, illegally selling tribal artifacts, and murdering the Red Earth tribal chairman.

"Ms. LaRoche, come in. Chief Bulieau called. I've been expecting you." His friendly manner was disconcerting. Renee expected something else.

"The chief said you'd have a package ready for me? Clothes and other stuff from the Native woman you buried as Jane Doe?"

With a name now for Jane Doe, it was hard not to confront the coroner about exactly what transpired in this case, but Ren had promised Hobey she would act only as a messenger this trip. Eyeing Dr. James Thorton keenly, she promised herself that someone would confront him later.

"Something else I can do for you?" Thornton's voice penetrated Ren's musing, and she realized she'd been staring at the man.

"What? Oh, sorry. No, no thank you. I was jus' thinking about how sad it must be to die alone like that," she lied.

"Yes, I would think so. That would be tragic."

"You did the autopsy didn't you, doctor?" Renee knew he had, but wasn't sure that was something she was supposed to know.

"Yes I did. It was pretty cut-and-dried, though. If you know what I mean."

"No, not exactly."

"Well, a bottle was found next to her and she reeked of alcohol," the doctor said, a condescending edge to his voice.

The thought of how her mother was found flashed in Renee's

mind. Dead in the snow with a half pint of Four Roses in her pocket. She'd left Trader Jack's, her favorite Rice Lake bar, and in drunken confusion apparently decided to walk the four miles home in sub-zero weather.

"Does that mean you can pretty much assume it was alcohol and the cold that got her?" Renee asked innocently.

"Well, not necessarily, but with the other factors, that was the most likely cause of death." He winked, grinning broadly.

Renee mirrored, though weakly, the coroner's smile, bristling at the wink and "other factors" comment. Of course she knew what he meant by *other factors*. The dead woman was Indian and was found alone in a field across the road from the reservation. What other cause of death could there be? Drunken Indians are the easiest to check off the list on a busy day.

"I understand you were pretty busy the day they brought her in?" A few more questions wouldn't make the chief too mad, she hoped.

"I'll say. We had one in from an auto accident. An eighty-seven-year-old from a nursing home who fell, and any time an accident's involved we have to determine cause of death, you know. To top it all off, we had a suicide from over in Isle. For an office that usually does only one, maybe two autopsies a week, four in one day made this a disaster area."

Renee nodded, trying to appear sympathetic, but all of a sudden she needed to get out of there. Friendly as the guy was—or rather, friendly as he seemed compared to the last guy—Thorton apparently held some rather ignorant views of Native people. Turning to the doctor, Ren announced, "Well, time to move on here. *Megwetch* for this stuff." She held up the bag of Rosa Mae Two Thunder's things. "I imagine the chief'll be in touch."

"*Megwetch*. That's one of your words?" Thorton hesitated, then added, "Chippewa, I mean?" The man was grinning as though he'd just discovered the missing link.

Renee nodded. "Ojibwa."

"Ojibwa?" He looked confused.

"We're called Ojibwa, not Chippewa." Then in a friendlier voice, she explained, "The French pronounced *Ojibwa* so it sounded like *Chippewa*, I guess, and that's what everybody started calling us." She turned then and hurried out the door before the doctor used her to try and get any closer to the local culture.

Driving back through Rice Lake on Hole In The Day Boulevard, Renee passed the new sign on Harley and Sarah's Fresh Meat Butcher Shop. A prosperous business in town, the butcher shop was a classic. Sawdust on the floor, a big double-glass door, walk-in cooler with sides of beef hanging inside. Harley and Sarah's was where Red Earthers who didn't skin their own took their hunted game, especially the big stuff, for skinning and quartering. The only things Ren could see they'd changed in the shop over the years were the halogen lights, the price of their meat, and now, the fancy neon sign outside. The two were long ago retired, and more recently dead, with the shop now run by their number-three son, Harry, and his family. The Samposes were one of the few white businesses on the rez trusted by Red Earthers. Most people attributed that to Harley Sampose's eyes. They were dark—some said brooding, others said haunted. Elders believed the look spoke of a pain nearly as deep as their own, and thus a man to be trusted, no matter what color he was. "No matter what color," Renee sighed aloud as she drove past. "No matter what color. Be nice if we had a coroner thought that."

Coming out of her daydreaming, Renee found herself pulling up next to the Eastern pine at her gram's. "Come on, Mukie, let's go in. Sure wish it was Friday—we could get some fresh fry bread, eh." Inside she found Gram and Auntie bent over their beading. Gram's deeply lined face bespoke of years working outdoors, and the trying, painful relationship Red Earthers had with the outside that took its toll over the years, stooping shoulders and creasing faces. Gram was the quiet sister. While the inside of silence scared Lydia, Gram thrived on it, explaining that the silence wrapped itself warmly around her. It was inside silence that she talked to other living things.

"*Boozho*, elders," Renee called. "How's it goin' with you two?"

Gram looked up and studied her granddaughter carefully. "You stop by, *nosijhe?*"

The warmth of Gram's words covered Renee, and she gulped for air as a river spilled from her lips.

"At first I thought this new coroner might be different, Gram. Then he starts in on drunken Indians and the same ol' tack *chimooks* get on, how it's so quaint to know an Indian, blah, blah, blah."

Gram looked out the big front window facing Gi sina Nibi Lake. The soon-to-bud oak branches were pressed against the window, as though listening to the conversation inside. "Before *chimooks* came, the People ripened as the seasons changed and time passed. The days of our history are long, my girl. *Chimooks* called their coming the manifest destiny; our elders back then called it the beginning of the season of suffering." Gram paused, staring out the window at the branches. "Since then, the People don't ripen any more...they weather."

The elder shook her head sadly. "Many white folks have forgotten their instructions from Creator, *nosijhe,* forgotten how to act," Gram added in her most serious voice. After another long pause she said, "They came to this land and forgot their original instructions. We haven't forgotten. The spirits, who live in every grove of trees, every turn in the river, every lakeshore of the north country, whisper to us not to forget." Gram patted Renee's hand. "But be respectful, granddaughter. Many white folks mean well."

Renee frowned at her gram.

"Anger is only productive, *nosijhe,* if it's understood. Get to know your anger before you run with it or it will run you." Gram leaned back in her rocker, closing her eyes.

Renee stood, passing between Gram and Aunt Lydia, and took a seat on an upright log next to the fireplace. She put a cap on her anger. A sick feeling grabbed the pit of her stomach as she watched her grandmother. Her translucent skin had thinned like the top layer of the birch bark—parchment thin in the sunshine. Ren had to face the fact that her gram was beginning the process of turning toward the spirit world. At ninety-two, the elder's hair had still been almost all black. Now, just a year later, it was mostly gray. Sometimes when Renee looked into her eyes it was as if her gram was gazing back through the curtain that separates the two worlds. And Gram was starting to dream about those on the other side.

"*Nosijhe,* I know why you look at me the way you do. It's not for you to worry. I'm getting ready to cross over, but not yet." Renee's gram offered a broad smile. "Though the thought of the trip pleases me."

Renee smiled a tiny smile, one that didn't reach her eyes and barely pulled up the corners of her mouth. She believed totally in the Ojibwa spirit world, but she wasn't ready to let her gram go. She did know that Gram wouldn't linger when her time came. She had once told her, "Surviving like a bug caught in amber is the white man's way of death, not ours." When it was Gram's time, Ren had to be prepared for her to go quickly.

"The day she gives away that ratty ol' wedding basket's the day I'll take the ol' lady seriously," Lydia giggled, giving her elder sister a gentle poke. The three Coon women laughed together, Lydia again having lightened the mood.

The station was silent of people sounds. Renee could only hear the buzz from the fluorescent lightbulb over Bobbi's desk. "She's been complainin' about that light for a month, eh Mukie. Must drive her crazy, listenin' to that buzzin' all the time." Then, from around the corner, Ren heard computer keys being haltingly assaulted. *No doubt about that sound.* Renee motioned with her lips, Ojibwa-style, in the direction of the noise. "Hey, Chief, type any faster'n you're gonna burn up the keyboard."

"Not funny, LaRoche. This is a pain in the you-know-what. With Bobbi out the last two days, the paperwork's way behind."

Ren checked her watch. "Okay, I've got a half hour before I've gotta get over to school. Me and the kiddies are goin' to the sugar bush with Esther Little Wolf to check the trees. See if they're ready to tap."

"Bless you, my child. Here, you can do this one." Hobey handed her his handwritten report for the FBI on Jane Doe.

"If we know her name now, do you wanna put it in?"

"Right, you said you know." Hobey grimaced as he stood and straightened his knees.

"Rosa Mae Two Thunder. Here's her things from the coroner's."

Renee handed him a brown paper-wrapped package. Opening it, they discovered her watch and a turquoise ring, brown cowboy boots, a jacket, and a set of clothes.

"Look at all the stuff on these clothes. Looks like she was dragged through a field," Renee started to brush the leaves, twigs, and thistles off, but then caught herself. "You got this on you too, remember? Who knows, could be evidence."

The two worked silently for the next half hour.

# 3

"Sammy, my love! I didn't know you'd be here." Renee called excitedly, hurrying to embrace her partner.

"Where you been?"

"Just finished with the kiddies at the sugar bush and sent 'em back to school on the bus with Esther. I forgot to give Hobey this list from the coroner's office, so I was gonna drop it off." She waved an envelope.

"The coroner's?" Samantha's startled look reminded Renee her lover probably wouldn't be happy to hear what she'd been up to.

"Later about all that, my love. You're home, and I missed you so much. Come here." Renee pulled Samantha to her.

"I made pretty good time getting home. The book signing in Bemidji went late last night, so I stayed over. I tried to call, but you weren't here. Went back to the store today, just to visit. Boy am I glad to be home now though." Samantha ran her fingers through Renee's hair, dwelling on the streaks of gray flowing out from her widow's peak.

Renee slipped her hands inside the back of Samantha's Levis. "Mmm, I like thinkin' of this little blue-blood, New England butt with no brookies on it, *saiagi iwed.*"

"You like my Dutch word?"

"*Brookies?* Mmm, and since we never had any such thing as underwear to give a name to, well..." She pulled Sam in close. "Missed you. That week seemed like a year."

"Renee LaRoche, you stop it now," Samantha slapped half-heartedly at her lover's hands. "Don't you be fondling my privates."

-27-

"But, Sammy, jus' look." Renee held her right hand like she was grasping a handle. "Pitiful I say, pitiful. This, my dear, is the shape of Eve's Garden's latest state-of-the-art sex toy handle. See," she held her hand up again, "slim and streamlined, leaving the thumb free to manipulate the slow—that's-better-and-God-don't-stop-now—speed button."

Samantha giggled, offering Renee an alluring smile, and walked her backwards to the bed. Renee stretched out, hands behind her head. "Is this it? The moment I've waited for for over a week? Take me, I'm yours."

Samantha nuzzled into her lover's neck. "Yes, I think I'll do just that," she said, her voice sliding down an octave. The Red Earther pretended to give Samantha's comment serious thought before rolling her partner over and diving toward her most ticklish spot. "Stop, Renny. I'm having a peak experience here!" Samantha pleaded through gales of laughter. Finally, after a few minutes, Sam gasped, "Be serious now, Renny. Enough. I've been gone over a week. I missed you so much one night I woke up kissing my pillow. So come, see what I've been dreaming about."

"Thank the Great Spirit Jenny went to spend the night at Gram and Lydia's after her softball meeting. There's a storm comin' in and I thought they might need some help." Renee traced the outline of Sam's ear before teasing it with her breath. They snuggled down further into the feather bed at the thought of all the snow predicted to sneak up on them under the dark of night. Mukwa shot them an annoyed look, stood and circled an area she determined was *her* bed, scratching and fluffing, then lay down with her back to them.

The ringing phone reverberated in the darkness. Startled awake, Renee stumbled to the phone, her heart racing. "*Boozho.*"

"Runner!"

Renee was instantly awake. Caroline Beltrain's voice had an edge of urgency. Back across the room Samantha switched on the light.

"Cal, what? What's the matter?"

"I've gotta see you."

"Now? What the hell time is it?"

"Six. Aren't you up? Oh right, white girl came home last night."

Renee ignored the remark. "How 'bout we meet for breakfast

in a couple hours?" Renee said sleepily.

"Couple hours! I've already waited a couple hours before I called. Come on, LaRoche. Get your brown butt outta bed. Girlfriend'll survive without you."

"Gimme an hour."

"Same place. Give her a kiss for me," Cal snickered.

Renee hung up and turned back to the bed.

"What was all that, love?"

"Well, like you said last night, you've been gone over a week."

"I should have known leaving you alone for that long could only be trouble." Sam brushed the hair off Ren's forehead and took her hand.

"That was a woman I knew a long time ago. She called the other day, asking for my help when a friend of hers turned up dead and the county sheriff's office buried her as an unknown."

"She didn't call the tribal police?"

"Doesn't trust 'em."

"No, of course not. How foolish of me."

"We were in the Movement together, Sammy." Renee sat on the edge of the bed trailing her fingers up and down Samantha's arm.

"Lovers?"

"It's a long story, *saiagi iwed.* Can we talk about it later? I'll come back soon's I'm done."

"Mmm, I guess." Samantha slid down into the warmth of their bed. "Go on then, get, so you can come back to me sooner."

Renee bent down and gave her partner a prolonged kiss, dressed hurriedly, and headed out the door, Mukwa at her heels. "Wowee," she turned back to Samantha and said, "look at all the snow we got."

"Not interested," the sleepy Sam mumbled, pulling the blankets over her head.

"Looks like we're on our own, Mukie," Renee hollered. "Let's go then." She led the way, pushing through the drifts of new snow. By the time they reached the jeep, snow globs hung from the dog's ears, under her belly, anywhere her hair was longer than half an inch. Renee brushed off as much as she could, but she'd long ago resigned herself to wet upholstery in the winter. "Thank the Creator Billy fixed the top, eh Mukwa? Otherwise there'd be more snow in here than you've got on you." Renee set the jeep into four-wheel drive, and the *nijis* backed slowly out the long drive praying they wouldn't veer off into either snow-filled ditch.

On the way into Mabel's Truck Stop Cafe, on the outskirts of Rice Lake, Renee took in the beauty of the new snow. She tried not to obsess about her meeting with Cal. Each twig on the trees and bushes holding its own mound of snow danced in the wind. From any angle at this spot on the rez, Renee could see what she loved about the north country—trees and water. Ojibwa were woodland Indians, and Ren couldn't think of another spot more soothing to a woodlander's soul. She knew the forests of Red Earth like a city girl knew her block. Driving through this back section of LaFleur's woods relaxed her. Crows screamed noisily above as they dove and flew at each other and the other birds.

"Cranky little devils, eh Mukie? But when the sun comes up our world's gonna sparkle like a gem field, and even the crabby ol' crows'll cheer up." The dog was too busy chewing a glob of snow stuck to her foot hair to care much what her *niji* was saying this morning.

Samantha tossed and turned for twenty minutes trying to go back to sleep, then gave up. She lay there contemplating the changing light in the cabin's east window. The dark gray was gradually brightening, until finally dawn shone as a light square on the wall facing the window. Rolling over, Samantha luxuriated in the smells and feelings of home, taking in the mare's nest of newspapers and magazines that had cluttered the cabin since she left. She was in too good a mood to let it bother her today. Sam smiled at her lover's earlier enthusiasm for the new snow. Being Renee included the outdoors. Rain or sunshine or snow, one-hundred degrees or thirty below. The Ojibwa woman didn't just love nature; there was a sensuality in the way she reacted to it, as though the environment enveloped her in the emotions of a lover.

The New Englander still couldn't picture herself on the Red Earth Reservation, but here she was: living the last three years with this Indian woman, her teenage daughter, and the dog who'd finally won her over—she being a cat person herself. Even her name—Samantha Salisbury—conjured up rolling country estates, polo ponies, long evening gowns, and coming out parties. The sweet-sixteen, not the I-like-girls kind.

Sam gave a huge yawn. How different her life as a professor would be now if she hadn't met Renee. Her nine-month visiting fellowship in women's studies at Granite Rock State College would have ended, and she'd be back in Minneapolis teaching at the university. There'd be no book about Betty, the Red Earth woman who'd lived a life of abuse and incest at the hands of her brother, the tribal chairman here. The woman with a story screaming to be told after she'd reached the end of her rope and paid to have her brother murdered. Samantha had hesitated to write the book, *The Broken Circle*, worrying that the people of Red Earth would not approve of an outsider—a *chimook*—telling a story about one of their own. But Betty's endorsement calmed most of the critics on the rez. The proceeds from the book were going to establish a battered women's shelter on the Red Earth Reservation. Sam couldn't help but feel pride at her part in it all.

She stretched out the length of the bed and pondered Renee's earlier life, previous partners. The woman she'd left their warm bed to meet—could she, or any of them, have loved Renee as much as she did? She doubted it, but she had to admit one disadvantage: all of Renee's other lovers had been Indian.

Mabel's Truck Stop Cafe was a good spot to meet if you wanted privacy; everyone went about their own business, no one hassled you, and you could sit for hours with one cup of coffee. Renee arrived first, or so it seemed. She didn't doubt Cal might be anywhere nearby, waiting 'til she saw Renee go into the cafe. Martha wasn't working today. In her place was a girl, not more than sixteen or seventeen, with Lucille Ball hair and an irritating habit of cracking her gum between words. "You wanna order?" Her bored tone interrupted Renee's gazing out the window at the dawning world.

"Water," Renee said pleasantly. "I'm waiting for someone."

"Whatever," the waitress growled, flipping a menu in front of the Ojibwa woman, who visibly stiffened at the last remark.

"Is that all this generation can say," she groaned, "*whatever?* Where is Martha when you need her?"

In a few minutes the waitress—Trish—gracelessly returned and plunked Renee's water glass down. Her long, red-nailed fingers hit the table, bringing the glass up short and spilling some onto the menu.

Renee agonized silently.

The cafe was almost empty, snow delaying many people. In a few hours, though, everyone would be about their business like it was a warm summer day. A foot of snow was not something that kept Red Earthers from their appointed rounds. "Let me know when you wanna order lady," Trish grouched, then chomped down on the wad of gum she'd been abusing the last ten minutes.

*Lady.* Hearing that always took Renee by surprise. Still hanging onto an image of herself as someone nearer the age of the waitress, *lady* forced her to admit she was old enough to be the young woman's mother. In fact, she had a daughter almost the same age. "Okay," Ren responded to the waitress, more congenial than she felt toward this barely-a-woman person in front of her. Trish withdrew behind the counter, cracking her gum as she went. Like all mothers of teenagers, Renee wondered occasionally about other mothers. Was Mrs. Trish living somewhere in the northwoods of Minnesota, blaming herself for her daughter's irreverent behavior? Would that be her in a few years? Ren took a big breath. Absolutely not. Jenny still actually liked her, and she was already sixteen.

Cal came in, interrupting Renee's reverie. "*Boozho,*" she said, as she sat down across from Renee.

"What's up?"

"This is gonna blow you away, Runner. It did me. I can hardly even say the words out loud because I don't want to believe that any of us could be involved in somethin' so ugly." Renee watched Cal intently, waiting for her to continue. After several minutes Caroline said, "We've got solid information, Renee, that a teacher, and somebody else workin' for the tribe, are involved in using foster kids from the rez in porn movies." Caroline whispered the last few words, glancing warily around the near-empty cafe. When no one appeared to be listening, she added, "I bet Rosa fell into some information on this and before she could get to us somebody got to her."

Renee stared at Cal in disbelief, wondering why the hell she'd come here. She didn't want to hear this stuff, but now it was too late. Goddamn fucking too late. "You said you've got solid information. What does that mean?" she heard herself saying, more irritably than she intended. Just then Trish came back and slouched against their booth. Renee turned her eyes up, but the young waitress was staring out the window chewing her gum, apparently to the beat of some song in her head. "Cal, you wanna order somethin'?" Renee turned back to her friend.

"I'd rather take you to meet someone."

"At this hour?"

"Trust me." The words startled Renee. She looked penetratingly into Caroline's eyes.

"You up for this, *washkobisid?*"

Renee nodded reluctantly.

Leaving the cafe moments later without ordering anything gave Renee a perverse pleasure, dampened only slightly by Trish's indifferent "whatever" in response to their departure.

They were following a highway plow as it cleared the foot of snow off Rice Lake's main road, giving Renee time to try and absorb what she'd just heard. After crawling along behind the plow for ten minutes in silence, she shifted in her seat. Mukwa, asleep on her lap, opened one eye at the movement. Then she went back to her favorite dream, chasing the *waboose* that feasted on their garden. Clearing her throat, Mukwa's two-legged began, "Cally, you've gotta stop holdin' your cards so close to the chest. I need more'n you're givin' me here."

Cal scowled at Renee, then turned back to staring out the window.

"I mean it, Beltrain, goddamnit. You trusted me enough to call, eh? So spill it, girl." Renee took in a breath, casting a brief look at her long-time friend, "or. . .I'm outta here."

"Okay, okay. You'll see in a minute. He's a foster kid stayin' at a white guy named Neuterbide's place. A brother was giving a talk at the middle school in Granite Rock about culture and stuff. You know, it's part of the educational program the Movement got instituted last year in the civil rights suit. Anyway, Bo said this kid came up to him after class and whispered to meet him after school, that he needed to talk to him. After Bo heard what the boy had to say, we started wonderin', maybe this was what Maesy'd stumbled onto."

"How?"

"Ned—that's the kid's name—told Bo he saw one of the girls from Neuterbide's talkin' to Rosa after a class she did the week before she was murdered. Said it looked pretty serious."

"Did Ned talk to the girl?"

"Naw, you know kids. Guess he forgot about it then 'til all this stuff about Rosa started comin' up." Caroline let out a long sigh.

"Holy shit."

Moments later, Caroline Beltrain led the way into a dark, three-story clapboard apartment building in the southeast corner of Rice Lake, just over the railroad tracks and down a dirt road off Hole In The Day Boulevard. Downwind of the new, tribally owned meat-packing plant, most of the twenty-seven workers at the plant lived in the renovated fifty-year-old building. Renee watched as several of the long, narrow windows lit up; the early shift at the plant was getting up.

Cal, Renee, and Mukwa entered an unlocked front door, past a *1 bdrm apartment for rent* sign. The halls of the building smelled like stale blood and guts, a smell Ren knew from family experience you never got completely out of your clothes. On the second floor, Cal stopped at the third door on the right, #206, slipped in a key, gave it a full turn, and nudged the door open. The apartment was sparsely furnished. A bean bag chair next to a wooden crate acting as a table hugged the east wall; a futon on the floor took up half of the west wall next to a couch. A thirteen-inch TV/VCR combination on another wooden crate stood in the northeast corner of the room by the front window.

"Grab a seat, I'll be right back," Cal said, disappearing around the corner and down a hall Renee could see led to the rest of the apartment. She headed for the futon after removing her Sorrels at the door. On a small stand next to the futon, Ren noticed a beaded medicine bag, an Inuit prayer stick, and a braid of sweet grass. Caroline's. She must be staying here, at least some of the time, anyway. The lone window in the room faced north, letting in little of the dawning light. Pulled up along the top of the window, a blue-flowered bed sheet was held up by four strings tied at strategic intervals. Renee looked around for a phone. She was about to follow Cal down the hall when her friend returned followed by a slightly built boy who looked to be about fourteen.

"Runner, this is Ned."

"*Boozho*, Ned," Renee nodded. "This is Mukwa." The boy offered a brief smile and sank onto the battered couch, just missing a protruding spring. He sat picking at the couch stuffing with his brown, still-chubby fourteen-year-old finger. Renee saw a frightened child stare up at her from somewhere deep inside the boy's angry, hardened eyes.

After some urging from Caroline, Ned started his story—in typical Ojibwa fashion—at the beginning. After several reports from neighbors about neglect and abandonment, Ned, at age seven, and his four sisters and brothers, were whisked away into the wintry night by Red Earth Social Service and taken to St. Joseph's Home for Children in Bemidji. Not long after his arrival at the home he was summoned to the director's office. The long, dark hall to the office was empty that night except for a table between two mahogany highbacked chairs outside the office door. Ned still remembered the faded red-and-yellow flowers embroidered on the cushions of the chairs the kids were only allowed to dust—never sit on. Each step down the hall had sounded like a cannon going off in the young Ojibwa's head. "The floor creaked every time I stepped on it and scared the heck outta me. All the way down the hall. I still hear it in my head sometimes." Ned's grin was frozen on his face.

The next thing he remembered was knocking on the door and the priest saying, "Come in, son." Stepping into the room, Ned had hugged the wall just inside the door. Down the hall a door opened and closed, footsteps hurried toward them on the oak floor. Another door opened and closed. The silence that followed swallowed up the last sound too quickly for young Ned to hold onto it for comfort. Motioning the boy to him, Father Jeremy had smiled as he said, "Come on now. You Indian boys are so shy. Come over here." The priest ran his hands through Ned's hair. "Of course we'll have to cut this. Can't have you looking like a little savage, can we," Ned remembered the priest whispering in his ear just before he kissed it.

The fourteen-year-old let go an involuntary quiver and Renee watched as he drew his legs up under him and crossed his arms over his chest. Mukwa, lying next to Renee observing the goings on, crossed the room and stood looking up at the boy. When Ned reached down and patted her, she jumped on the couch, laid her head in Ned's lap, and began licking his hand. A ghost of a smile crossed his face, so quickly Renee almost missed it. After a few minutes the teenager seemed to relax and went on to recount years of being moved from foster home to foster home, with stops in between at St. Joseph's.

Stops that usually included visits to Fr. Jeremy. "I still hate the smell of furniture oil and floor polish," the boy said in a hushed tone. "That old house stunk bad from it, and so did we after a while from polishin' the damn stuff." In Ned's telling his story Renee recognized the familiar *I'm scared to death by these surroundings* that reservation kids experienced in their treks into the outside.

Occasionally, Ned would run into one of his siblings when they were passing through St. Joseph's at the same time. He'd take them aside and counsel them on how to get along in *chimook* foster families, on the importance of not skipping school—even though he skipped himself—on what to do if they couldn't stand where they were living, and especially about drugs, alcohol, huffing, and, as they got older, sex. All the things a big brother in a family without functional parents did for his younger sibs. Things Renee remembered hearing from Ben. The only one Ned ever lived with again was brother Kevin. Two years ago, along with Kevin, two years his junior, he had landed at Floyd Neuterbide's house.

"Did you ever tell anyone what happened at St. Joseph's? A school counselor, police, anyone?" Renee asked.

Ned stole a glance at Cal. "Who'da believed me?" he retorted. As the young Ojibwa tried to pick up on his story the words lay on his tongue like rocks, unable to roll off and make a sentence until suddenly, a waterfall of words spilled out, one over the other in rapid succession. Renee and Cal felt the impact like spray at the bottom of the falls—shocking, sobering words about a dirty behavior the People had learned from their *chimook* invaders. Standing in the face of that spray, listening to what Ned said, was chilling. He told of Floyd Neuterbide, the abusive foster parent, "gettin' funky" with the boys. "It's just bogus," the teenager spit out, falling back against the lumpy couch. Ren recognized the edge of sadness in the boy's eyes. He was peering out from that empty spot in his heart. It was the kind of look that, when Renee had gotten it as a child, prompted the comment she had old eyes. Now she understood what it meant.

After a long pause, Renee asked, "How 'bout this guy. Have you reported him?"

"Granite Rock's Robocops wouldn't do a damn thing. The ol' man's friends with practically every cop over there."

"How 'bout somebody on the rez?"

"Neutie never lets us over here," the young Indian said, barely above a whisper.

His voice went straight to the back of Renee's heart. The boy's description of Neuterbide was a shocking revelation to Renee. She knew him as part of Granite Rock's conservative elite. Unlike some midwest college towns, Granite Rock was not a magnet for the country's most exciting students. It was a state college catering to reservation students, first-generation collegians off the farm, and any other students too afraid or poor to leave the northwoods. The brightest of these had been drawn away to other colleges. A number of professors taught part-time at the college and owned community businesses on the side. Floyd Neuterbide taught in the history department and owned, with his wife, the Lone Loon Resort, located at Eelpout Point on Sturgeon Lake, two miles west of the college campus. They were both active in the evangelical church and the local college circle.

The Lone Loon Resort billboard on Highway 7 boasted, *A Family Resort, home of the largest stuffed eelpout in the world: 5lbs. 13oz.* Despite its bulging eyes and large floppy mouth, everyone agreed the eelpout tasted amazingly like rock lobster—"poor man's lobster"— the locals in the Loon Bar promised visitors. People poured into the area, and especially to the Lone Loon, for the Eelpout Ice Fishing Festival every year in early February. Ice fishing off the Point was the best spot for attempting to break the record and catch the biggest, ugliest, but tastiest fish in America. Apparently, however, Floyd Neuterbide was involved in something far uglier than the eelpout.

Renee hadn't crossed paths with Professor Floyd Neuterbide regularly, but she knew of his reputation; most Red Earthers did. He'd been vocally expressing his opinion almost from the first time he drove into town more than thirty-five years ago. Her last face-to-face with the man had been at a county board meeting this past winter. Renee had gone representing the Odeima Anishanabe Kikinoamading school's field trip interests.

"I've been to meetings with this guy," Renee said to Ned and Cal after an extended silence. "When he's not tending bar in the evening at the Lone Loon Resort, ranting and raving about his favorite topic—the freeloaders of society—he comes to county meetings and beats up on the reservation." Renee spit the words out. "He bragged about carrying a pistol at one of the meetings. Said they'd have to bury him six feet under before he'd give up that right, then took the pistol out and showed it to everyone." A huge man, Neuterbide's voice had bounded up the register as his excitement grew, then plunged to a level Renee didn't know existed as he finished his point.

Owning the resort and holding a respected position in the community placed the Neuterbides at the top of the list for foster kids of all colors. Despite the Indian Child Welfare Act, which stated Native American children must be placed with Native American families, county social services routinely placed Indian kids with non-Indian families like the Neuterbides. If tribes didn't have enough staff or money to challenge the county placements, that's where they stayed.

From what Ned told Renee and Cal, life as a Neuterbide foster child sounded grim no matter what color you were. Five boys shared one floor of a bunkhouse attached to the main house—three Indian kids, one white, and one Vietnamese. The other floor housed four girls, three Indian and one white. Ned described how they often had to stand at attention by their beds at night and listen to this man with a booming voice lecture them about how they were all good-for-nothings and would never amount to a hill of beans without his help. "He tells us about all the kids who've left and ended up dead, or in jail. The old man's hands move constantly, and ya never know when he's gonna haul off and whack ya." Ned laughed cynically, "I jus' stand with my head down. If I get it, I get it," he shrugged. Renee hated the image of the kids standing by their beds scared to death of this huge man. She had seen Neuterbide's way of pounding out points in regimented order as he scythed the air furiously, and she agreed that he was a scary man.

Ren and Cal finally called for a break and went into the kitchen.

"Jesus Christ, Beltrain, we gotta get him outta there, get all of 'em outta there," Renee whispered.

"How? Bust 'em out?"

"I don't know. Somethin'. I gotta talk to Chief Bulieau." Renee shook herself like a dog shaking water from its fur and took a deep breath. "You livin' here, Cally?" Ren asked, looking for relief in another subject.

"You know me, Runner. I don't live anywhere, really."

"Stayin' here then?"

Cal nodded.

"Ever think about settling down, goin' into a different line of work?"

Cal's eyes slid away from Ren. Tongue in cheek she said, "You askin' me to marry you?" Cal caught sight of her friend's expression and laughed out loud. The full belly laugh Renee remembered filling up whole rooms in the past.

"Very funny."

"Not tryin' to be, Runner. Been thinkin' a lot about us. We were good together." Cal touched Renee's cheek.

"Now there's selective memory if I've ever seen it. You mean between the frantic, midnight car trips across country, with the break-downs and flat tires? Between the brawls with tribal councils and arrests by tribal police, the escapes and wild car runs to hide in the mountains or up here in the woods? And how about the fights and pseudo-romances with the men, the fights between you and me? Are you remembering those momentary flashes of uncomplicated, romantic love?"

"Yeah, those." The smile that crossed Cal's face went directly to Renee's heart, taking her breath away.

"I thought I'd never see that smile again," she whispered.

"I save it just for you."

"Come on, Cal, think about it for a second. You could never settle down, and with Jenny I can't be a nomad anymore." Renee's heart was beating so wildly she felt a little dizzy. This was totally unexpected. She had figured Cal was all business, that the kiss the other morning was a tease, nothing more. "Besides," she said somewhat breathlessly—"there's Samantha—"

"You're right, Runner. Don't get yourself all in a tizzy over this." Cal gave Ren a quick hug. "You're a married family woman now, I know, and I could never stop what I'm doin'. Every time I think about it, I remember what Delores Brings Her Back said to us. Remember? We'd just had a sweat. It was around midnight, and there was a full moon. We were talkin' about the Movement, our responsibility to our unborn relatives..." Caroline paused.

"I remember." Renee's voice was barely audible.

"'It's important we learn to walk lightly, because the faces of unborn relatives are looking up at us, relying on us to care respect-fully for their inheritance.' I'll never forget that."

The silence was prolonged. Finally Renee said, "You've done that, Cally. Always. Your commitment to preserving our ways is somethin' I've always respected. Look at you now, jumpin' right into this mess." Renee stepped to her friend and embraced her. "Auntie calls you a dragonfly," she whispered. "Best description I've ever heard." They stayed in the embrace for a long time before Renee reluctantly stepped away.

When they returned to the living room, Ned started again. "One night, about four months ago, the old man came up to me and Kevin and asked if we wanted to earn some extra money—we get five dol-lars a week workin' around the resort. I said maybe, wadda we gotta do?" Ned swallowed hard. "Kevin's younger, so I gotta look out for him. That ticked Neutie off—me not sayin' okay right away—and he smacked me upside my head."

Ned recounted how he and Kevin were picked up by an Indian and taken to a house on the edge of the reservation. Ned told about the liquor and drugs they were plied with, and the sex acts they were both sweet-talked and forced into performing. Things they did to themselves and to each other while the men videotaped them.

Renee's rage grew as she listened to the boy describe the event. "Who was there, Ned?"

"Couple of skins and two *chimooks*." Ned spit the words out like they were a bad taste in his mouth.

"Neuterbide didn't go with you?"

The boy shook his head.

"Can you describe everybody?"

"Skins were both old. Maybe in their thirties, forties. One was a Shanab, one not. The one that wasn't had long hair, tied back. The Shanab had boots I'd recognize, definitely recognize. Red and black. Fancy."

"Did the Anishanabe have short hair?"

Ned nodded. "Really short. Military type. He was dark." Ned stood and began to pace.

"How 'bout the other Indian?"

"Long hair, like I said. Thin, no pot belly. He was dark, too. Mighta been a dog-eater."

Renee smiled at the boy's use of the nickname Ojibwa had for their Lakota neighbors. "There's a couple Lakota at school. One's a teacher, name of Crocker. He's got long hair, but...," Ren's voice trailed off, "I can't imagine it'd be him. He's such a quiet guy." She glanced at Cal and Ned, a distressed look on her face. "Didya get any names, Ned?"

"Naw, didn't really notice."

Renee was fascinated with the boy's body language. He'd go from hugging his knees to his chest to slouched and sprawling carelessly on the couch, depending on where he was in his story. At the moment, he was sprawled on the couch, looking like any other teenager, without a care in the world.

Next Renee asked, "How 'bout the *chimooks?*"

The fourteen-year-old arched his eyebrows and, with a half-smile, said, "They all look alike don't they?" The burst of laughter amongst them relieved the mounting repulsion they all felt. Renee was glad to see Ned hadn't lost his sense of humor.

After relating several more incidents at the house, the boy looked completely drained. "I think we'll stop, Neddy," Cal intervened. "We don't have to hear everything now. And you gotta get home soon," she added. The teenager was back standing at the window. "Bo's comin' back to get ya."

"Be better off dead," Ned responded in a fragile voice.

"Come on, Ned. You don't want that," Renee implored the boy.

"Wouldn't be so bad. Bullet goes whack an' you go black. All over in a second, eh?" He shrugged his shoulders.

Renee could see that he was at least half-serious. "Where do the Neuterbides think you are, Ned?" Renee asked, changing the subject.

He turned away from the front window. "Neutie took Mai to the University Hospital in Minneapolis to get her club foot checked. Mrs. is easier to get around."

"Do you like her?" She hoped there was at least one adult in his life that was treating him decently.

The young Ojibwa shrugged. "She's okay."

"Does she know what's goin' on?"

"Don't think so. He's mean to her too."

"Is there a way we can be in contact with you, Ned? You know...so we can get you if we have questions, be sure you're okay? I don't want you forced into any more videos or anything else you've had to do with that pig."

"I can take care of myself," Ned countered defensively.

"Right. I know, I jus' thought—"

"We've got a signal, Runner," Cal interjected.

"Good, good."

Ned went to gather up his things, and Renee made ready to leave. Shrugging into her jacket, she turned to Cal, who grabbed her lapels and pulled her close. "Runner, you gotta get this pig Neuterbide arrested. I know this is what Rosa stumbled on. I bet the asshole killed her."

"Slow up, Cally. I'm gonna talk to the chief. Are you sure Ned and the others are safe there for now?"

"Asshole's not due back for a day or so."

"We're gonna have to move fast then. Are you willing to talk to Hobey? Cause he's gonna need some clear solid stuff to get the Feds goin' on this."

"What? I talk to him and he gives me up to the FeeBees. No thanks, that's what you're for, girlfriend." Renee could feel Caroline Beltrain pull away.

"How 'bout on the phone?" It was quiet for several minutes before Cal nodded and grunted a reluctant yes. "So, we'll be in touch then, eh? Soon." Renee gave her old lover a hug, separating quickly. Just to be safe.

Leaving the apartment, Renee and the *animoosh* almost ran into two neatly scrubbed white men in their early twenties. Their starched white shirts, black pants, and black ties gave them away. The "Mormonaries" was how they were known on the rez, because Mormons came to Red Earth on two-year missions to convert the red skins. Renee doubted they had much success, but they always had smiles on their faces, so Renee returned the pleasantry. She smiled wider at the thought of them knocking on apartment 206. Cal didn't cotton much to outsiders.

With a pause in the emotions of the morning, Renee recognized the gnawing in her stomach as hunger. It was almost noon. She picked up the police cell phone in the jeep.

"*Boozho*, Tribal Police."

"Hobey? Answerin' your own phone now?"

"Bobbi's still out with the flu."

Renee drew a deep breath. "We gotta talk. Jus' came from seein' Cal and she's got some stuff that's gonna blow you away."

"Sounds serious."

"Somethin' I've never had to deal with before. You got time now?"

"I can't now, Renny, tribal council meeting."

Agreeing to meet after she taught her afternoon class, Renee hung up, then dialed home. Two rings, three, before a breathless Samantha picked up.

"Hello?"

"Ah, my sweets, it is I. Shall I return from the wilds for lunch?"

"Come on ahead, I've shoveled a path for the two of you."

"How sweet. Hold that feeling, my love, I'll be right there." Renee sighed and turned on the car radio. "Brown-eyed Girl" was playing. "Oh God, Mukie, Caroline used to sing this to me." She flipped the song off. More stress was not something she needed right now. Second-guessing perverts, crazies, and the *ef-bee-eye* made her feel weird enough. She took a deep breath and prayed the morning out of her mind. When she turned the radio back on, pow wow music filled the airwaves and she daydreamed about Samantha the rest of the way home. Most of the roads were cleared and the drive was pleasant, the sun glinting off the new snow. "Sun keeps shinin' like this, snow'll be gone again in two days, Mukie." Renee reached over and rubbed the cocker's belly. "Spring's on the way. Can you feel it?"

Renee and Mukwa trudged in the back door of their two-room log cabin, Ren shucking her parka and Sorrels on the way to the kitchen. Opening the refrigerator, she stood staring into it and drifted off. That was where Samantha found her. "See part of your new investigation in there, or are you watching a k.d. lang performance?" Sam whispered in her lover's ear, sliding her arms around her waist.

Ren could feel the heat from Samantha's body on her back. She turned around, enveloping her in a bear hug. Images of Sam's naked body floated before her eyes, and Renee had a sudden need for some normal passion. Pulling her lover over to the bed, Ren gently laid her down and began exploring Sam's body with the curiosity of her first time. Opening Samantha's blouse, she gently touched her breast. A groan started deep in Renee's belly, and she'd just about fumbled through removing Sam's blouse when she heard Jenny outside thanking someone for the ride. "Oh my God, Sammy, Jenny's home." They scrambled to redress and rearrange, managing to get all four feet off the bed and onto the floor by the time JJ banged her way into the cabin.

"I'm home," she yelled.

Mukwa bounded off the bed and into Jenny's arms, licking her face excitedly. *Thank God you're home, JJ. These two are so boring when they've been apart for a while.*

"Hi honey, *anin*," Renee called in a croaking voice, trying to erase the passion in it. "Welcome home. We sure did miss you last night," she added, winking at Samantha. Then, clearing her throat, she said, "You're home early."

"Teachers' meeting and no basketball practice today 'cause of the tournament last weekend," Jenny said, seemingly unaware of how nervous her parents were. "And softball meeting was postponed 'til tomorrow 'cause of all the snow. What's to eat around here, anyway? I'm starving."

Renee and Samantha looked at each other. "Jenny's home," they said in unison, before busting out in belly laughs.

# 4

Renee trudged into the cabin hauling the last of the night's wood supply. It was quiet except for the crackling of the fire. Before closing the door she glanced out at the narrow crescent of the Budding Trees Moon, hanging like a lantern in the leafless branches of the tallest birch tree. Dropping the wood into its bin, she joined Samantha and Jenny at the table. "Wow, smells great in here." Over the rim of her thick white mug, Ren studied Sam's face as it danced with the fire shadows, putting her expressions first in the light, then the darkness. Sam shifted in her chair, and the fire flared in her deep-blue eyes, making them flash and sparkle. The scene brought a contented smile to Ren's face.

"So, Mom, how's your old girlfriend?" Jenny's question halted Renee's mug in mid-air.

"Old girlfriend?"

"Yeah. What's her name, Caroline?" Jenny winked at Samantha.

Ren looked from her daughter to her partner. "Why do I get the feeling that I'm being set up here?"

Sam and JJ shrugged in unison, continuing to eat their supper.

"Well?" Renee persisted.

The ringing phone drew Jenny, with a shrug of her shoulders and an impish grin, to the living room and back into her teenage world.

"Old girlfriend. Now there's an interesting phrase," Samantha said, after minutes of heavy silence. Picking up her and Jenny's dishes, she made her way to the kitchen sink.

"It's a boring phrase," Renee said, trying to put a tone of finality on the conversation.

"Oh, I don't know."

"I do."

"Are you avoiding this discussion?"

"What discussion?"

"Renee Morning Star LaRoche!"

"Okay, okay."

"Okay, okay what?" Sam returned to the table and drew a chair up snug against Renee's.

"My relationship with Caroline Beltrain was over eighteen years ago."

"Did you love her?"

"I loved what we were, the purpose of our lives. The Movement. Sharing it with her increased the excitement. You know how that is. You believe in somethin' together, you plan an action around it together, you do the action together, then you talk about it and rehash it over and over together."

The expression on Sam's face turned wooden, again stopping Renee's mug half-way to her lips.

"I know this investigation is something you feel you have to do." The dirgelike sound of Sam's voice startled Ren. This wasn't funny anymore.

"Sammy, I have to look into this for Caroline. But I'd never betray us. You have to believe that."

Samantha's nod was heavy. Ren took a deep breath and closed her eyes. "I promise, *saiagi iwed.*"

"I believe that's what you want to do, Renny. Whether you can or not..." Sam's voice fell off.

Renee sighed. "Have you ever noticed how loud silence can be sometimes?"

In a barely audible voice Samantha said, "I can't compete with all that, Renee. Plus the fact she's Ojibwa."

"You don't have to compete with anyone. Where's all this comin' from?" Renee leaned over and laid her arm across her partner's shoulders.

"Sometimes I see you as the Catcher in the Rye, Renee, standing at the edge of the cliff trying to save the world." Sam ran her hand down Renee's cheek. "I know how you get on this stuff, Renny. Doing it with Caroline can bring back a lot of good memories and feelings."

"It'll be okay, *saiagi iwed*."

"You're setting me up, Renee. I don't like you doing this kind of thing. I worry. She's in it with you so you get support from her. I don't dare say anything about my fears because I'm afraid it'll drive you further into her arms."

"I already told her I'm crazy about you. That you're my one and only." Renee's voice was soft and loving.

"You did?" A hint of the familiar teasing whine was creeping into Sam's voice, raising a cautious smile on Ren's face.

"Uh huh." Renee gave Sam's lower lip a little pinch, then took her face in her hands. "I love you now. What I had with Cal was a long time ago, in a different life."

They sat staring into each other's eyes. Finally, Samantha said, "Can you understand how it could make me a little insecure?"

"Yes, I can."

The night spirits were busy in the LaRoche cabin the rest of the evening.

The squeak of the ladder the next morning startled Renee awake. A question pushed at her. She laid her left arm across Sam's side of the bed, then smiled. It wasn't a dream; her lover was back. Ren's next thought was of the conversation from last night, and her smile evaporated. Groaning, she rolled over and slid out from under the covers, careful not to disturb her sleeping partner. If they were going to take up where they left off last night, she needed a run and morning prayers first. Grabbing her medicine bag off the table, she glimpsed her reflection in the tiny, round mirror hanging next to the east window. The sun was just coming up, and the slant of the sun's rays caught the brush of gray hair at her widow's peak. "You're either tired or gettin' old, LaRoche," she muttered to the sleepy image. "Get your butt movin'," she added, squinting out the window. "Grandfather Sun's been up a half hour already."

Renee slipped quietly from the cabin, Mukwa at her heels, into the silence of the dawning day. Ankle-deep in snow, she walked slowly around the yard offering her morning prayer. When she finished, Mukwa thrust her cold nose into the two-legged's hand. Ren rubbed the cocker's ears vigorously, then slid the medicine bag into her anorak pocket and set out on the tree-protected running path. At the section of the trail where the land fell away into the deep, long valley of the Journey River, she slowed to revel in the gloriousness of the sunrise, pushing the memory of Jed Morriseau's body on the river flats below far back in her memory.

Renee stomped her feet on the entrance rug of the tribal police station, trying to shake loose the wet snow. "Mornin' everybody. Big storm so late in the season, eh?"

"Pretty big," Hobey said, in his usual less-than-garrulous way. "That why you look so tired? Snow keep you up shovelin'?"

"Huh? Oh, no. Me and Sam, we...oh, it's complicated."

"Joyce's one who likes to talk late at night, too. Darkness makes her think of all her problems, she says." Hobey offered Renee a brief smile. "One of the southwest tribes has a tradition that if you have troubles, you dig a hole and talk into it, giving your troubles to Mother Earth. Then you fill the hole and leave them there." Hobey smiled again. "Buddy in Korea told me that."

"I'll remember to tell Samantha that. Any call back from the FBI?" Ren piled her winter jacket, scarf, and cap on the clothes tree in the corner.

"Our favorite, Agent Lawton. Bless his little white heart."

"Well, I woulda blessed somethin' a little lower, but is he gonna help us?"

"He's comin' by. So long as Neuterbide's outta town right now and the boys are safe, I'm jus' gonna feel Lawton out, see what we can do without the FeeBees." Hobey stared out the window. "All that jurisdiction crap. Neuterbide's off the rez, but he sure as hell seems to have our kids."

"Same problem with Rosa Mae."

"You said her dad's a Cree healer?"

Renee nodded.

Hobey looked pensive. "I was thinkin' we could combine a new autopsy with digging her up to send her home." The chief glanced at Renee. "Got a number I can get Mr. Two Thunder at?"

"Ellis."

"Ellis."

"I'll get it from Cal."

"I'd like to talk to your friend, too."

"I told her you did, Chief."

"And?"

"And well, she's not too trusting where cops are concerned. You know the Movement's had some bad run-ins with tribal cops."

"We'll have to work it out, LaRoche. I wanna talk to her."

"Okay, I'll set it up." Renee agreed to do it but dreaded the actual event. "Not to change the subject but...Hobey, do ya think it'd be unethical if I looked at Caroline Beltrain's rap sheet?"

"I don't know. Have you asked yourself why you want to?"

The chief peered up from the paper in his hand. "Okay, Bobbi, looks good. Thank God you're back. I'll need this by one o'clock." He handed the 10-34 BCA autopsy requisition form back to her and turned to Renee. "That's when I meet with the judge to see about gettin' Rosa's body back up top so we can take a look." Hobey finished his coffee, tossing the empty paper cup at the basket as he passed it. Missing, he stooped, picked it up, and this time effected a right hook. The shot was on target, raising a big smile on his face and a whistle to his lips. "Say, LaRoche, got Two Thunder's hand blown up. You remember, the picture?"

Following Hobey into his office, Renee examined the blow-up of Rosa Mae's left hand. The enlargement displayed the crude reservation tattoo, LOVE, across the woman's fingers. The dark mark on the back of her hand was faint and blurry but unmistakable. "A bear, Chief?"

"That's what I see, too."

"The stamp of a bear's head. Someplace with a cover charge? A bar, maybe...over on the campus?" The pause was brief. "How 'bout the Bear's Den?"

"I'll go along with that." Hobey tilted his chair back, clasped his hands behind his head, and crossed his cowboy-booted feet on top of his desk.

"Recent, too, or it'd be wiped off."

Hobey grunted, regarding Renee carefully, and grinning.

"What're you smilin' at?"

"Why aren't you a cop, LaRoche?"

"Me?"

His smile broadened. "Yeah, you."

"Never happen."

"Why not?"

"Jeez, Chief, if I was a cop, I'd have to start obeyin' the law." Renee smirked.

"That'd be a stretch for you, eh?"

"Plus, don't you have to be of high moral character?" Bobbi called from the front room.

"All right, all right. Impugning my character—or whatever that word is—jus' because I didn't give you sympathy about bein' sick?" Renee walked out to the chief's assistant and gave her shoulder a slug. "I'll check on the Bear's Den, Chief. Let ya know."

"You know I love ya. How ya doin' girl?" Bobbi looked up from her desk.

"Pretty good. Samantha's back. I never knew a week could feel like such a long time. Me and Jenny and Mukwa been rattlin' 'round the house without her. Then Jenny left for a few days with the basketball team, their last tournament of the season, so it was jus' me and Ms. Blackness here." Mukwa gave a high-spirited bark.

"Samantha gonna have to do this much now that she's a famous author?"

"God, I hope not! But she loves it, you know, major extrovert that she is."

"Did ya tell her your old girlfriend's back in town?"

"That's what kept us up last night."

"Jealousy's a mean-spirited tramp, eh?"

"I guess." Renee was still caught off-guard when Bobbi's teasing included her lesbian relationship. With Gram's help, though, Bobbi'd come a long way on that subject.

"By the way, LaRoche, I talked to Jesse about that call to the sheriff's office to ID Rosa's body," Hobey said from his office. "Jesse said they should have a tape of that call. If they say they taped over it, she told me tapes have somethin' called ghost prints left on 'em even after they've been used again. You use a decoder that slows the tape down and you can hear the ghost print under the voiceover, I guess. We jus' gotta figure out how to get the tape. We're gonna have to ask the Feds for help on this one, too, so prepare your friend Cal. The *ef-bee-eye*'s comin' to town!" Renee grinned at the reference. It sounded matter-of-fact, but she could hear the edge in the chief's voice. There wasn't a tribal police unit in Indian Country that liked working with the *chimook* FBI except the corrupt ones that were already in bed with them.

Just then Officer Jesse Johnson stumbled headlong into the office, buried in her Iditarod parka, mad-bomber cap, and Canadian Sorrels. "Here comes the pride of Red Earth tribal police now," Hobey hollered out uncharacteristically.

"Hi everybody, *boozho.*" Jesse tugged her parka off and tossed it onto the already overloaded clothes tree.

Chief Bulieau had come to rely on Officer Jesse Johnson a great deal the last two years. Her college degree in criminal justice was a valuable addition to the eight-member Red Earth tribal police force. Jesse was the one Hobey usually picked to send to conferences and police training up-dates. She'd just returned from an advanced course at the Minnesota Police Academy Training Center that included a section done by the FBI on its relationship to local police departments.

"So, you think we can verify what Caroline told me about calling the sheriff's office?" Renee queried.

"That's what they said at that fancy training Hobey gave up Las Vegas for."

"You get all the perks, eh?"

"She deserves 'em," Hobey chimed in. "Done more to clean up the rez in the little time she's been here than we did for five years before."

"Our hero," Bobbi laughed.

"That's right."

"You're our hero too, Chief," Bobbi added.

"Not me. Saw Will Rogers once when I was in the army. He said, 'We can't all be heroes. Somebody has to sit on the curb and cheer.' That's me, a curb-sitter."

The women in the front office looked from one to the other shaking their heads. The chief might be a curb-sitter, but he was a good guy. Always thinking of the other person. He'd used money designated by the tribe for his continuing education to send Jesse to the training with the FBI. Money that other tribal police chiefs gladly used to "attend conferences" in their favorite vacation spot, Las Vegas.

"Jess, think you could give me a lesson on what you learned about the NCIC?" Renee asked. "I know the politics, but not the technical stuff. Thought maybe we could use Beltrain's file."

"Well," Jesse sneaked a peek at Hobey—

"LaRoche's practically one of us now, even though she'd never admit it." Hobey winked at the three women. "I think we can give her this...no questions asked."

Renee could feel her face getting hot.

"Now?" Jesse reached for a cup of coffee.

"That's good for me."

"Okay, I can do that. Let's see. How about an overview first." Jesse moved to the computer. "The National Crime Information Center, NCIC, was set up in 1967 by the FBI as a way for local PDs to have almost instant access to a national criminal list. There's about 110,000 terminals around the country now. At the training the Feds told us they do about a million and a half transactions a day, providing lists of stolen property, wanted fugitives, criminal records. Hoover was against it at first. Said it was too expensive."

"Sounds like that tight old fart," Renee interjected. She watched the comment bring red into Jesse's cheeks. Poking her playfully, Renee grinned, "Not used to my word choices yet, eh?"

"Anyway," Jesse cleared her throat, "the Feds told us they authorize who can use the system, but I talked with local cops who said the code words the FBI gives to locals find their way onto a lot of PI rolodexes. So although the FBI claims the system's never been cracked, the human factor contradicts that."

"You just type in a name and wait for a response?"

"That's about it, then put in the code from our office. Why don't you type Caroline's name in and let's see what happens." Renee took a deep breath. It felt a little sneaky, but curiosity about Cal's last eighteen years had gotten the best of her. After Renee entered her friend's name, Jesse added the Red Earth Tribal Police code and they sat back. "Shouldn't take too long," Jesse said, leaning forward and grasping her crossed knees with both hands. A few minutes later the printer began to whir, indicating a response was coming. It was slow at first, almost self-conscious about what it was sending, but soon the speed picked up. Apparently having resolved its conflict, the printer released one line after another in rapid succession:

Caroline S. Beltrain, aka Cal Beltrain, aka Sue Beltrain. Arrested by Minneapolis PD; Bemidji, MN PD; Rapid City, SD PD; Hennepin and Chippewa County MN SD; Pine Ridge Reservation TP; Red Earth Reservation TP.

The rap sheet listed charges with convictions for carrying a concealed weapon, possession of marijuana, inciting a riot, disorderly conduct, and auto theft. Additional charges included DWI X3, parole violations X4, plus failure to appear and flight to avoid prosecution. Renee knew the rap sheet would've been another three pages if her juvenile records had been included. She read the main printout, then started on Appendix B, Cal's parole jacket. It included a detailed report from her Chippewa County parole officer. Ren could tell the officer didn't like her friend much, adding statements to the report like, "This Indian woman continues her shiftless, nomad, drinking lifestyle. She's never held a job more than two months." Renee assumed the last comment meant the parole officer didn't consider Cal's four-year executive director position with the Movement, or her three years before that as Movement Secretary, real jobs. The report ended stating Caroline Beltrain was a sociopathic personality and could never be rehabilitated. Cal's last contact with her parole officer had been three months ago. She had failed to show up for her last two appointments. "Who can blame her?" Renee muttered. Intense pressure changes things, she thought to herself, like carbon into diamonds. The system had never given her friend the respect and honor she deserved. From their point of view, the pressure had not produced a diamond. Renee disagreed.

A wave of memories about life with Cal, most of them on the back of Caroline's motorcycle, washed over her. There'd been a sexuality exuding from the black-and-chrome chopper, and watching her lover swing her leg over the saddle and settle in had sent a quiver through Renee's pelvis—from the very first time she rode with her. Sitting behind Cal scared Ren to death, feeling the power of the bike as the heat oozed up from its growling engine and over her thighs. She remembered the thrill as Cal gunned the motor, popped the clutch, and leaned the bike over sharply at the first turn out of Sparky's Bar parking lot, just off the rez on Highway 7. It was one of those times so terrifying, it sucked the fear out of the moment and left an exhilaration that made Renee scream with ecstasy. Then there was the time they tried to take the curve at Sucker Creek. They must have been doing fifty. Ren guessed Cal put the Harley down at about thirty, and they flew straight off the lip of the road into the creek. Creator was with them that night—the creek was full with winter run-off and the high water saved their lives.

"Renny? You still with us?"

"What? Oh, sorry. Daydreamin'."

"By the look on your face it must of been a good one," Jesse replied, giving her friend a nudge. "Seein' old friends'll do that to ya, eh? Cal's history's pretty colorful."

Renee's distant look returned. "I can't decide if she's a criminal or a hero of the People." Renee tossed the report onto Bobbi's desk. "I know I wanted to see that, but now I'm not sure it did me any good to be so curious."

Jesse and Bobbi looked at each other knowingly. "Just remember, Renny," Bobbi urged, "she's the same person now as she was before you knew all of that. You know the woman's heart."

"Dragonfly."

"Huh?"

"Nothin'. Somethin' Auntie said. You're right," Renee nodded. "I can do that. We've been friends too long to let a little—or even a big—rap sheet get in the way. Besides, it's the *chimook*'s view of her, not mine." Ren paused, then whispered, "What do you think the chief'd say?"

"I say don't give the chief something to say about, if you get my drift." Bobbi winked.

"Got it." Renee picked up the report and stuffed it into her pack.

"Where you off to, Renny?"

"You know how every once in a while you meet somebody and they scope out a little spot in your heart and jus' kinda settle there?" Both women nodded. "I've gotta follow up on somethin' a kid like that, a young boy with a very old soul, told me."

Ned had a good memory for directions to the house he and Kevin had been taken to, and getting in was easier than Renee anticipated. Of course, the lock pick set she got a hold of while doing Movement work and, at times, had to use to get into places where she wasn't invited, was a big help. "Wayta go, LaRoche. You haven't lost your touch," she whispered, as the lock clicked and she cracked the door open.

An uninvited entrance presented several problems, not the least of which was that you never knew who, or what, might be on the other side of the door. Even if you thought the place was empty.

Once inside, Renee eased the door shut until she heard the familiar click. Her heart was racing, sweat beginning to bead on her forehead. Lifting her booted foot, she warily stepped away from the door. For several long minutes Ren surveyed the living room, listening with a tracker's ear for noise she prayed she wouldn't hear. Once certain the only sound was her nervous breathing, she took another step into the room. It was in total disarray, as if someone had gotten there before her. Whoever it was seemed to have been after specific items. It wasn't the usual break-in—the TV, VCR, and stereo were untouched. At the darkly painted archway between the living room and the rest of the tiny, crumbling house, Renee hesitated. She caught sight of three doors down the hall. All closed. One, she figured to be a closet; one, no doubt, the bathroom; and the last one probably a bedroom. "Pray to Creator there's no one behind one of those damn doors, LaRoche," she muttered to herself, wishing she hadn't left Mukwa and her woods dog nose in the jeep.

The Bear Clan sleuth made a rapid visual sweep of the clutter. Overturned chairs, books pulled from their shelves, a broken lamp on the floor, CDs and video tapes strewn from one end of the room to the other. In the middle of the floor was what appeared to be a carrying case just the right size to hold video cassettes. It was open, with four commercial movie videos tossed next to it. Renee picked the case up and set it aside as possible evidence.

She walked to the first door and paused to listen. After several seconds, she grasped the doorknob with a gloved hand. Turning it slowly, Ren waited for the anticipated click as the knob released its inner workings from the doorjamb. The door opened into a bathroom. A quick perusal found the small room empty, so Renee moved across the hall to the next door. A closet full of towels and cleaning supplies. "All the trappings of home," the Indian woman grumbled, tiptoeing down the hallway to door number three. "You have to be the bedroom," she whispered to the last closed door, not sure why she was still being so quiet. "Is this where it happened? Where all the ugly, sick things Ned talked about took place?" It took Renee three attempts before she could force herself to open the door.

The bedroom door was not shut tight, and a small push slid it open. A scene from an X-rated movie studio greeted her. Strobe lights were situated around the room. The bed was made up with red satin sheets, a teddy bear perched on top of king-size pillows. A dream net hung on the wall above the bed. Renee stood paralyzed, staring at the scene. Here it was, the center of a disgusting storm that had sucked two young Red Earth boys up, then deposited them back into their ordinary, everyday lives like they were friends of Dorothy's returning from the Land of Oz.

A video camera sat on a tripod near the east wall. To Renee's dismay, it was empty. Mirrors overlaid the ceiling. The closet door was open, the closet also empty. As she left the bedroom, something caught her eye. Sun streaming in the east window was shimmering off an object on the windowsill. Upon closer inspection, Renee found a single key dangling from a key chain sporting a gold-plated *J* and a tiny emblem of some sort. Ren stood for a few minutes examining what she'd stumbled upon, realizing Creator's hand in her discovery. An hour or less either way, a cloudy day, a different turn of her head, and she might never have noticed the shiny object. Renee swept it off the sill into a baggy retrieved from her pocket.

Back in the living room, the Ojibwa lowered herself into an overstuffed chair by the windows, next to the phone. She punched the buttons with a pencil. "Chief? Renee here." She gave a brief description of the place.

"How'd you get in there, LaRoche?"

"Jus' come over, okay? It's on the southern edge of the rez. Take County 3 south to Little Fork. Jus' past the turn-out there's an overgrown road, only goes left. The house is at the end. The bedroom's exactly like Ned described it, so's the rest of the house. Not much of importance left though. I don't know how they knew I was comin', Chief, but looks like somebody got here before me."

"Stay put, LaRoche. We're on our way." Renee heard Hobey grumbling about her being there alone as he hung up. All she could hope was he'd cool off by the time he got there.

Waiting for the tribal police, Renee ran over what she knew so far. Rosa Mae Two Thunder had been murdered. That was almost certain. Ren didn't know how yet, but she was convinced she'd been killed, taken to that remote spot on the Jaspers farm, and left there. Dumping the victim's car nearby, the murderer—or murderers—had tried to cover their tracks, make it look like a suicide, or an accident. To Renee that said Rosa Mae must have been on to something. Why else would they go to all the trouble of disguising her death? Those involved might have felt threatened by what she knew and worried her death would lead back to them. "She was getting close to something," Renee affirmed out loud, "and somehow they knew how close she was. Maybe she talked to one of 'em but didn't know it." She made a mental note to speak to Jesse about going over Rosa's car, and soon. Renee figured the murderer was a *chimook*. One of the few things the autopsy did report was finding strands of blond hair caught on the ring on Rosa Mae's right hand. Cal could be right. Rosa Mae might have uncovered what Ned was involved in, and that's why she was murdered. The videos the men were shooting apparently were not just for themselves; Ned had overheard them talking about advertising in papers.

"Did they know I was comin'?" Renee groaned, returning to the current itch she couldn't scratch, "And who is *they?*" But someone had definitely been here, and not to rob the place. This was a deliberate kind of messiness. The only videos still around were commercially made movies. And one video carrying case was missing. She could tell there'd been two by the dust markings on the shelf near the VCR. Who? How? "Goddamnit," she muttered, disappointed she hadn't gotten to the house first. She'd see if Bobbi could trace the owner of the property.

She back-tracked over and over in her mind, going through what she'd done after first hearing about the house from Ned. Finally, it hit her: she and Hobey had talked about Ned and this place on the police band radio yesterday. Anyone with a police scanner could've heard their conversation and put two and two together. "The sheriff's department, maybe. They could've monitored our calls and picked it up," Renee speculated, not worrying about anyone hearing her now. "If they thought I'd come here, they coulda beat me to it and cleared the apartment out."

The only thing Renee hoped the intruders might have left was a fingerprint or two. She could still pray for that at least. "But if they're pros, we won't find one. Goddamnit, and it's my fault. A real cop would've thought of that. I already knew the sheriff's office was suspect. I should've been more careful." Renee threw the pencil she was still holding full force across the room. It was a dead hit on the TV power button. Channel 3, the CNN news channel, flashed on. *Not bad, LaRoche, good shot.* Renee grinned. *You'd of been an excellent knife-thrower in the old days.*

It took another minute for her to realize what had just happened. The people using this place were probably not having intellectual discussions about the news of the day or watching CNN for their personal enlightenment. The TV was set on Channel 3 because it had to be there in order to watch a video.

Stumbling over the mess in the middle of the room, Renee dove for the VCR. She pulled her finger back moments before she smeared her fingerprints on the control buttons. *For chrissake, LaRoche, get a grip.* Retrieving the pencil from where it had landed, she was about to turn on the machine when there was a knock at the door. Renee sucked in a big breath.

"LaRoche. It's us. You in there, girl?" The door opened a crack and Hobey peeked his head in. He spotted Renee on the floor. "Bored?" he smiled, as he and Jesse stepped into the small box of a living room. "You look like you're about to watch a little TV."

"It's a long story, but I was about to check the VCR. As you can see, the place's been tossed. All the videos are gone except—"

She crossed her fingers, pushed the VCR button with the pencil, and hit PLAY. The two Red Earth police officers took seats on the battered couch. Silence, except for the clicks and whirs behind the black plastic of the VCR, filled the room. The screen was robin's egg blue. A white tracking message ran along the bottom with a tiny asterisk bouncing from dot to dot.

"Come on dots, you can do it, give us what we're afraid you've got." Renee spoke softly, through prayerful hands.

Everything was suspended for a millisecond, as though the universe was deciding whether the ends justified the means, whether showing this video was worth it to get the people who made it. Then the music started. "A B C D E F G..." The children's alphabet song stopped on *K*, the *K* expanded to KIDS, then KIDDIES, in a child's handwriting across the screen. The lights came up in what Renee recognized as the bedroom down the hall with the red satin sheets. The teddy bear sat on the pillows, and the dream catcher hung on the wall. She looked up at Jesse and the chief. "Thank the Creator, they forgot the one in the VCR," Renee said grimly. "Almost missed it myself." The three Ojibwa watched another few minutes before the images on the screen of their young, naked Ojibwa brothers were so disturbing that they turned it off.

"We can look at the rest of this later," Hobey said, "but I think I'll jus' turn it over to the Feds. Let that stiff-necked Lawton look at it. It's his people that invented this crap," the chief snapped. After a long pause he added, "This house bein' on the rez, at least we've got some jurisdiction now."

Officer Josh Fairbanks arrived with the fingerprint kit. Renee chose that moment to leave. "Gotta get to Gram's before Auntie pulls another one on Samantha."

"I wanna talk to you, Renee." Hobey followed her out of the tiny run-down plywood house.

"You'd never know what's been goin' on in there by the looks of this place, eh Chief?"

"And you never know what's goin' on in your head by lookin' at you, LaRoche. Why in hell did you come out here alone?"

"I know, it was stupid. You said you had that hearing with the BCA folks, and Jesse had to be at school for that safety week thing. Guess I jus' didn't wanna wait." Renee gave a slight shrug.

"If you're gonna keep takin' on these cop-like jobs, I want you to get yourself a gun." Hobey put on his stern, you-listen-to-me-now face. "The thought of you comin' to a place like this unarmed and alone," he growled, "makes me very nervous."

"Oh DAD, come on now. I don't need a gun. You'll protect me," Renee kidded, trying to lighten the mood. They'd talked about this before.

The chief's scowl deepened. "We're going into Thunder Lake and buy you a gun. And not one of those little Lady Smiths, either. Jesse's gonna teach you how to fire a Smith and Wesson Chief's Special, or a .44 Magnum."

Renee turned and made a face at Hobey. "Not in this lifetime," she called, as she got into her jeep. Rolling down the window, she added, "Jeez, Chief, first ya make me carry around a cell phone. Now this. The stuff you give me keeps gettin' heavier and fancier, more and more ominous. Next thing I'll be strapped with grenades and haulin' an automatic Tech DC 9 assault weapon."

The chief gave a loud *harrumpf* and strode back toward the house. Opening the door, he called over his shoulder, "Jus' remember what I said, LaRoche, and don't forget I want to talk to Caroline Beltrain. And very soon."

"I'm workin' on it, Chief."

# 5

Renee pulled in next to the giant Eastern pine. She killed the motor and sat staring at the house built by her Grandpa Coon almost eighty years before. Though located across the field and woods from the LaRoche family home, this was where Renee really grew up. And for sure, this was where almost all her good memories came from. She stepped out of the jeep as smells of supper drifted across the melting snow in the yard. Smells that, growing up, always drew her and Mollie there to eat because Gramps hunted and trapped most of their food. You could count on moose liver and onions; elk heart, fried potatoes and fiddlesticks; or backstrap steaming on the cookstove any day but Friday. Fridays, Gram simmered fish with a rice and raisin dish, in case any Catholic friends dropped in.

"You know, stillness is something I've learned since I've been here." Renee heard her partner's voice almost before she was in the door. "Gram, you told me once about a year ago that the gifts of stillness never end, and that it's the cornerstone of character. I'm beginning to understand what you were saying." Samantha's smile was one Renee had never seen before. "Stillness as a quality, I mean," Sam continued, "or even as an art form. It was a foreign concept to me." She looked up at Renee, who was shucking layers of winter clothes in the corner between kisses from the cocker spaniel.

"We're pretty foreign here all right," the Ojibwa woman smiled at her partner.

"Please, Renee," Samantha insisted, "no jokes. I'm trying to explain something." Turning back to Renee's grandmother, she continued, "Someone wrote once that writing is like having a baby: it makes you pay attention. My writing up here has made me pay attention to something really important. Stillness."

Renee sat down on the couch next to Samantha, Mukwa on her lap. "I'm all ears and stillness, my dear." Sam's scowl prompted Renee to purse her lips, making a locking motion with her fingers.

"Thank you. All right, as I was saying, Gram, I never forgot something you told me, that in stillness you can filter life through your heart, observe it through the eyes of your soul. I thought about that a lot on this last trip and discovered I am seeing stillness differently now," Samantha continued. "I know it has its own importance, even though I still see it as contrast to movement, or action. Like the stillness in a modern dance piece, for example, a kind of pause between the action, with no value itself."

Renee's furrowed brow said she wasn't quite tracking with her partner yet.

"Anishanabe are taught stillness has a value all its own. It doesn't have to be compared to anything." Gram rocked in her chair and stared out the darkened window.

"A light went on for me when I realized how much I've changed these last few years, but I was disheartened to see how far I have to go." Samantha shrugged.

"Sammy, it seems you use big words like *disheartened* almost like shields to your real feelings," Renee offered. "And you're always lookin' at how far you have to go, so you're not happy with where you're at right now."

"But I'm better. Look at the revelation I've just had. Aren't you proud of this dyed-in-the-wool WASP?"

"Yes I am, *saiagi iwed*. Yes I am." Renee put an arm around Samantha. The elder *ikkwe* smiled.

If there hadn't already been a trickster in Ojibwa tradition, Renee was sure her auntie would be the prototype. Ojibwa tricksters learned their role from Coyote, and Lydia took her position as family contrary seriously. Her latest antics started at supper when Samantha complimented her on the meat she served.

"Is it beef, Auntie?" the New Englander asked innocently.

"You could prob'ly say that," Lydia said with the tiniest of smiles. Renee groaned as Samantha pursued it. "*Probably?*"

"I learned this kinda huntin' a long time ago," Lydia began with a straight face. "Drivin' into town I move every dead squirrel, rabbit, coon I find off to the side of the road." She winked at Renee. "Comin' back I pick up all the new ones. They're the fresh ones." Lydia gave Gram a poke, motioning with her lips at Samantha.

Sam's mouth was open, her fork poised halfway between her plate and her lips. The three Ojibwa howled with laughter as Samantha slowly set the fork down.

"She did say *fresh*, Sammy," Renee hooted.

"Coon today," Lydia added for effect.

"Very funny," Samantha scowled, but allowed a small smile to creep in.

Gram patted her arm. "Never mind that old woman," she said between giggles, "she loves to torture city folks with that story 'bout Ford Motor Company's country buffet." Samantha nodded as she slowly joined in the laughter, but everyone noticed she'd laid her fork down with a sense of finality.

On the way home, during their quick stop at LaFleur's Trading Post, the women ran into Hugh O'Leary.

"Hey, O'Leary."

"Hey to you, LaRoche. How's it goin'?" the bear of a man with a bushy head of carrot hair called.

Hugh O'Leary had taken over as head ranger at the Chippewa National Forest when the ranger before him got his long-awaited transfer to the Florida Everglades. The appointment, at thirty, made O'Leary the youngest head ranger in the National Forest Service. The first thing he'd done was come to the reservation and ask for help, especially from the elders, to lead the nature walks and evening cultural programs at the campground. When he celebrated his fortieth birthday a month ago, over half the sixty people in attendance were Red Earthers.

"Been to any meetings with Floyd Neuterbide lately, O'Leary?" Ren and Hugh had labored through several county meetings with the boisterous, overbearing professor. Sturgeon Lake bordered the eastern edge of the Chippewa National Forest, making the Lone Loon Resort one of several privately owned establishments grandfathered into the forest when the Feds made it a national park.

"County Fish and Wildlife Commission luncheon last week."

The ranger set his bag of groceries into the forest service GMC.

"How's he seem?"

O'Leary shrugged. "No different than usual. Had a petition for people to sign opposing Native spearfishing in the lakes. When I asked him what we should do about the 1867 treaty, he sneered and said, 'Burn it.'" The ranger ended the sentence with a shrug. "He's an ornery cuss. Ya know, Renny, the guy's like that element in chemistry—what's it called? Cesium, I think. It's basically harmless with its own kind—other metals. But it's got this problem: it only has one electron on its outer shell, one electron aching to jump to any other atom lacking a full outer shell of electrons. It's a bomb in a suitcase if it leaves the neighborhood. On contact with oxygen, cesium is explosive. Put it with chlorine or iodine, for instance, and look out!"

"Interesting, O'Leary, so who are *we*? The iodine I suppose?" They all laughed, but it was without much enthusiasm. The underlying significance of what had been said had not gone unnoticed.

"How'd the meeting go otherwise?" Ren offered a quick smile.

"The professor did bring a proposal for a cooperative college-county summer youth program. Then it was the usual. Blah, blah, blah, let's take a vote. Blah, blah, blah, let's take a vote. Blah—"

Renee held up her hands in a defensive motion. "Okay, okay, I give." The ranger laughed a hearty laugh and threw a freckled beef-steak arm over her shoulder.

"Well, I'm off to sign up some volunteers over at the college. It's trail clean-up time. Almost, anyway. Snow'll be gone off the forest in a week or so."

"Take care, O'Leary. Keep an eye on the professor, eh?"

The sun was getting low in the sky when they turned down their long drive and stopped next to the woodpile. Renee's late-afternoon sleepiness disappeared, erased by the chill in the air as she stepped from the jeep. Shivering to wake up her heat cells, she tucked her chin into her jacket and began piling split wood in her arms. She'd daydreamed on the drive home about the long, slow removal of Samantha's clothes, one piece at a time. After depositing the wood in the bin next to the stove, Ren turned, her skin burning with passion for the woman standing in front of her. She took a step forward, pulling Samantha toward her onto the couch and burying her face in Sam's throat.

Tipping her head up, Samantha kissed her partner with enthusiasm, then shifted so she could snuggle in closer and lay her head on Renee's lap.

"I'm glad we've got some quiet time together, that JJ's in bed. I wanna talk to you more about Caroline."

"Okay, my love," Sam said, looking up at Ren's chin. "Just don't feed me some wild story like at supper."

"Promise. You gotta admit though, that was pretty funny. You know Lydia 'specially likes teasin' the ones she loves."

Samantha smiled warmly. "Now, on to you and Cal. Are you trying to tell me something?"

Renee giggled, more uncomfortable than she cared to admit, but said, "No. I wanna tell you about my past with her, not my future."

"You're keeping your future a secret?"

Her eyes slid from Samantha, her expression mockingly mysterious.

"You can't fool me, I know you love me," Sam sighed, "so, tell me about you and Ms. Cal. Is there another book in it for me?"

"You never know, *saiagi iwed*. You never know."

Gray ash covered the still-smoldering coals the next morning, and it required extra kindling to re-ignite the fire. Renee talked to it, feeding it bits of birch bark until the fire leaped up, ready for larger fuel. "*Megwetch*," she whispered gratefully. Early morning chill was not her favorite. She put water on for Sam's tea, then sat down at the table.

"Whadda ya think, Mukie? Is this gonna be a good day or not?" Mukwa's assenting growl told Ren she was paying attention. Then the cocker padded over and stuck her nose into Ren's hand. "Cold and wet." Ren rubbed the dog's nose. "Guess you're healthy. Okay, my friend, let's make girlfriend some breakfast. See if we can get the bad taste of last night's conversation-turned-sour out of her mouth."

A half hour later, Samantha was at the table, sitting down with a copy of the nearly week-old Minneapolis Sunday paper. Her bathrobe was tucked tight around her. Moments later she set the paper down to concentrate on the plate Renee put before her. Cheese and mushroom omelet, buttered whole wheat toast, and moose sausage—

something she never thought she'd learn to eat. Sam lifted the heavy white mug to her lips, carefully sipping the hot blackberry tea.

Trying to fend off the tightness that stress always settled there, she twisted and stretched her back. This latest crime involvement of Renee's, plus Caroline Beltrain, wasn't making for a smoothly running relationship at the moment. But then, whoever said relationships weren't a contact sport? Sam wondered if she'd ever get that easy, secure feeling back. She sure as heck was going to try. *Just because I've never had to fight for what I wanted, just because things have come easy for me, doesn't mean I can't—won't—learn. That woman's not going to get her without a fight. That much I know for damn sure.*

Renee watched Sam tugging on the hair behind her right ear and couldn't help the smile crossing her face. Seeing Sam's eyes she swallowed her comment, though. *She'd be a terrible secret agent.* Ren chuckled to herself instead.

Ten minutes later Samantha sat back, pushing away the nearly empty plate. When she spoke her voice was sad. "You're not hungry, Renee?"

Renee shook her head, a mug of tea steaming on the table in front of her. She pushed the twinkle in her eye back, in honor of Sam's gloomy expression. Sam set her nearly empty mug down, and Ren nudged her hand between the mug and her partner's palm, picking it up and kissing it. Which is how Jenny found them when she slid down the loft ladder, sleepy and not quite dressed.

"Gross, you guys. Kissey-face at breakfast?" The teen grimaced and went into the bathroom. Minutes later, the cabin door opened and Jenny's friend Jody peeked her head, in announcing a prearranged date with Jenny to work on a dance routine for culture class at school.

Renee and Samantha moved to the couch with newly filled tea mugs. Soon, from JJ's loft, a drum beat out a rhythm, sounding at first to Sam like one monotonous pattern, the singing like a chanting monotone. As she continued listening, though, her ears, or some part of her soul, grew accustomed to the sounds. The singing became mournful, then joyous, then reflective. The drumbeat took on the sound of a heartbeat—steady, comforting, vibrating through every cell of her body. Sam looked at Renee and nodded toward the loft where the two teens had started to dance. "Listen to their feet, Renny, their beautiful, wonderful feet," she whispered. *This is what I can't share with her, not totally anyway.*

"'To see us dance is to hear our hearts speak of who we are,' Gram says."

To Renee's amazement, tears welled in her partner's eyes. "Sammy, Sammy." Ren engulfed her lover in her arms.

"It's just so…" the silence was short but charged, "poignant," she finished.

"What's goin' on, *saiagi iwed?* Why so teary?"

"Just hold me."

Upstairs the song continued and the girls danced. After a prolonged period of quiet Renee said, "You 'bout ready to take up dancing seriously?" She leaned over and laid her head in Sam's lap.

"Me?" Samantha suppressed a blush as best she could, but soon the redness crept over her collar and fanned out.

"Yeah, you."

"Seriously, ready?"

"Seriously."

"I don't know. Would you like that?"

Samantha leaned over and stared at Ren, a multitude of expressions crossing her face—serene exhilaration, confusion and puzzlement, sadness, and finally anger. The pause in reality was over. Sam was back to last night's emotion. Renee saw it all and let her next words drop slowly into the waiting stillness. "Sammy, you don't have to be Indian for me to love you. I love you exactly the way you are. I just thought you might wanna try dancing."

Samantha couldn't speak. She could barely reach out to Ren and hold on tightly before her anger gave way to sobs, great racking sobs assaulting her body. Renee changed positions, laying Sam's head on her chest and letting her cry.

"Whadda ya think, Hobey?" Renee and the chief were walking down the hallway, on their way to the bedroom of ninth-grade Red Earth teacher, Joe Crocker. "We wondered why he wasn't in school this morning. I took his history class."

"Got a call jus' before you came to the station. Jesse and Josh took it," Hobey said over his shoulder.

Around Joe Crocker's neck a one-inch-thick black belt had made an angry-looking welt. The other end was tied to a pipe, painted white to blend in along the outside wall at the ceiling. A chair, presumably used by Crocker, had fallen, or been kicked, to the side below him. His once-handsome Lakota face, partially covered by long raven hair, had been replaced by an expression Renee judged to be more one of terror than despair. Ren's eyes moved down, perusing the rest of the body. His arms hung limply at his side, and a closer look by Jesse revealed what appeared to be rope burns at the wrists. They were faint, half hidden by his shirt, but there. Ren noticed that only one of Crocker's shoes was on; the other was still sitting by his bed.

"Strange, eh, he decided to hang himself right in the middle of putting his shoes on...or taking them off," she said to no one in particular. "Any note?"

"None found here," Jesse said. "You know him, Renny?"

Renee nodded, thinking back over the conversations she'd had the last few days that included Joe Crocker's name.

"Family?"

"Joe's from South Dakota. Pine Ridge, I think. You know I'd never take Joe for this kind of exit." Renee realized she was talking in a whisper.

"How so?"

"He's a quiet guy...was a quiet guy. Shy. This seems so bold. I mean it's not just suicide, it's thumbin' your nose, especially at whoever finds you."

"Mrs. Rawley down the hall."

"Huh?"

"Found him. Mrs. Rawley found him. Guess she cleans for him. Came in and here he was."

"Yeah, see. That doesn't fit with Joe. Why would he put Mrs. Rawley through that? He's too polite, plus, he's had Melvin Leaper livin' here the last few months," Renee added. "He wouldn't want Melvin to find him like this."

Walter Leaper's Vietnam vet son, Melvin, had left the family home in early winter. For a while he lived under Old Bridge in a cave that the huffers, over the years, had dug out of the Journey River bank. When tribal police got tired cleaning up their empty spray-paint cans and paper bags, and ran them out, Melvin took up residence in an abandoned bus out at Morriseau's Reclamation and Junk Yard. One night, three months ago, after Melvin almost burned himself up using old tires to keep warm, Joe Crocker bumped into him being treated in the emergency room at the reservation hospital. It turned out Melvin hadn't been unconscious from the fumes of the fire but from all the Lysol he'd consumed right before it. A Vietnam vet himself, Crocker took Melvin home with him, cleaned him up, and had been more or less taking care of him since.

Renee recounted what Ned had told her about an Indian with long hair being involved with the pornography video. "He also said he was dark and thought he was Lakota."

"He does seem to match the description," Hobey said.

"Unfortunately. Ned said he was from the school, but I jus' can't see Joe Crocker involved in anything like kiddie porn." A look of disgust crossed Renee's face.

"It's hard to imagine anyone involved in that crap." The chief reacted with a face of his own.

"Well, whoever it is who murdered Rosa Mae could've done the same to Crocker. Maybe he got outta line. They tried to make Rosa's out to be a suicide, too." Crocker's death seemed to shed new light on Rosa Mae's death, although it revealed little.

"Before we go any further with this idea, we need to check the apartment thoroughly. Make sure this isn't suicide. Then we'll show Ned a picture of Crocker," Hobey began, "and even if he IDs him, it still doesn't mean he was murdered. But it's a start. Then we'll talk to Neuterbide. We're gonna have to be careful, though. I did some checking on him since yesterday, Renny. He's got somethin' funny in his past," Hobey said with a ghost of a smile. "Indecent exposure, somethin' about him and a minor. Can't get the specifics because it was sealed as part of a plea agreement—after he went five years without gettin' in trouble again. Happened back in Chicago. He was about thirty, I guess."

Hobey leaned against the kitchen counter. "I know he's got a lotta influence around here so I want our ducks in a row before questioning him." Hobey paused, clearing his throat. "To get this guy we're gonna have to make a direct hit, I think. Once we know more I'll bring Lawton and the FeeBees in."

The apartment seemed unusually cluttered. Half-empty Coke and Dr. Pepper cans, a partially eaten TV dinner—several days old, judging from how dry and hard the remaining noodles looked. Next to the TV dinner was Joe's briefcase, open, school papers strewn about on the kitchen table and the floor around it. Dirty clothes waited in a half-hearted pile near the bathroom door. Anxiety, it seemed to Renee, lacked concern for tidiness.

That's when they heard it. Faint at first, but in the stillness the sound got louder. They moved into the front room. Huddled behind the couch, in the corner, a tabby kitty was issuing a plaintive cry. "Chief, look, she's scared to death. Come here, kitty." Renee reached the kitten and lifted her up, petting and talking to her. As soon as she was settled in Renee's lap, the cry changed to a purr.

"What should we do with her?"

"Take it to the shelter, I guess."

"How 'bout if I take her? Samantha's been wantin' a cat. Be a nice peace offering." Then Renee hesitated. "I don't know, though. Look at the hair—it's sheddin' all over me."

"Go ahead, take it, Renny. I'll let you know if anyone has a problem with it."

Renee rummaged through Joe's closets until she found a carton she could use as a cat box and set the kitty in it.

"Where you headed?" Hobey followed her out into the hall. "The BCA came through for me on exhuming Two Thunder's body. They'll be here in about an hour to do the second autopsy."

"Damn, I'd like to be there for that. I mean, well, you know what I mean. Ren held up her hands and shrugged.

"I know what you mean, Renny." Hobey smiled at the younger woman. "You're welcome to tag along."

"I've gotta give Caroline a call. She was gonna try and get in touch with Rosa's ex, or her dad. Then me and Jesse are gonna go check out Rosa's car."

"I talked to Ellis Two Thunder and everything's set. Rosa Mae's going home today." The chief finished in a barely audible voice. "I took Esther tobacco and she said she'd do the ceremony. It's basically the same one she did when we reburied the stolen bones from the caves last year."

"That's good, Chief, that's good," Renee said, imitating his whisper.

"Okay, I'll be in touch. And this weekend we shop for that gun, LaRoche."

"We'll talk."

Renee left with the kitten. An elderly woman was just coming in the front door of the apartment building.

"Mrs. Rawley? Hi, Renee LaRoche."

"Well, my, my, Emma Coon's *nosijhe*. Look at you," the elder chortled.

Renee smiled sheepishly, uncomfortable as always being identified as a Coon grandchild. Like she had some impossible standard to measure up to.

"I was just up at Joe Crocker's place," she said to the elder. "Thought I'd take his kitten home with me." Ren nodded at the box.

"Isn't it a shame? He just got the kitten yesterday. Found it down by the creek all wet and dirty. Told me the kitty looked like he felt." The tiny woman shook her head sadly. "I'm gonna miss Joey. He was a Sioux," the Ojibwa elder smiled sweetly, "but he got to be like one of my own."

Renee opened the door of her jeep and introduced Mukwa to the new addition to the family. When the cocker spaniel refused to give up her front seat, she set the box behind the dog, then stretched and leaned back in the driver's seat. "Times like these, Mukie, I could sure use a drink, or a toke, or somethin'. Anything to take the edge off. This clean and sober crap's a pain in the butt sometimes."

Mukwa raised an eyebrow and glanced at the box. *Did you hear that you rangy little feline?* No time like the present, she thought, for the pipsqueak to learn how important she was to the two-legged. She gave Renee a self-satisfied *woof* and licked her face. Then, smiling to herself, she fluffed her bed and lay down.

"Well, Ms. Blackness, what was that about?"

*Just staking territory,* niji, *just staking territory,* the cocker replied, with one last raised eyebrow into the back seat. Renee gave the dog a disapproving look, but Mukwa was unconcerned.

# 6

Winter's translucent sky, with its crystal clarity, was merging into the brilliant blue of the summer heavens. The small southerly wind gusts of early April, a precursor to the big winds of May, were melting a sizable portion of the new snowfall. April's wind was the kind that blew just above the silence, not intruding, not interfering, whispering to the people of the awakening of Mother Earth.

Encouraged by warm breezes, living things emerged from their houses, nests, dens, holes, and trees. The wind brought with it such a cozy feeling that saps ran, buds bloomed, cocoons opened, and hives buzzed. April's winds heralded the biggest snow melt in the northwoods, and as Renee drove through a corner of the Chippewa National Forest she could already see the morel and scarlet cup mushrooms peeking up through the wet and soggy earth. Trillium and trout lilies, red clover and chicory had also pushed through the snowy forest floor, exactly the signal male bears needed to leave their dens. You could always tell when their wintering was over, Gramps had told the young Renny, pointing to the aspen and willow trunks scraped high up for food. Later on, with the spring's full bloom, the bear's choices increased and the trees healed.

Renee had seen wood ducks at the pond west of the cabin, and the kids' favorite turtle, the painted, had begun its seasonal pastime—sunbathing on handy logs and rocks. The first turtle every spring reminded Renee of the rule about never helping turtles cross the road. The one time she'd done it, Gramps made her stay and watch as the turtle walked back out to where Renee had picked him up, then turned around and finished his trip across the road. Apparently they liked doing things themselves. The snapping turtle, unlike its painted sister, awakened from its winter sleep and kept to the anonymity of the pond's floor, where it fished undisturbed. Canadian geese were back, incubating eggs along the Journey River, while above them a host of returning birds sliced the sky of their summer home. With barn swallows constructing neat, orderly nests, and robins building their messy ones to birth first families of the season, the wingeds' *nibin* had begun in full force. Renee reminded herself to toss cut hair from her family out in the grass. When a bird picks up some of your hair and includes it in their nest, Gram had taught her, all the little birds wake up every morning with your scent and remember you forever in their songs, their flight, and their death. Gram said that wherever you left your hair, living things remember you and talk to the spirits about your journey. Given what she was involved in now, Ren figured she needed all the spiritual help she could get.

Alongside the wetlands, off County 3 on the rez side of the *You Are Now Entering Red Earth Reservation* sign, green and leopard frogs were up from their winter homes at the bottom of the wetland pond, and the banjo-plunking call of the green *omakaki* could be heard throughout the marshland. Renee noticed the red-winged blackbirds atop cattails swaying in the marsh breeze. The first-of-the-season blue herons flew over the emerging bulrush and pond lilies as though on reconnaissance for their friends.

Spring mating season brought dancing and preening with a myriad of sounds, led by the fancy drumming dance of the ruffed grouse to his mate. The small sounds—squirrels, chipmunks, birds, leaves in the wind—were what Renee missed most by the end of winter, and what she noticed first in the spring.

Under all of this, the plant family was bursting on the scene. Dandelion bulbs bloomed, daffodils peeked their heads out next to asparagus tips, and lilac bushes leafed. Having been up for a few weeks already, the rhubarb relaxed and chuckled at the late bloomers. Life, Renee ruminated, was in high gear in springtime. She loved the celebration of it all.

In her mind's eye, the Ojibwa woman recalled the bustling activity of her Odeima Anishanabe Kikinoamading class on their field trip to ready the sugar bush behind her cabin. Soon the LaRoche woods would be split by the cacophony of dripping sap into metal pails, and filled with the smells of burning wood and cooking maple sugar. "This is no time to be working on this disgusting pornography stuff, Mukie," she mumbled. "This is a time for life, for celebrating life."

She continued down County 3, past spots where she'd gathered medicines with her gram. She hadn't known back then the importance of the gathering and preparing, of the prayers said while picking things like the black poplar tree buds. The strong odor of the buds and the messiness of gathering them was one task she especially remembered not liking, but inconveniences faded once young Renny was old enough to understand the sacredness of the work. The labor was intense, back-breaking, and time-consuming. Gram still did it every spring with the commitment of a mother bear. Stories from the old Ojibwa played across Ren's mind now, as they did each spring when the life force of Mother Earth infected her, too, with the same passion her gram felt.

Healing was a Coon tradition. Gram had been called in a dream to be a healer as a young girl. Having heard that story her whole life, Renee developed insomnia as a teenager for fear she'd have a similar dream. The thought of being called to a life demanding such sacrifice and commitment scared her. After three sleepless nights, however, she finally collapsed in math class. When she didn't dream that time, or the next, she relaxed a little; then, embarrassed at how egotistical she was thinking Creator would summon her, she forgot about it. Sure enough, the call never came.

Renee came out of her reverie just in time to avoid hitting a rabbit loitering at the turn-off from County 3 onto Anishanabe Circle. The white coat of winter, not yet replaced by its multicolored summer browns, almost cost the *waboose* her life. Road kill. Renee smiled, remembering Lydia's teasing of Samantha, but she hated road kill and was grateful she'd avoided making a contribution. "Ugh," she said, "though when ya think about it, vultures do eat better than probably everybody else." A bark of approval came from the passenger seat.

Renee released her daydreams of spring as she pulled up next to the station and killed the motor on her jeep. She dialed the number Cal had given her on the cell phone and waited as the number of rings climbed. Five, six. "Hello?"

"*Boozho,* ah, I'm lookin' for Cal. She gave me this number to call."

"Never heard of her," came the hostile response, a millisecond before the click.

"My, my, a little testy today are we?" Renee winked at Mukwa. "Okay, I'm cool. I'll jus' call back." She dialed again.

"Hello." The disembodied baritone voice sounded angrier this time.

"Don't hang up, I'm Cal's friend. Tell her Runner's on the phone." She didn't hear the click this time, so she didn't know how much Man With An Attitude on the other end had listened to before hanging up. Renee set the phone down in her lap and leaned back. Looking over at Mukwa, she said, "Who is this Neanderthal? He's starting to ruin the good mood I jus' cultivated." She scowled at the phone. "I'm gonna try this once more, and then I'm gonna drive over there and—" She punched the number into the phone. Mukwa looked away from the window and back over her shoulder as Renee dialed. "What're you lookin' at?" Ren glared at the dog. "She gave me this number to call and then I get treated like the enemy? I don't think so!" Mukwa offered a brief whine and toss of her head, glancing to see if the little orange runt was paying attention to the conversation, then went back to gazing out the side window of the jeep. This time the phone rang once and Cal picked it up.

"Runner?"

"Jesus Christ, Cal, call off your doberman! You need a better class of friends, girl."

"He's just watchin' my back."

"Back watchin's gotten a lot nastier than in the old days. Listen, I'm callin' because Chief Bulieau still wants to meet with you."

"And?"

"And, I'm waitin' for you to say when."

"Why's it so important he talk to me?"

"Come on, Beltrain. You know why. You're the whole reason he got involved in all this. You owe him that much."

"Tribal cops. I don't figure I owe tribal cops beans."

"He's not like the others, Cal. Give him a chance."

"God, you're a pest, LaRoche."

The call intensified Ren's sadness over the death of Rosa Mae

Two Thunder. She was becoming a real person, someone Renee, more and more, wished she had known. Cal said Rosa's father had had a dream the night of his daughter's death. She had been running along the Fork River that cut through the Cree Reserve. It was winter, but she was barefoot and without a coat as if, her father said, she had left someplace in a hurry. The next day, in the sweat lodge, a message had come to Ellis Two Thunder from Owl: his youngest daughter was dead. When Cal told him what the coroner had said about cause of death, the Cree healer had replied, "I will pray for that man to open his heart."

The fact that Ellis Two Thunder did not believe his daughter's death, was a suicide motivated Renee even more to get to the bottom of it. "I won't let this rest, Cally, I promise," she had reassured her old friend. "Hobey's got the BCA up here today to do another autopsy. That'll tell us a lot."

"We're countin' on you, Runner. You know that."

Renee arranged for Cal to pick up a picture of Joe Crocker from the Red Earth school. It was more perfunctory than anything at this point. Renee was convinced Joe Crocker was involved.

Leaving the kitty and a message for Jesse at the tribal office, she headed for the reservation border. As she pulled into the parking lot at Sparky's Bar ten minutes later, Ren almost hit one of the Red Earth panhandlers populating the lot this time of day. Two of the men staggered up to her window before the jeep even stopped, smiling near-toothless grins and mumbling about money for chicken pot pies and Dr. Pepper. She recognized one of them as Rudy Bouchard, an alcoholic who ran with Melvin Leaper. He had on a pea-green cap, fur earflaps pulled down over his one and a half ears—having lost the lower half of the left ear along with two toes from his left foot to frostbite. His flimsy blue nylon windbreaker advertised the new tribal meat-packing plant. They'd given the jackets away to the first fifty attendees at a community picnic last fall, sponsored by the plant. Red Earth homeless now looked like some kind of bedraggled athletic team as they wandered the rez wearing jackets with *Wiiassike* emblazoned over the left breast and an outline of a building with *Red Earth Ojibwa Meats* encircling it on the back. Renee nearly gagged at the powerful smell of Lysol, urine, and sweat as she stepped from the jeep. Although her stomach lurched at the thought of someone drinking Lysol, at seventy-nine cents a bottle it was the cheapest high around.

"Hey, Rudy, how ya doin'?" Renee smiled.

"Good, good. How *you* doin'?" Out of place as it was here on the edge of the rez with this crowd, Rudy was shaking Renee's hand like he'd just finished the used car salesman's school of greetings. Ren could tell by the friendly but blank stare that Rudy didn't have a clue who she was but was too polite to say so.

"Renee LaRoche," she offered, "a friend of Melvin's."

"Sure, sure." Rudy shook her hand a little harder. "Good to see ya, Renee," he said enthusiastically, but Ren knew he was still confused about who she was.

"Seen Melvin lately?"

"Melvin? No, not lately," Rudy slurred, still holding onto Renee's hand.

"It's pretty important that I find him, Rudy."

Renee could see she wasn't getting anywhere. Even if Rudy had seen Melvin a half hour ago, he wouldn't remember now. The only thing working his brain was the overwhelming need for another drink. She didn't see anyone else amongst the half-dozen men who she thought might know where Melvin Leaper was, but it had been worth a shot to try and track him down here. Renee handed Rudy a ten-dollar bill.

"*Megwetch* for your help. Get something to eat, eh, and if you see Melvin tell him I need to talk to him. Okay?" she said, letting Rudy think he was doing something for the ten bucks, though she knew he'd forget the request before she left the parking lot.

"Sure will, Rosie." Rudy's half-toothless grin had broadened.

"*Renee,* Rudy. It's Renee."

"Right, Renee." Rudy stumbled over her name. Then he and his friend stuck out their hands.

After more handshakes around, Renee got back into the jeep and watched as the two stumbled toward Sparky's, jabbing and poking at each other, thrilled with their newfound wealth. "At least tonight they won't drink that brain-pickling Lysol," she said to Mukwa, watching the retreating figures. "You know, Mukie, no matter how out of it Indians get, *winiwa kaginig niningishka onindijima gigi kin.*" Renee looked inquiringly at her four-legged friend. "When did the handshake ritual get to be so popular amongst the people of the first nations?"

Mukwa had a bored expression on her face. *You got me,* niji. Not interested in chatting since that kitten was no longer there to impress, she turned back to watching a cluster of men near the dumpster. *There's somethin' interesting goin' on over there, though.*

Melvin sometimes hung out under the Black Duck Road bridge with other huffers. At certain times of day just walking over the concrete-and-steel bridge could get you light-headed off fumes from their spray-paint cans. The stale breath of hopelessness enveloped the area. They popped the cans with the tip of ivory-handled French hunting knives—a favorite Vietnam souvenir of the underbridge dwellers in the forty-to-fifty-year age range—then sometimes used the knives to stick holes in each other. After a few huffs from their paper bags, even pals could believe their only friend was the last huff from the can.

The riverbank along here was thick with willow, ash, choke-cherry, and cottonwoods, concealing the group huddled around burning tires along the shore. Renee pulled off onto the shoulder, and she and Mukwa headed down the embankment.

"*Boozho,*" she called, as the group came into view.

They looked up without comment or change of expression. Renee had lived in the middle of hopelessness and anger that felt like this. It hunched you over and squeezed your stomach. Nurturing that kind of rage tended to make you jittery and, as Ren remembered it now, prone to life-threatening behavior. Her breath released in a short gasp; the flashback made her nauseous.

As she reached the group, Renee recognized two as former classmates. "Suck it up, LaRoche," she muttered. "Jimmy, Brenda, how's it goin'?"

"Renny LaRoche, well how 'bout that. Hey, how are ya, lady? What ya doin' down here?" Jimmy grinned. "I thought you gave up the sauce?"

Renee nodded. "One day at a time, Jimmy. You know how that goes, eh?" She poked her old classmate playfully, putting down the large bag she had carried from the jeep. "I'm lookin' for Melvin Leaper right now. You prob'ly know, he's been livin' at Joe Crocker's and well, Joe's dead and I jus' wanna make sure Melvin's okay."

"Joe's dead?" Jimmy looked around at his buddies. "What happened?"

"Not sure, maybe suicide." Renee tried to read their faces. There was a lightness to Jimmy's question that sounded a little forced.

"Suicide, eh?" Jimmy looked away.

"At least that's what it's set up to look like."

"I guess you could make a death look like anything you wanted to, eh, if you had a mind to." Jimmy shrugged and kicked a piece of ice at the shoreline.

Ren was sure of it now. Melvin knew something, and he'd told his friends. At least Jimmy. "You know," she began carefully, "if it wasn't suicide, Melvin's own life could be in danger, and Chief Bulieau wants to protect him." Renee let the silence extend.

"Anybody seen Melvin?" Jimmy called to the rest. No one in the group responded. Renee glanced at Brenda. She was clutching a paper bag, and Renee could see flecks of silver paint around her mouth and on her fingers. Telltale marks of the huffer. That and the glassy eyes Brenda stared back at her with. Renee turned away quickly. Too many of us end up like this, she lamented to herself, too goddamn many.

It was funny how much of an outsider Renee now felt to this kind of life. She thanked the Great Spirit that she'd gotten out before it sucked her in, too, and spit her out all twisted and empty.

Renee picked up the groceries she had brought with her and handed them to Jimmy. "These are for Melvin. Thought he might be hungry. There's some sterno in here and some foil to cook the hamburger, so maybe you guys better eat it. It'll spoil if it's not eaten pretty soon."

A couple of the others, their interest piqued, came over to help Jimmy empty the bag. Brenda sat off to the side staring at the rest, clutching her paper bag. Renee never had figured out why metallic paints were the huffers' favorite. She helped them set the food out on a shelf they'd fashioned under the bridge, overhearing one woman she recognized but didn't know whisper to the rest that she remembered Renee from the Movement. After that, there was considerable warming amongst the under-the-bridge crowd.

Things loosened up enough during the next half hour that they all agreed to bring Melvin by the next time they saw him. Renee felt confident Jimmy and Sylvie, the woman who had vouched for her—the two most sober members of the group—would follow through on their promise. The others wanted to help too, she could tell. She just wasn't sure they had it in them.

Pulling Jimmy aside, Renee said, "You've seen Melvin, eh?"

Jimmy's nod was imperceptible.

When nothing more came from him, Renee touched his arm. "Okay, Jimmy, I understand. I'm countin' on you to bring Melvin to me though, okay?"

Jimmy stared back at her.

Ren left them with her home number and the number on the cellular phone, then she and Mukwa trudged back up the hill. "Hear from ya soon then, eh?" Renee called to Jimmy, who grinned back like he'd won the lottery, waving a cheese sandwich in one hand and a bottle of juice in the other.

*Smart move, LaRoche.* Renee smiled, getting into the jeep. "Food's always an ice-breaker, eh Mukie?" She rubbed the cocker's belly. "At least for you."

"*Boozho.*" Renee lifted the ringing phone up from between the seats.

"Runner, it's me. I've thought about it and I'll do it."

"What, Cal? What the heck you talkin' about, girl?"

"Come on, Runner, don't make me say it."

"Oh, okay, I get it. Hobey, right?" Renee heard what she took to be an affirmative grunt from the other end of the line. "When?"

"Soon as possible, before I change my mind," Caroline snarled.

"I'll see what I can do, but you're gonna have to perk up a little. The chief won't like it if you're all puffed up and snarly, girlfriend."

"Okay, okay. Let's jus' get this over with."

"See you in a bit, sunshine." This time Renee thought she heard a laugh from her old friend. A quick call to the station canceling her plans with Jesse and setting up the meeting with the chief, and Renee breathed a sigh of relief. Caroline was lucky Hobey was such an easy-going guy and took into account her history with tribal cops. Now, Ren prayed, if only her two friends could meet and not end up screaming at each other. Her confidence rested with Hobey's side of the conversation.

"So, Chief Bulieau, Runner says you think you can help us," Caroline said. There was little friendliness in her raspy voice.

Hobey's stoic facial expression revealed nothing, giving Renee the sick feeling the conversation was in danger of stalling before it began.

"Well, I can say this," the chief finally responded, an edge to his own voice, "this is something you can't fix yourself. Not only that, but your actions so far haven't helped the investigation...much."

"What in hell's that supposed to mean?" Renee's friend glared at her, then turned back to the chief. "I'm talkin' to you, ain't I?"

The silence extended before Hobey said, "Yeah, Caroline, you're here. Sort of. Maybe half of you's here. But we've wasted a lotta time, haven't we?"

"I don't know, have we? Or is your ego jus' upset 'cause I didn't jump when you yelled?"

"Cal," Renee interjected, but then she saw Chief Bulieau shake his head.

The stillness in the room was heavy. "Caroline, past experiences do not make up today's reality."

"That's how it's been for me with the tribal police." Cal was slouched in her chair with a belligerent look on her face.

"So, you make up your mind before you meet someone?"

"With you guys I do. Clones," she grunted.

"I remember—" Hobey cast about for the right words before finally settling on, "I've learned a lot from my uncle over the years." Chief Bulieau's voice had taken on the sound of a father, or elder teacher. Renee watched his face soften. "You, as I, have to live with our questions until we live into our answers. My answers are not yours...just like yours are not mine." Hobey flashed a quick smile. "And you have to trust them. Thought-out, prayed-on answers that are yours are the right ones for you. The key is *thought-out* and *prayed-on*." The angry silence saturating the room was dissipating.

Caroline Beltrain felt a strange tingling at the base of her neck, then realized she hadn't taken a breath in quite a while. Tears welled at the corners of Renee's friend's eyes, gave into gravity, and flowed full force down both cheeks. The tears stopped everyone in midthought. Renee put an arm over Cal's shoulder and massaged the back of her neck. She wasn't really surprised by Cal's emotions; the woman had been moving at supersonic speed for the past week, barely pausing to grieve Rosa Mae's murder. And Renee knew Cal felt responsible for the young foster kids at Floyd Neuterbide's. She looked over at the chief, sending a prayer to the elder for some special words.

Hobey caught Renee's glance. "Caroline," he offered quietly, "my uncle asked me once what I thought about Coyote."

This brought Cal's head up and slowed her tears.

"That's jus' the look I prob'ly gave him." The chief smiled. "He told me then what I'll tell you now. What does Coyote call us to think about? To pay attention to orderly behavior, to the importance of family relationships. And that Coyote wants it both ways." Hobey took a breath. "That was my lesson to learn. We can't have it both ways. Coyote lives on the edge between chaos and harmony. He's the hero and villain, the trickster."

The chief went on to tell a story about Coyote's dual personality, reminding the women, "I only tell this story because there's snow on the ground. Do not tell it out of season unless you're prepared to change the weather.

"Coyote helps us learn balance, something to remember at times like this. If any of us go off half-cocked, or refuse to work as a team, we're gonna be in trouble." Hobey paused for effect and waited until he saw them both nod. "Caroline, you and me, we don't trust each other much. That's gotta change. So, I'm gonna start trusting you. After all, first and most important of all, we're Anishanabe."

Time seemed to stand still. When Cal got up, Ren realized she hadn't moved a muscle since Hobey started talking. Her sudden intake of air caused everyone to jump. Renee shrugged sheepishly.

Cal offered a half-hearted smile, turned, and held out her hand to Hobey. "You've got my trust, Chief. No tribal cop's ever talked to me the way you just did. Told me a story about Coyote, talked to me about what they learned from their uncle."

Hobey nodded and laid his other hand onto the handshake.

Renee watched in amazement at what was transpiring before her. She'd known this woman for a good part of her life, and if she'd had to bet on how this meeting would go, she'd have put her money on the opposite result. That would teach her to underestimate Chief Hobart Bulieau.

"So...who's the Thought Police you guys deal with?" Cal's query was hesitant.

"Henry Lawton's the top agent."

"He doesn't seem to be one a the ones Daddy Hoover slapped butt on," Renee laughed. "But there's a couple of ones under him that are definitely living out—how do they say, 'disciplinary transfers'—up here." The three Ojibwa laughed, almost like old friends.

"Lancaster's definitely a dress-code violation, wouldn't you say, Renny?" Hobey asked between laughs.

"I'd say."

Renee was excited about the plan they'd devised to work together. Glad the chief agreed, for the time being, to keep Caroline away from the FBI.

"I want you to promise me, though, you'll talk to the FeeBees when this is all over," Hobey said in his fatherly voice. Caroline gave her word.

"I'm feelin' like a drop of water on Gram's hot skillet holdin' this thing." Renee held the pistol up for Samantha to see. Setting it down on an upturned cut round, Renee fell into the circle of her lover's arms, grateful Sam was finally home. "Thought you guys'd never get here."

"Had to take Jody to her gram's," Jenny answered.

Renee picked up the pistol. "Let's go inside and I'll tell you about this," she said, dangling it between thumb and forefinger.

As she hung her jacket in the closet, Ren noticed her grandfather's old .30-.30 Winchester for the first time in quite a while. The light glinted off the worn steel ring on its side, a remnant of the days it was secured to a saddle scabbard. Lifting it reminded her how Benny had had to help her hold it to her shoulder. Its weight, and the loud boom when she pulled the trigger, had been awesome to her at age ten. Touching it now, Renee thought about its use and the intended use of the pistol on the table. A sick feeling tightened her stomach. How could she practice shooting that pistol? She'd never be able to use it on another human being.

"Whatcha thinking about my love?" Samantha came up behind her partner, hugging her around the waist.

"That Smith and Wesson .38 and the hollow-point bullets

Hobey gave me are really gettin' to me." Renee rolled the bullets—the kind that spread out on impact and do the most damage—around in her hand. "Why am I practicin' shooting that? I'll never be able to shoot someone. Look at my gramps' old .30-.30 He used that to feed his family. And, he used it respectfully. I don't think I ever saw him shoot somethin', Sammy, without puttin' down tobacco and sayin' a prayer first. And he used every part of the things he shot. What we didn't eat, he and Gram made stuff out of." Sam squeezed Renee tighter and kissed the back of her neck. "What am I gonna do, Sam, tell the bad guy to wait while I say a prayer and put out some tobacco? Then skin 'em and make moccasins?"

"Renee LaRoche."

"And then," Ren grinned, "we'd have to eat him too, I guess."

"Renee LaRoche, stop that!" Sam poked Renee in the ribs.

"Okay, okay. Jus' don't tell Gram I said that."

"Will you be good then?"

"Promise."

"Seriously, Renee, what are you doing with that gun?"

"Hobey was gonna buy me one. Then this one turned up so he gave it to me. It's a .38 Smith and Wesson's all I know so far." Renee and Samantha walked around it to the couch.

"Why does he want you to carry it?"

"He doesn't necessarily want me to carry it—jus' have it for this case 'cause of the people we might be dealing with."

Sam's face went ashen. "*The kind of people you might be dealing with?* What does that mean?" She emphasized every word.

Ren shrugged. "I don't know. You know Hobey. I'm jus' doing this to keep him happy. Don't think I'll ever carry it." She picked up Sam's hand. "I love your skin, *saiagi iwed*," she said, touching the hand to her cheek.

Jenny's noisy descent from the loft interrupted their moment. "Ma, Ma, Jody and me got free tickets to the Indigo Girls concert in Bemidji."

"How'd you do that?"

"Jody's auntie told Jody about them lookin' for volunteers to help at the concert. You know, take tickets, sell stuff?" Jenny was dancing excitedly around the couch where Renee and Samantha sat, Mukwa at her heels. "So we signed up."

"Sounds fantastic, J. You goin' over with Jody's auntie?"

"Well, not exactly. It's Saturday night and she's busy. We need your jeep. Can we borrow your jeep?"

The next fifteen minutes alternated between Jenny saying, "It's not fair," and Renee saying, "Life isn't fair, my girl," until Jenny stormed back upstairs.

"Thanks a lot, Sammy. Why didn't you back me up on that?"

"The Pips couldn't have backed you up on that."

"You agree with her?"

"Yes, I do. Jody will be with her. She's seventeen, Renee."

"Not for two weeks."

"They're only going to Bemidji."

"Fifty miles away."

"Still, she's a good kid. All moms should be as lucky as we are."

After a long silence, Renee said, "All right, you're right. She can go." Out of the corner of her eye she caught Samantha looking up to the loft and giving Jenny a thumbs-up. Ren yelled to no one in particular as she headed into the kitchen, "Why do I feel like this was rehearsed?" Secretly, though, the thought of Samantha and Jenny conspiring together made her happy.

As they walked in the door and the familiar smell of cigarette smoke and stale beer hit her, Renee regretted having talked Samantha into this little excursion. The Lone Loon Bar crowd looked like nothing unusual for a rural resort bar: some resorters up north early, local friends of the owner, a Kiwanis club holding its regular weekly meeting, and serious drinkers who belly up anywhere near home at 10:00 A.M. opening and stay through to closing.

Renee and Sam took chairs out of the way near the door, hoping no one would notice the lone person of color in the place. The crowd noise was pleasant, the laughter easy and friendly. Ren marveled at the bar society, noticing both how familiar and how unappealing it felt. The clumping of people drawn together because of similar interests, or similar pains. She observed Neuterbide, his bartender's skill at philosophizing, drawing listeners in, plying them with mind-loosening beverages until the right moment to pounce. And then he had them agreeing with his narrow-minded, hateful view of a world necessarily singular in its pale appearance. Tonight, when

Neuterbide started in on "today's kids"—how they needed more discipline, how if girls couldn't stop having so many babies there should be forced sterilization—it took all her determination and Sam's calming hand for Ren to stay in her seat. When the conversation escalated in volume and grew to include most of the adjourned Kiwanis club members, the women decided they'd had enough and took their leave. There was still time to salvage the night with a walk by the river.

# 7

The Chippewa County sheriff was a tall fellow with a closely cropped head of red hair and a neatly trimmed mustache. Ronny Davidson was newly elected. He had recently been sworn in to his job protecting the 51,249 residents of the county, including 1,027 college students, and, occasionally, 747 Ojibwa Indians. The population fluctuated little when college let out for the summer because within days vacationers from the city escaping to the north country lakes and woods invaded the county. Today, at the Eat & Meet Cafe in Thunder Lake, the off-duty sheriff sported tight black jeans, a white cowboy shirt with pearl buttons, and well-worn black cowboy boots. He'd been sitting with one of his deputies, Rod Johanson, a Granite Rock football star thirty years ago turned deputy sheriff. Rod's hair was as blond as Davidson's was red. The testosterone that passed between the two of them as they joked with each other and the woman behind the counter filled the diner.

"Bunch of drugstore Indians at that place, Jeannie. No see um, no talk um." Sheriff Davidson noticed Renee and Jesse standing in the doorway just as he finished the sentence. "Oops, sorry there, Johnson, LaRoche," he said to the women, with not much sorry in his voice.

"No problem, Davidson. Wooden Indians are inventions of your culture, not ours," Jesse replied, stealing a look at Renee, who was glaring at the officers.

Renee had a sudden urge to turn around and go out the way she'd come, but she stayed, eyeing the sheriffs suspiciously, the potential criminal involvement of their department higher on her mind than their racism.

Davidson got up from his counter stool, hitched up his jeans, and flung a shearling jacket over his shoulder. "See you tonight then, Jeannie." He flashed the young, dark-haired woman behind the counter a toothy grin, and she returned the pleasure.

"Just the man we're looking for." Officer Jesse Johnson approached Davidson, adding her smile to his. Renee took a seat at the counter near the door.

"What brings you to the poor side of the county?" The appeal that won this man the recent sheriff's election was apparent; he definitely had a charm about him.

"Poor, right," Jesse sneered. "Want to compare salaries?"

"Now, now, be nice, Officer," the sheriff smiled playfully.

"We need directions to your impound lot now that you've moved it again."

"The fire those juveniles lit did some major damage to that old lot, but this one isn't too far from there. Goin' out to check the Two Thunder car?"

"Why would you ask that?"

"Only thing I can think of of interest to you out there. Or did I miss somethin'?"

Jesse shook her head. "I hope not. Say, Davidson, did you guys check the registration on that car?"

"It was registered to a dead person. Somebody named Hamilton, I think."

"No one at the address on the registration?"

"Far's I know, it was an abandoned house on the reservation."

"Trashed by reservation kids got nothin' better to do than destroy property," the until-now-silent Johanson interjected.

Jesse ignored the remark. "Just wondered if someone followed up on that as a possible way to ID the body."

"Now, Johnson, you know if we'd had a name we would of followed up, yeah?" Davidson peered at Jesse and Renee over the top of his sunglasses. "We like to help. Isn't that right, LaRoche?"

"Let's see. I'm from the government and I wanna help? Funny, that line never caught on on the rez," Renee replied. She glanced at Jesse, who was giving her a *don't say anything* kind of look. Ren turned away from her friend, again eyeing Davidson and Johanson suspiciously.

After getting directions to the lot, the two Ojibwa left the cafe.

"Kind of weird havin' a twenty-six-year-old sheriff, eh?" Jesse said to Renee as they watched his six-foot-three frame stride past the jeep.

"Takes up a lot a space, too."

"At least from what the chief says, this one seems honest."

"And where does Cal's call about Rosa fit into that honest image?"

"Well," Jesse pursed her lips, "we don't know who answered the phone in the sheriff's office, Renee, so don't jump the gun on Davidson."

Renee glowered at her friend. "He is the boss, Jess, but you're right. Forgot myself there for a minute. J. Edgar did say justice is merely incidental to law and order. How 'bout we confront Davidson on that call?"

"The chief already did a check. Indirectly. He asked him something like, 'If they'd gotten any help from the community to ID the woman.'"

"And?"

"And, I guess he said no."

"Whadda ya know about Johanson besides how he feels about reservation kids?"

"Not much. Married, eight kids I think. Catholic boy."

"I guess. Either that or he likes his women barefoot and pregnant."

"Seems harmless."

"If you're not his wife." Renee frowned.

Minutes later she was following Officer Johnson on Squaw Lake Road, heading north out of Thunder Lake. "Shoulda seen that cute little white boy fawning all over Jesse, Mukwa. Rather, that cute, big ol' white boy. A sight to behold." Renee looked over at her four-legged *niji*. "Thank the Great Spirit we're lesbians, eh?" Mukwa offered a short whine, opening one eye. "Come on you ol' rez dog, you know you are. If you don't admit bein' a two-spirit, I'm gonna sig Gram on you. She'll get it outta you jus' like she did me. So let's see a little enthusiasm here. You don't even look like you'll be able to go for a run later." With the last comment, Mukwa stood and pawed the window, her stubby tail wagging the rest of her body. "Oh, I get it. You're bored, eh?" Renee slowed, pulling in next to Jesse in the county impound lot. "Hop out then, my girl." She opened the door and the cocker spaniel sprang out.

"Guess those Canadian Injuns got the same taste in cars we do," she called to Jesse as the two came to stand in front of a beaten-up '76 Thunderbird. Mukwa ran by like a streak, ears flying and a smile on her face.

"Must be the common genes between Crees and us, eh?"

They each opened a front door on the rose-and-cream T-bird. The inside showed definite signs of being gone over. "Caroline said Rosa'd only been back down here a few days before she was murdered. She thinks Rosa mighta stumbled onto a name, or some evidence of Ned's situation, and they killed her."

"Seems possible," Jesse nodded.

"When Hobey and I talked with Cal earlier, she told us word was that Rosa tried to contact her, couldn't find her, stopped at Heart of the People next, but didn't visit anyone. Just hung around the school. Left there late afternoon. Nobody saw her after that, at least nobody we've found so far. Bobbi's got her friend Jean, the school nurse, askin' around on the Q.T."

"Trail stops there? That might suggest she was checking up on someone from the school. Crocker, maybe?" Jesse paused in her rifling through the glove box to look up at Renee. "One of the lecturers at the training quoted Dr. Edward Locarde—king of criminalists—who said that every criminal takes something away from the crime scene and leaves something behind. No matter how tiny. All we have to do is find it." Jesse turned back to the glove box. "By the way, how'd your visit go? You, the chief, and Caroline? Hard to imagine."

"Pretty good, actually. They were both on their best behavior," Renee laughed, "or rather, Cal tried to bite but Hobey dropped a marshmallow in her mouth." Jesse joined Ren's laughter, each conjuring their own image of Caroline Beltrain and Chief Bulieau standing toe to toe and talking about ways they could help each other.

"What's the plan?"

"Hobey's gonna run interference for Caroline with Lawton. I think he really believes her, Jess. I mean about not bein' involved in that bombing at Prairie Peninsula." Ren gave her friend a big grin. "I was proud of Cal for finally dropping her guard."

"Seems like she's risking being arrested herself to help clean up this mess."

Renee nodded.

"It's kind of eerie in here, isn't it?" Jesse said after an extended silence.

"No kiddin'. Everything seems so calm. Hard to imagine this is part of a crime scene." Noticing a tear along the driver's door pocket of the Thunderbird, Renee slid a gloved hand in and retrieved a light blue three-by-five Mead memo book with a stub of a pencil tied to the spiral. She leaned back in the seat and flipped up the cover. The first entry, written in a neat hand, read: "Talked at GR school today. Heard JC at rez school's into M/B stuff. Check ad in last week's *Collegian*." She flipped to the next page and the neat penmanship continued: "No luck yet. Will try the school tomorrow. Haven't gotten C yet." Another page turn. "Meeting someone at BD—might help." It looked like someone was writing in haste on the next page: "Wonder about SS in TL and on the rez. Think they've been funneling kids for years. Heard a rumor FN at GRSC involved. Can't prove anything—yet."

"Awful quiet over there, Renny. Got something?" Jesse slid over next to the other woman. "You're getting saucer eyes."

"This's gotta be Rosa's, maybe some of her last writings. But I'm not sure what any of it means."

"Let's see."

"Take a look at the last page. I think what she's written is: "B/B porn. Got to be JC, PA involvement or someone at SD maybe. Probably FN too. Haven't contacted DW yet. Wouldn't trust—" Then it stops. That's it, except for a scribble after trust that I can't read. Think she was writing this when something spooked her?" Renee and Jesse stared at each other, imagining what might've happened to Rosa as she made this last entry before storing her notebook back in her hiding place in the car door.

"Glad those white boys don't think like us Injuns. They'da found this," Renee tapped the blue book on the steering wheel. "You find anything?"

"Book of matches under the passenger seat from the Lone Loon Resort."

"The Lone Loon? You gotta be kiddin' me. That place?"

"What? You know something bad about that place, Renny?"

"That's Neuterbide's place."

"Oh, that's right. Where Ned's staying."

"Ned—he's a brave kid. Breaks my heart he's never really had a childhood. What is it with people, Jess? Especially straight white men who see kids as property?"

"I guess it's the same way they see women as property," Jesse responded. "Where's Ned now?"

"He's at the Neuterbides'. The professor's out of town and Ned's gonna call Cal when he comes back."

"This is serious stuff." Jesse paused, shaking her head. "I don't know much about this Neuterbide guy."

"Well, imagine a wall with pictures of Rush Limbaugh, Ronald Reagan, David Duke, and Charlton Heston on it. Limbaugh and Reagan autographed. That's the Lone Loon Bar. Neuterbide owns it. Samantha and I went there last night to check it out, and I almost got sick to my stomach. Neuterbide's still a history professor at State. He's been in these parts about thirty-five years or so. Wife's a local farm girl, Sylvia. He got polio in the '50s. Everyone says after that he took the pull-yourself-up-by-your-bootstrap philosophy and turned it into a battering ram. Claimed if he could do it with fifteen pounds of metal strapped to each leg, then all those goddamned lazy bastards in line down at welfare could do it too."

Jesse let out a noisy breath and the moment snapped it up like it was gasping for air. "Am I mistaken, or are this guy and his wife the ones that won Chippewa County Foster Parents of the Year last year?"

"One and the same," Renee nodded. "How can he be honored for helping kids get to college and—"

"And be the same guy that shipped Ned and his brother off four times to the bedroom with the red satin sheets?"

Jesse's lament was loud. "It's hard to grasp it. You know, Renny, at least in nature the dangerous ones, the poisonous ones, are brightly colored so you know who they are."

"Think we should paint a yellow stripe down the back of the guy's head?"

"That'd be my vote. Think Rosa mighta gone to the Lone Loon?"

"I'd bet that'd be a no," Renee answered confidently.

The sweet, reedy sound of honking geese drew Renee's gaze upward. Canadian honkers were moving in a V across the sky, another flock completing its round trip back home to the north country. Every so often the lead goose fell off and drifted to the back of one of the lines. Renee smiled over at Jesse. "Now that's a community, eh? Reminds me of Gram's stories about how we learned from the *awessi* in the old days. Animals are our teachers, she says. Our ancestors watched how they lived in harmony and set up communities. They watched *maingans* and learned how to be families. They watched *mukwa* and learned about medicines and about protecting the people. Gram says we learned about how to hunt, what was okay to eat in the wilderness. Bunch of stuff. And now the world's losing six species an hour to extinction."

"But you know, Renny, the new predators out there seem to be a breed all their own. What can the old ways teach us about dealing with them?"

Renee returned her gaze to inside the car, her mind circling on the thought her friend just expressed. "Maybe, Jess...and maybe that's the mistake we're makin'," she paused, looking back up at the geese, "thinking that the times now are so different that we can't learn anything from the old ways."

They sat quietly until the geese were tiny dots in the sky.

Renee leaned back in the seat and stretched her legs.

"Jesse, did you notice this seat?" Ren sat up behind the wheel. "Look at this," she said. "I'm five-feet-six-inches tall. The autopsy ID'd Rosa at five-five. I couldn't possibly drive this car with the seat in this position. Whoever drove it last had to be at least six foot, wouldn't ya say?"

Jesse stretched her legs out in front of her. "I'll check with Davidson to see if they moved the seat, and tell him about this other stuff we found." Turning her attention to the matchbook in her hands, she flipped up the cover. "Look at this." Jesse held the matches up. "The name Mark here on the inside of the cover, with a phone number."

"That could be somethin'. Wonder how tall Mark is. Mrs. Jaspers said the car was towed from where Rosa's body was found. If so, they didn't move it then."

"Might've moved it when they were looking through the car."

"I'd like to hold onto this stuff for a while without tellin' the *chimook* fuzz." Renee's eyebrows spiked down at the thought of sharing any evidence with the sheriff.

"Oh God, Renee...I don't—"

Renee held up a hand. "I jus' don't trust 'em over there since what Cal said, and then the condition of the porn house when I got there. At least 'til we find out who took the call, I say we don't give anything to 'em."

Jesse tapped lightly on the back of the seat with her fingers, finally nodding her agreement. "The chief'll probably have my butt—both our butts—but what the heck. Just a few days, though."

"You keep usin' those awful words like *butt* and *heck,* Jess, and he'll be washin' your mouth out with soap."

The women laid their arms over each other's shoulders and shared a hearty laugh.

After checking the trunk of the car and collecting some of the burrs, twigs, leaves, and other debris, Jesse said, "I'm heading into the station after I dust the steering wheel and dash for prints. You coming?"

"Think I'll head home. That time Samantha was gone seemed more like three months than just over a week." Renee raised her eyebrows a few times and an elflike smile crossed her lips. She watched a blush starting at Jesse's neck, but didn't say anything.

"I envy you having someone to go home to," the tribal officer said, giving Mukwa a pat. "Going to the funeral for Crocker?"

"I'm goin'. Gonna sit in the back and observe the comings and goings of the mourners. Take some pictures. Be less conspicuous than one of you folks doin' it."

Samantha's head was cocked to one side as she listened intently to Renee's re-creation of her day. The teasing smile frolicking at the corners of Sam's sensual mouth throughout supper had disappeared. "Let me see those notes, love," she said, determined to be helpful and as involved in the investigation as she could stand. She held out a hand to Renee, who stood up from the table with a mug of tea in hand and retreated to the couch, the kitty at her heels.

"Whadda ya gonna call this little thing?" Renee called back over her shoulder.

*Scrawny,* Mukwa muttered, following the kitten to the couch.

"Renny."

"What?"

"Renny."

"WHAT!"

Samantha burst out laughing, coming up behind her partner and kissing the top of her head. "You are so cute. I was teasing, but I guess you're too tired."

"Oh, *Renny.* I get it." Renee offered a little giggle.

"Okay, okay. Forget my jokes and let's work on this notebook." Samantha came around to the front of the couch and sat down. "What do you think? I'd say the initials are probably people or places, nouns," Sam offered. "You agree?" After Renee's concurrence Samantha continued. "So we've got JC, M/B, PA, RJ, FN, SS, DW, TL, B/B, GRSC. The ones in twice are JC, PA, and FN. I don't think M/B and B/B are a person or place—you wouldn't put a slash between. Then there's that lone C."

The nightly news was on in the background. Renee had been listening with one ear when she heard, "Today at Granite Rock State College students protested…," and looked up at the TV. A student holding a sign that said *GRSC Unfair to Women Professors* was talking to the reporter. Renee's eyes moved from the TV, to the notes, and then to Samantha. "Sammy, what about that? On the TV." She pointed to GRSC on the paper. "Granite Rock State College—GRSC? Make sense? FN at GRSC. FN. Floyd Neuterbide? Jesse found a matchbook from the Lone Loon in the car. That's Neuterbide's place." Renee didn't mention Ned's story. She hadn't yet told Samantha about that.

Samantha patted Renee's cheek, "My little investigator."

"Bear Clan."

"Yes, Bear Clan. You're very good at this."

"Details, my dear. Noticing details. In my drinking days I could tell if a glass was clean by the head on my beer."

"Excuse me?" Samantha grimaced. "Beer foam?"

"Yeah, if a glass is greasy, the beer doesn't foam very good." Renee's response took on an edge.

"Okay, okay," Sam held up a hand. "Don't get testy with me."

"What's the matter, Salisbury? Too lowbrow for you to relate to?"

"Renny, hold on. I was just kidding around." Samantha cleared her throat. "Maybe we should just see what else we've got."

"I'm sorry, Sammy. I'm so damned tired. You're right, I am getting testy." She leaned over and gave her lover a kiss, then tapped the paper. "Let's get back to this. How about the C?"

"The C?"

"C. Caroline. Cal said she hadn't talked to Rosa, and here on the second page Rosa wrote, 'Haven't gotten C yet.' And then this one, JC."

"Yes?" Samantha's throat tightened at the sound of Cal's name, but she pressed on.

"JC. Joe Crocker."

"Joe Crocker. That fits, doesn't it? And it makes sense, Renny, from what you've told me. He's involved, worries they will be found out, so he commits suicide."

"Or maybe he was murdered. Like Rosa. Maybe he was gonna confess or blow the cover. Ya know, Lydia gave me an article about a squirrel solving a crime. Tol' me to read it. I'm jus' starting to get why she gave it to me."

"Why a squirrel?"

"Well, generally the squirrel has a diet of over one hundred different plants, and even under a foot of snow they can find nuts they've buried. Maybe that's because they don't roam very far. They live within a two-hundred-yard area, except, of course, when the male's lookin' for a mate." Renee nudged Samantha. "We don't have to worry about that. Anyway, this article tells how a squirrel had picked up and stored some bullets and casings that the cops were lookin' for. It helped break the case." Renee sighed. "Guess Auntie wanted me to see that digging is important, not giving up. Keep sniffin' around, uncovering pieces of evidence." This time Renee laughed heartily. "Those old ones are sneaky, eh? Gram talks about the animals teaching us. Auntie gives me articles about squirrels. It's a painless kind of learnin', that's for sure."

"They put a lot of stock in you. There was a time I didn't understand that. Even I can see a little of the draw of this kind of investigating now. The excitement of it. It reminds me of the kaleidoscope I had as a kid. You turn it and turn it, watching the little glass pieces falling into place, making a complete picture." Samantha smiled at her partner.

"'Specially when it's in your genes." An impish smile crossed Renee's face. "And it's gonna be even more stimulating when I use that .38 Hobey gave me. I can blow someone away—I mean, cap someone—if they get outta line." Renee mimed drawing a pistol from a shoulder holster.

"Renee LaRoche, wait until I tell your grandmother how you talk."

"Okay, okay. I give up," Ren said, arms raised. She returned the imagined gun to its holster, blowing smoke from the barrel.

Another half hour passed before the two stopped going over the initials. "Think I've squeezed everything I can from this little pea brain." Renee tapped her head. "Better call Hobey, though. At least give 'em what we've got." Renee stood, stretched, and moved to the phone.

"Say, by the way," Samantha interjected, "did you eat at home at all while I was gone?" She hoped Renee didn't get the underlying question about how much she'd been seeing Caroline.

"Well," Renee glanced over at Mukwa, "J.J. and I ate here one night before she left with the basketball team to go that tournament at Turtle Mountain..."

"And?"

"And Mukwa and I ate here for breakfast two mornings after our runs."

"And?"

"And, well, you know me. I hate eating alone. But I didn't eat out. I jus' didn't eat."

"You like doing everything else alone."

"Everything?"

"Well, almost everything. Although you did mention something about acquainting yourself with a new product from Eve's Garden—" Samantha had no time to finish before Renee placed a finger over her lips and followed it with a kiss.

"Now hold that thought. I'll be done talkin' to Hobey in a flash, my love."

Samantha stretched out on the couch and closed her eyes. The muffled sound of Renee on the phone, Jenny's music up in the loft, and the kitty purring on her chest gave her a comforting feeling. Stuffing her fears for Renee's safety, and her jealousy, had been touch and go, but overall she thought she was coping. For a first-time effort at least. "It'll get easier," she whispered to the kitty, who shifted contentedly on the warm body under her. She wished she hadn't asked so many questions at supper about Cal's meeting with Hobey, and she definitely should not have taken Chief Bulieau's side when Renee repeated some of the nasty comments Caroline had made to him. Sam fell asleep smiling at Ren's disappointment in Cal. Score one for my side, was her last conscious thought.

Hanging up the phone a half hour later, Renee moved sheepishly out of the kitchen. "*Saiagi iwed,* I'm sorry it took me so long. I had to set up a time with the chief and—"

She looked down at Samantha. She was too late. Her partner was sound asleep with the kitty curled up on her chest and a big smile on her face. Ren thought about waking her, but knew she could rebuild the cabin and hold a housewarming party around Sam without disturbing her. Besides, it was great to see that smile. Renee left her to her dreams.

# 8

Rounding the curve by Goodbears' on Old Bridge Road, Renee almost ran into Melvin Leaper and Jimmy standing at the road's edge in the early morning fog. Jimmy waved and pointed at Melvin as soon as he recognized the jeep.

Once they settled in, Jimmy offered, "Melly's got somethin' ta tell ya 'bout Joe."

Renee waited while Melvin stared out the window. The ride was quiet until Renee said, "Good food the other night."

"Great. We all pigged out, then fell asleep." Jimmy turned to Melvin, "Mel, 'member I tol' ya Renny came by lookin' for you?"

Melvin nodded, but Renee wondered if he'd even heard his friend. He continued staring out the window, absently petting Mukwa, who'd settled on his lap, sensing the man's need for affection. They pulled onto Anishanabe Circle, and Renee stopped in front of the Red Earth Circle Restaurant.

"Jimmy, wanna grab some breakfast for yourself and then bring some over to the station for Melvin?" She handed her former high school classmate a twenty.

"See ya in a little, Melly." Jimmy hopped out on Renee's side and strode up the walk.

"Yeah, okay," Mel mumbled, long after Jimmy was out of hearing range.

Once inside the station, Renee took his jacket, showed him a comfortable chair, and got coffee. "Bobbi, tell Hobey we're in here when he gets in, eh?"

Bobbi held up crossed fingers.

"Comfortable, Mel? Can I get you anything else?" Melvin looked up as though just realizing there was someone else in the room. "This's gonna be tough," Renee muttered, taking a deep breath. "Mel?" She knew she couldn't ask questions that put words into a potential witness's mouth, much as she wanted to. So she said, "Jimmy said you've got somethin' to tell me about your friend Joe's death?" She flipped on the tape recorder. If Melvin did have something to say, she wanted it word for word.

After a pause, long even for an Ojibwa, Melvin whispered, "I was there."

"You were there?"

"*Gigi* Joey, there with Joey. In the *tchibakwewigamig*, in the kitchen, in the kitchen, in the kitchen, in the—"

Renee reached over and laid a hand on Melvin's arm. He jumped out of the chair and crawled behind the desk. She found him crouched with his arms covering his head. Kneeling beside but not touching him, Ren said, "It's okay, Mel, it's okay. You're safe here."

Mel rocked back and forth and covered his ears. He mumbled, "*Ondis nissaii, ondis nissaii*, he's gotta gun, get down, he's gotta gun."

"Who's got a gun, Mel?" Renee asked softly.

"The kid, the Indian. They all have guns. Gotta watch out. They all have guns."

"Who, Mel?"

"In the village, they all have guns."

Renee sat on her haunches, realizing that Melvin was back in Vietnam, a grunt in the army. After several attempts to penetrate the wall he'd dropped, she decided all she could do was wait until Jimmy returned with breakfast. Maybe he could bring Melvin back. But she had to wonder—what set him off? He said, "the Indian kid, the kid with a gun." Was that who came to Joe's apartment, a kid? If so, the kid must have come with someone. She doubted a kid could have pulled off hanging Joe Crocker up by his belt like a bagged deer. Even so, what kid? And what about the gun?

Jimmy came in with breakfast. This seemed to bring Melvin back to the present.

"Jimmy, did Mel tell you what he saw at Crocker's?" Renee asked, watching Mel wolf down the food.

"He said somethin' about a kid."

"That's what he said to me, too. Anything else?"

"He was hard to understand, Renny. He mumbled a lot, kept goin' back and forth between here and Nam. I don't know if there really was a kid there, or if he was rememberin' Nam."

"Me either, but this could be important."

Renee heard some noise in the front office, then Hobey's voice, "What the heck's that smell, Bobbi? Somethin' crawl in here and die?" After whispers, there was a knock on the door. Chief Bulieau peeked in. "'Scuse me, didn't know you folks were in here."

"I'll be right back," Renee announced. She shut the door to Hobey's office behind her. "'Member I told you Jimmy said Mel Leaper saw somethin' at Crocker's the day he died?" Renee briefed the chief. "I was jus' tryin' to get him to stay in this decade and time zone so we can find out what he knows."

"Sorry 'bout the crack, LaRoche. Didn't know it was them," the chief whispered.

Renee shrugged. "I better get back to Mel. I think if just Jimmy and me try and talk to him we might get somewhere." The chief nodded and Renee added, "Cross your fingers. He's talkin' about a kid being in the apartment. I hope to heck it's not Ned or one of the other kids at Neuterbide's."

Back in Hobey's office, Jimmy turned to Renee, "He's back, Renny. Think you can try again."

She nodded. "Breakfast okay, Mel?"

Melvin gave Renee a big grin. "I was pretty hungry."

Renee smiled. "Mel, can we get back to Joe Crocker's apartment? You said something about there bein' a kid there. What'd you mean?"

"Joe answered the door. The Indian kid came in and said he was there to give Joe a message from somebody. They started arguin'. The kid pulled out a gun. I hid."

"What happened then? Do you know who the kid was?"

"The bedroom, they went in the bedroom. I heard screamin', shoulda helped Joe." Mel looked at Renee with such a pained expression on his face she wanted to take him in her arms. "Screamin'." Shaking his head, Mel put his hands over his ears. "Screamin', don't like screamin'." Renee held her breath, but when Mel looked up she knew he was gone again. They weren't going to get anything more from Melvin Leaper today. And really, Renee didn't want to—she could see how painful this was for him. It sent him back to Vietnam, and no reason seemed valid enough to keep doing that.

"It's okay, Mel. You don't have to remember anymore today. It's okay." Renee turned to Jimmy. "Let's bag it for now. Need a ride, can I drop you somewhere?"

"We'll manage. Walkin's good. Clears the mind." Jimmy smiled. "I'll come by if I find out anything else."

Renee slid a twenty into Jimmy's pocket. "*Megwetch*, Jimmy. You've been a lotta help already. 'Preciate it."

After the two men left, Renee and Chief Bulieau turned their attention to Joe Crocker's autopsy.

"Melvin said somethin' about a gun. I don't know if he was talkin' about now or Vietnam, but we should probably assume here, eh?"

Renee sat in a chair in front of Hobey's desk. She was glad the autopsy had been done by the BCA, with the chief observing. It was complete and detailed, and just as they had suspected, Crocker hadn't committed suicide. The report identified signs of resistance. The buttonholes on the Lakota's shirt were strained, and the buttons were loose. Signs of someone tugging on them, tossing or dragging the person around. It also showed that Crocker's neck had two strangulation marks: the belt burn was laid over a thinner mark, made by something the width of a shoelace, or wire. The report went on to say: "There is a small ecchymotic area at the left temple and a trammeling on the right clavicle and in the right kidney area consistent with the victim being struck with a cylindrical object of some weight." It identified the marks that Jesse had seen on Crocker's wrists as rope burns, as if his hands had been tied.

"No mention of a gunshot, but the bruise at the temple could be from the butt of a gun. Whadda ya think about this trammeling business, LaRoche?"

"What could've been used? A cylindrical object. Wait, Chief, I saw a baseball bat there. I remember thinking that every guy in the U.S. must keep a baseball bat in his bedroom."

"A bat would do it okay. So how'd he get the guy into the belt and hanging there—beat him into it? Crocker wasn't a big guy, but still, dead weight's dead weight."

"I was wonderin' that too."

Chief Bulieau shrugged. "One more thing to look into, but I'd say it took two people at least."

"Yeah, one more thing, one more thing," Renee laughed. "I'm starting to sound like Melvin. Kinda gets to be a mantra."

"Whatever you say, but aren't you and your mantra due over at school?"

"Oh my God, you're right. What would I do without you?"

"Jus' protectin' my interest's all." The chief smiled.

"And speaking of your interest—after class I'll follow up on that phone number on the matchbook Jesse found in the car."

The Jablonskis lived on a working-class street of small, one-level, one- and two-bedroom homes with the sameness of early '50s tract construction. The housing development in Granite Rock took up most of the north end of town, just off Highway 7 to the east and the 35 freeway to the west. The only thing distinguishing the Jablonski house from the others on the block was that the two Ojibwa women wanted to talk to someone inside that one. Up the hill, around a curve and over the proverbial railroad tracks from the Jablonskis', individually designed and built homes of the Granite Rock upper crust, set back from a wide, maple tree-lined street, smugly overlooked the town.

Tracing the phone number on the Lone Loon matchbook had been easy. Discovering it belonged to the woman standing in front of them now was a surprise. The way the woman lowered her eyes while listening to Renee convinced the Ojibwa she knew nothing about any Lone Loon Resort or pornography group. The mail on the table near her front door, however, indicated she had a son who lived with her—Mark—who might. When Renee first called the number and asked for Mark, Mrs. Jablonski had been friendly. Now, face to face with Renee and Caroline, questions about her son were met with tight-lipped silence as Mrs. J's thin lips got thinner, and what color she'd held in her cheeks drained away. The color stalled in blotches at the woman's neck, haloing her Saint Christopher's medal. When Renee repeated her request to talk to Mark, adding it was police business, Mrs. J's eyes became vacant. Her face crumpled like a discarded newspaper. She still managed to stammer out, "I want you to leave now." Walking to the door to underscore what she'd said, she added, "My son isn't even here."

"When will he be back, Mrs. Jablonski?" Renee asked in a respectful tone.

"I don't know." The mother hesitated, looking at Renee as if she were going to say something else. Then she changed her mind. At the door, Mrs. J. stood with her back to the two Ojibwa women. Renee motioned Cal with her lips and they left the crackerbox house.

Cal's state of mind, once they were back in the car, made Renee regret bringing her. She had wanted to come, thinking if she helped locate Rosa's killer, it might relieve some of her pain. Her involvement didn't seem to be having the hoped-for effect. The shivering began at the tips of Cal's toes, moving in waves up through her thighs. "It's all so pointless," she stammered, trying to block out the image of Rosa Mae alone with her murderer, possibly this Mark Jablonski. Renee urged her friend to take some deep breaths, but the shivering continued, along with a cramp beginning in her right calf. It pulsed with a grief that was now blurring her vision. Ren watched Caroline wind herself tighter and tighter, and was helpless in her attempts to reach her friend. She seemed beyond listening.

"Runner, stop the jeep. I've gotta get out." Caroline Beltrain felt the muscles behind her eyes letting go, blurring reality. As Renee brought the jeep to a quick stop, Cal shoved the door open and pitched herself out into the bright sunshine. The combination of the sun's warmth and the northwind chill was like a slap in the face, and Caroline looked around as if she'd just awakened from a long dream. Dropping to her knees, the Ojibwa woman began to sob.

Renee rushed around the jeep and took her friend in her arms. Cal looked stunned, and Renee watched as her face closed over itself like a folded shirt. Renee had gotten to her a fraction of a second too late. She recognized the look and knew once Cal retreated behind it, she was gone, her way of saying, "I can't deal with this." Renee drew her friend close, keeping her silence now, not wanting to interrupt the woman's tears. They sat together for a long time. Cal sobbed loudly; Renee wiped away her bugle bead tears.

Caroline was exhausted when they resumed their drive back to the rez, but she refused Ren's offer to come home with her. This despite Renee's promise that Samantha would be okay with it. Renee reluctantly dropped her off at the corner by the meat-packing plant

and watched as she made her way slowly toward the apartment building where she was staying.

Laying her head on the back of the seat, Renee stared up at the
royal blue of the heavens. The summer sky was returning to the north
country. Winter's pale, remote, cold sky was changing to a summer
sky that invited you to reach out and touch it. Even in the dark of
night you could feel its closeness as Grandmother Moon slid up over
the horizon and hung suspended, observing the other night-spirits.
The sky would stay like this until the harvest moon of late summer,
until it began its winter retreat. "Sometimes," Renee sighed, "I really
want the days when Nikomis was more central in our lives. When we
lived with the rhythm of the moon and the seasons."

Renee had to motivate herself to move off down Hole In The
Day Boulevard. At the stop sign, she noticed Janice Walking Bear
struggling in the approaching darkness with two bags of groceries
and her eighteen-month-old daughter. "Need some help?"

"*Boozho*, Renee. Billy's comin', he's in the store. Thanks, though."

"Janice, your mom still workin' with the tribal social service?"

"Yup."

Renee had a momentary flash that Janice's mother, Donna
White, might be able to give her some details on the number of foster
kids placed off reservation. She'd become an essential part of the Red
Earth social service office since sobering up ten years ago. Getting
some history about off-reservation foster placement practices might
be helpful—Renee had a suspicion that this had been going on for a
long time, probably to someone's financial advantage, although certainly not for the benefit of the kids. "Say hi to Billy for me, eh?" she
called to Janice as she made her turn and continued on to Anishinabe
Circle.

At the tribal office building Renee got directions on where to
find Donna White out in the field, along with a brief history on how
Ned Sayer and his brother ended up at Floyd Neuterbide's house.
Their dad had died young, even for an Indian. They found him when
he was twenty-eight, curled in a fetal position, the rope around his
neck also tied to his ankles. It wasn't until twenty hours later, until
rigor mortis released him from its grip, that his chest revealed the
stab wounds that had ended his life. The murderer was never found.
Brenda Sayer, the boys' mother, cleaned the houses on the hill for

Granite Rock's elite, doing occasional baby-sitting for a package of tobacco and cigarette papers, or a box of powdered milk for the kids. By the time welfare stepped in her spirit had been broken. Food stamps were traded for alcohol, and eventually the kids were whisked off in a county car.

It made Renee think back to her own childhood memories. With Gramps, Renny and her friend Mollie had walked through the woods picking wild asparagus and mushrooms, and, in season, all the berries. They played hide-and-seek in the woods and, except in the spring, in the sugar bush structures. Their own special launch spot was in the small bay of Gi sina Nibi Lake, just down from the Coon family home, where they stored their raft a short distance from the treehouse they never quite finished—the Cardinal's Nest. Summer vacation started every year with the pig riding contest, the winner getting to choose how they spent the money from their first bottle-return hunt. Renny and Mollie ate almost all their meals together, at whichever house had the most sober parents. But since most families on the rez spelled *steak* S-P-A-M, they both preferred Grandma Coon's place. Gramps still trapped and hunted most of their meals. Even killed slow elk once in a while, though not often, because Gram didn't approve of shooting white people's cows. "There's a big difference, Mukie," Renee sighed, "in Ned's comin' up and mine."

Renee pulled into Rice Lake's newest government housing project on the west end of town. The prefab box structures had gone downhill fast in the twenty years since their construction; most of the houses were badly in need of repair and paint. Their style alone discouraged upkeep. The landscaping consisted of a few new-growth trees planted after the area had been clearcut of the full-growns, and that was about it. The front yards were worn bare from kids' play and no upkeep. The people were in similar shape. It was the first place tribal police expected to be called on Friday nights, the area having come to be known as "score corner" because of all the drug parties and sexual activity.

"*Boozho,* Donna, how's it goin'?" Renee called as the social worker returned to the official tribal staff car. Their conversation was congenial but guarded after Renee explained what she'd come to talk about. She was able to get a general picture of Donna White's work, work she had to admit she'd find difficult to do herself. White talked of one case after another of kids ignored, abused, and neglected. She talked of her initial belief in the Indian Child Welfare Act, voted in by Congress in 1978 to stop Indian children being removed, many times without reason, from their families by nontribal public and private agencies. White agreed the law was thought by Indian Country to be a survival tool for the culture. "But I don't see it that way, not anymore. If people wonder why I resist this so much," Donna said, "I tell them about Angela and how I thought I was doing the right thing helping her keep her daughter who ended up running away at sixteen and dying soon after of a drug overdose. Her mother was too stoned to attend the funeral."

"That musta been tough, but that's one case, Donna. The basic purpose of the law is to try and stop our culture from seeping away. Don't we lose 25 to 35 percent of our kids to non-Indian families? That can't be good for us as a people, and for the kids especially." Renee peered into White's eyes, trying to read what was really going on.

"On the surface it looks bad, Renee, but kids are suffering by being forced to stay in sick families here on the reservation."

"What about all the kids that go to non-Indian families to suffer and be abused there? I bet there's a lotta cases like that. Plus, they're away from their people and their culture. They look different, and you know that means they're treated different." Ren could feel her blood pressure rising. She reminded herself that tolerating Donna's opinions was the price for free information.

"You don't understand 'cause you don't do the work," Donna replied.

"Maybe so. Let's jus' take a few examples on this block." Renee pointed to the corner house. "How about them?"

White relayed the story, without giving a last name, of a single mother whose son, Chris, was taken from her when he was four and placed in one foster home after another until age twelve, then was placed with a prominent white family in Granite Rock. At age fifteen he ran off to Minneapolis and tribal social service lost track of him.

"Do you think he's happy?" Renee asked.

"Last I heard he was living on the streets," the social worker admitted.

The silence that followed bounced off the two Ojibwa like acorns hitting the forest floor. Donna looked from the files she carried, to

Renee, and back to the files. "You've given me something to think about," she said, getting into the tribal car.

Renee left feeling she understood Donna White a little better, but with the sick feeling that White's involvement in kids leaving the reservation was feeding a pornography ring—intentionally or not.

"J.J., you ever talk in class about kids bein' sent to *chimook* foster homes off the rez?" Renee had just dished up venison, potatoes, and a crowd of peas on Jenny's plate. She sat examining her daughter, thanking Gitchi Manitou that Jenny was almost through adolescence and doing well.

"No. I don't know, Ma, whadda ya mean?" Jenny's face displayed a mixture of confusion and boredom.

"I don't even know, I guess. I'm jus' looking into foster home placement and it seems like most kids are sent off the rez. Thought it might be somethin' you talked about at school."

"Jeez, Ma, I'll be good. I promise." The plaintive cry brought a burst of laughter from both Samantha and Renee.

"It's for the case she's workin' on, sweetie." Sam patted Jenny's hand. "Besides, I'd never let her get rid of you."

"Thanks, Mom."

"Seriously, J., any thoughts on this?"

"There's a boy in my current events class who wrote a paper a few months ago about a cousin who got sent away as a little kid. Willy's uncle went to prison and his aunt couldn't take care of the kid, I guess."

"Do you remember the cousin's name?"

"Naw. Oh, wait. Cliff, or Chris, or somethin'."

"Did they live over by score corner?"

"*Score corner?* Whoa, Ma. Pretty hip." Jenny flashed a smile.

"All right, all right. Very funny. Anyway, did he live over there?"

"I think so. I don't know. Why?" Jenny asked between bites of venison.

"Donna White mentioned a Chris from over there." The wind outside had picked up. It sounded like someone crying.

"He was pretty bad off for a while, I guess. Ran away to the city, lived on the streets, into drugs. Even did some funky movies, I think Willy said. Then some big shot over in Granite Rock took an interest in him and I guess he's been doin' better."

"Well, good for him," Renee smiled. "Sounds like he might be all right, eh?"

"I guess," Jenny shrugged. "Gotta go, Ma. Good dinner," she said, getting up from the table and grabbing the phone.

"Okay, my girl, jus' keep your ears open over there, will ya?"

"Ma!"

"Okay, okay. I'm not askin' you to snoop or anything."

"Whatever."

"Puberty," Samantha whispered, smiling.

"Honey, you made it through that," Renee giggled. "It's not gonna come back."

"Very funny, Renee Sue. I meant Jenny."

"I know what you meant." Renee sat back in her chair and sighed. "This stuff about foster kids—it's gettin' to me, Sammy."

Samantha leaned over and turned up the volume on their radio. "Listen to the music, my love. Chill out, as Jenny would say."

Renee closed her eyes. "Oh, I like this song. Come on, Sammy, lighten my mood. Dance with me."

"Guess I could do it in the privacy of our own home." Sam took Renee's hand and slid into her arms.

Leaning over the loft railing, Jenny watched the two of them, then called, "Sammy, who said you couldn't dance?"

"I'm doing better?"

"Yes, she is. She's close enough to the beat now, she can see it as it disappears around the corner." Renee grabbed Samantha in a big hug and swung her around as the three laughed uproariously. "This is better, much better," Ren said between laughs.

# 9

Caroline called just before Joe Crocker's funeral. Ned had ID'd the picture of Crocker. Renee had initially held out some hope that the Indian guy with long hair Ned described that day at Caroline's apartment wasn't Joe Crocker, but the call wiped out the last sliver of it. The boy also told Cal that Floyd Neuterbide was back and "in a major fit," ordering Ned to get Kevin ready because tomorrow they were taking a trip. Renee didn't like the sound of that. They'd have to draw the pieces together, and fast. The boys couldn't leave town with that man, and they only had a day and a half to stop him.

Renee sat in her jeep watching the people file into church for Joe Crocker's funeral. The Lakota man had led a circumscribed life: respected ninth-grade teacher and Little League coach, volunteer at the Elder Center, Vietnam vet who took in a brother in trouble. Only the circle of friends as debased as he knew his underbelly.

The funeral was held at Holy Rosary Catholic Church, Fr. Philip Murphy presiding at the Mass. An old friend of Renee's family, Fr. Murphy had retired, but he still said Mass once a month and offici-ated at special events for friends. Jenny and her classmates loved the new priest, Fr. Jason Demmay—J.D.—assisting Fr. M. today, but Renee had told Fr. M. that he was the last Jesuit for her. She was done with the Church. As far as she was concerned, it could pack up and leave the rez. An idle wish, she knew, but it stemmed from rage at a church that invaded her people's lives two hundred years before, wreaking havoc on a culture that had been doing just fine without it.

Renee sat at the back of the church. People from school, Indi-ans and a few whites, sat in the front nine pews; the first two were full of Crocker's ninth-grade class. Red Earthers and white folks from around the rez, including some Renee didn't know, filled up the rest. It saddened her to think what would happen when everyone found out about Joseph Crocker's hidden life. A lot of people were going to be very disappointed, especially his students. And many more would be furious. Ren noticed two *chimooks* take seats across the aisle. She snapped a few pictures of them. The one closest to Renee must have been Catholic. He knew when to kneel, but neither one seemed very interested in the service. They spent most of the Mass whispering and pointing at people around the church. She wished she'd seen a picture of Mark Jablonski at his mother's house.

The recessional, led by the drum and pallbearers wheeling a simple wooden casket, snaked its way up the center aisle and out the front door. Renee exited her pew as the two white men across the way walked by. "Mark?" she said softly, nodding and smiling at the first man. He flashed her a quizzical look as he moved past, leaving Renee to speculate if the look was because he wondered how she knew him, or because that wasn't his name. *Not too smart there, LaRoche.*

The morning air was warming outside as the April sun tried to maintain its advantage over the cumulus clouds. They raced across the sky, driven by a southwesterly wind. It was shaping up to be a beautiful day. Baneberry and bluebird lilies bordering the church-yard had begun to sprout, the extra springtime moisture from the snow aiding their efforts. The scent of loam, pine, and a faint aroma of mint filled the air. Life was budding everywhere. What a contrast, she thought, watching the casket being loaded into the hearse. The Ojibwa woman let out an involuntary cry as they closed the door on Crocker's final ride.

Hobey was in the crowd of mourners, talking to the Red Earth school principal. After checking that Jesse was ready to lead the funeral procession, he came over to Renee. She was standing at the edge of the crowd. "Comin' to the cemetery?" Hobey kept his eyes on the mourners.

"Not unless you think it's necessary," Renee responded. "Say, I don't see Crocker's parents."

"Couldn't afford to come from South Dakota. Plus, I think they're pretty old. See anything during the funeral?"

"A couple of guys near the back. Never seen 'em before, and

they seemed more interested in lookin' around and gossiping than participating in the Mass. I had a feeling one was Mark Jablonski, but I blew talkin' to him on his way out. They provided several photo ops, though." Renee patted her backpack. "Thought I'd run the film over to that one-hour photo on campus, if it's okay with you."

"Good idea. Jesse and I'll meet you at the station after you do that and we finish up with this." There was an edginess to the chief's voice that Renee assumed came from the erratic spring weather. Lately it was making everyone a little crazy. One day sunny and warm, the next below freezing and snowing. It was the time of year even northwoods winter enthusiasts were ready for shirtsleeve temperatures.

"Maybe if these pictures come out we can identify the *chimooks* involved and turn the heat up a little," Renee whispered.

"Good time to do it. Funerals tend to bring out the serious side of folks."

"Amen to that." Renee looked back at the hearse as it slowly pulled away from the front of the church.

Renee stopped down the street at Ole and Lena's, an art deco coffee bar on campus, while she waited for the photos. It was a typical coffee bar, with half the long counter displaying bins of coffee beans from which to choose, and the rest filled with a variety of cookies and pastries. Renee chose a pink marble table by the window and turned her chrome-and-black leather chair so she could people-watch, one of her favorite pastimes. The room had a mirrored wall opposite the windows. That, together with a ceiling lined with reflective material, expanded the relatively small space to feeling nearly twice its size.

Not a coffee drinker, Renee had to ask her waitron for suggestions on coffee beans. "Chocolate cappuccino'd be a good choice," the young Asian man hurriedly replied. Renee added a piece of chocolate mousse cake to his suggestion. As he retreated behind the counter, she marveled at the physical similarities between those from the land of the yellow people and the folks from the red nations. *I can see how those Bering Strait theorists get their ideas*, she thought, *but I'm stickin' with our story about comin' from the megis ess.* Watching the white folks coming and going, Renee wondered what they'd think about the Ojibwa belief that the People came from Creator breathing life into the megis shell. The thought almost made her laugh out loud.

Renee retrieved two papers from a giveaway stand at the coffee bar's entrance—the *Collegian* and an underground paper called *Footsteps*. She turned to the *Collegian* personals. It was the section Rosa Mae mentioned in her notebook. Not knowing for sure what someone interested in pornography, especially kiddie porn, would be looking for, she started at the top of the first column and worked her way down. Near the end of the section she came to an ad using some of the abbreviations she'd found in Two Thunder's notebook. "Out of the ordinary taste in fun? Like M/B activity, B/B viewing? PO Box 77, GR, MN." Right below it was, "Father Figure, 50, int. in BD spanking. Discreet. #25834." And, "Looking for boyish escorts? Avail. out or in calls. Call 643-Boys." "Welcome to Northwoods. Like M/B action? B/B watching? Look no further S/M, BD optional. #2473." She circled the abbreviations M/B and B/B. And finally, "Check the Internet. Beautiful Orchid Club exchanges. All style pics." "Goddamn perverts," she heard herself growl. "People actually respond to these?" She set the paper down as her coffee and cake came.

The sight of the chocolate mousse, moments earlier looking mouth-wateringly delicious, now made Renee want to vomit. She wasn't sure what most of the stuff in the personals meant, but she knew enough to want to run away from it all as fast as she could. It was the thought of Ned, his young innocent brown face and old eyes, that kept her in her seat. That, and remembering the photos of a woman she'd never known but felt a growing kinship with, dead in the morgue. Aside from the fact that Indian people usually feel a connection to each other, she wasn't sure what drew her to Rosa. Maybe she was overdoing it because she wanted to have something real with Cal, wanted to be able to relate to her last eighteen years. "And maybe that's jus' so much psycho-babble, LaRoche," Ren mumbled, "and you feel connected because it's something oppressed people feel for their own." Ren smiled at herself. *I agree with the dog—sometimes I do go on about things.*

Ren dropped some money on the table next to her untouched order, picked up the newspapers, and walked out of Ole and Lena's. With time left before the funeral photos were done, she tucked the newspapers in her backpack and headed down University Avenue.

The Bear's Den was at the end of an open air hallway housing small art and novelty shops. During the day the Bear's Den doubled as a deli, serving hot and cold sandwiches, soup, sodas, and coffee. Quick lunches for busy Gen X students who felt less passionate about eating healthy than they did about their coffee, the current obsession in *chimook* society.

Renee stepped through the open French doors into a space that looked more like a greenhouse than a bar or deli. Vines and ferns hung from the ceiling, and tall big-leafed plants stood along the brick walls. To her relief there was no stuffed bear, or bear's head, mounted on the wall. She approached the cashier, waiting while the woman finished with a pale young man wearing a sleeveless denim jacket over a sweatshirt and tight faded Levis sporting well-placed holes at the knees. His blond hair was in serious need of a washing and hung in his face down to the ring in his nose and the one in the middle of his upper lip. A chain connected the two.

"Can I help you, ma'am?" The cashier's voice rose. "Can I help you?" It finally penetrated Renee's gawking at the young punker. "Oh, sorry. I just...," she took one last glance over her shoulder at the departing chain and rings, "...how does he eat with that on?" The cashier stared, unresponsive, and Renee suddenly felt a very large generation gap.

"Can I help you?" the woman tried again.

Renee took out two photos, the close-up of Rosa's hand and a portrait Caroline had given her. Holding up the one of Rosa's hand, she asked, "Is this the Bear's Den stamp?" The startled look on the cashier's face after seeing the picture prompted Renee to explain why she'd come, but the explanation seemed only to heighten the woman's anxiety.

"Just a second," she stuttered, "I'll show this to my boss."

"Here," Renee held out the other photo, "maybe your boss will remember her. She would've been in a few weeks ago."

The cashier looked from Renee to the pictures and back. She gingerly took the photos and backed into the kitchen, moments later returning with a thirtyish white man she introduced as Tom.

"So, what's this about?"

"Well, like I told...," Renee glanced at the cashier's name tag, "...Amy, we're trying to retrace the steps of this woman right before she died."

"*We're?*" Tom looked her up and down.

"Red Earth Tribal Police."

"Well, well, you're in luck, sweetie." Tom smiled seductively at Renee. "Just so happens I remember her. Talked to her for a long time one night a few weeks ago, though I'm sorry to see she's dead." He paused before saying, "Name's Roseanne, right?"

"Rosa."

"Rosa, that's right. I noticed her right away." Tom gave Renee another big smile. "I'm kinda partial to you gals from over there." He winked. "Brown skin's my favorite."

When he licked his lips Renee wanted to ask, "And this is supposed to make me feel good?" But she needed information from the guy, so instead she said, "You talked to her?"

"Sure did. She came in about 5:00. Alone, so…," he shrugged, "what's a guy to do? I bought her a coffee and we talked." Tom paused, then continued. "She told me she was meeting someone here. We talked for a long time, but no one showed up."

"Did she say who she was meeting?" Renee was growing tired of the guy's condescension. He hadn't given her much for all his bragging about being able to help. Lydia'd say he was "emotionally frostbit," Ren thought, lightening her mood as Tom droned on.

"She was pretty tight-lipped about that. She did say something about an ad in the paper, though."

"Which paper?"

"The *Collegian*, I think. Yeah, I'm pretty sure, the *Collegian*."

"Remember what day it was?"

"Well, let's see, musta been Wednesday 'cause the *Collegian* comes out on Wednesday."

Renee's heart skipped a beat. It had been estimated that Rosa died on Wednesday night or early Thursday. "Can you remember anything else?"

"About 7:00 she got a phone call and left," Tom answered.

"You don't know who the call was from?"

"The guy workin' the bar that night said it was a man. Not an Indian, though. 'Cause, well, you know, you guys do talk a little different." He winked again.

Renee sucked in a breath for one more question. "You didn't

happen to get a name, did you?"

"What do you think, I'm nosy?" Tom laughed enthusiastically at his own joke, then added, "If I remember right, the bartender thought she called him Mike, or Mark."

"Mark? You sure?" Renee still hadn't mastered the art of keeping her enthusiasm in check at times like this.

"Someone you know?"

Renee shook her head. "You got a fair amount of information about Rosa that night, didn't you?" On the one hand, Renee was glad; on the other, the implications made her a little sick and a little suspicious given what happened to Rosa after leaving the Bear's Den.

"Like I said, I had a special interest in the lady." For the first time, Renee saw something in the man's eyes other than narcissism.

"Thanks for your help." She picked up the photos and turned to leave.

"Hold on," Tom said, grabbing her hand, "how 'bout you and me have some coffee?"

She had to give the guy credit—he recovered his self-absorption quickly. "Gotta go," she said, pulling her hand free and stepping off. *Slicker'n spit on a window,* Auntie'd say.

"You sure?"

Nodding, Ren turned and hurried out.

The chief and Jesse were going over details on the funeral. "Get anything, Renee?" Jesse set her coffee cup down and slid a chair over for her friend.

"God, how can you guys drink that junk?"

"Huh?"

"Coffee. I tried to drink a cup while I was waiting for the pictures, at that art deco coffee bar on Main. Interesting spot to watch people, but a coffee bar, I don't get it."

"It's an acquired taste." Jesse smiled.

"Or jus' somethin' you drink to stay awake," Hobey added.

Taking the photos out of her pack, Ren spread them on the chief's desk.

"This guy here," Jesse pointed at one of the white men in the second photo, "he looks kind of familiar."

"He's the one I thought might be Mark Jablonski. And," Ren

touched the picture, "what's this on his pants?"

"Looks like lint or something. Chief?" Jesse handed the picture to Hobey.

"Need a blow-up to really tell what it is."

Renee dropped another shot in front of Hobey. "I aim to please."

"Why should his dirty pants mean anything to us?" The chief examined the picture of the man's cuffs closely.

"I noticed this stuff on the guy's pants in church. Tried to figure out a way to get a sample of it, but short of fallin' down at his feet or tacklin' him, I couldn't come up with anything." Renee looked from Jesse to Hobey.

"That would've been a sight." Hobey chuckled.

"Anyway, I'm wonderin' if it's cat hair."

The tribal officers stared at the close-up. "Jeez, Renny, it could be, eh? You thinkin' what I'm thinkin? Crocker's cat?" Hobey peered at Renee over the top of his reading glasses.

"Remember when I picked the kitty up? I got hair all over my jeans. Well, what if he rubbed against it when he was there?"

The chief and Jesse nodded in unison.

"I say we show these to Ned. Try and get an ID on this fella—" Hobey jabbed his finger at the blow-up—"and his friend."

"And if it's Mark?"

"If it's Mark, we go talk to him and get a search warrant for those pants," the chief said.

"Mrs. Rawley told me Crocker just got the kitty, so if we can ID this as cat hair from *his* cat," Renee held her hands up in a *what-if* gesture and grinned, proud of her observation and the potential evidence she'd found. "Maybe he was there with the Indian kid and Melvin didn't see him or forgot about him." The tribal officers nodded. "Let's go," Ren said, gathering up the pictures. "I'll call Cal."

"Hold up, Renny. I want to review what we've got so far. Sit down and let's talk."

Hobey began after Renee was seated. "Renny, you said Neuterbide's planning to take the boys somewhere on the weekend?"

Ren nodded.

"That means we've got little more than a day to get enough evidence to arrest him and put a stop to this." The chief slouched in his chair, the silence extending as he fiddled with his coffee cup. His gnarled, slightly chubby fingers danced noiselessly on his thighs, an uncharacteristic show of nerves, but he felt like he'd been hit with a 12-gauge shotgun. Noticing his nervousness increased Renee's growing apprehension. She knew Hobey was worried this case could blow the reservation wide open for the world to examine in an endless finger-pointing odyssey while *chimook* involvement, central as it was, could easily be set aside or lost. Most people held deep prejudices against Indian people. The chief didn't want that reality to get in the way of the horrific child abuse, but Renee was sure that it did. Hobey knew his community was not a hotbed of violence against its own children, that it was only a few sick ones who'd been sucked into this perversion. And he would see they were punished, severely punished, but he didn't want the whole of his Red Earth to be painted with the same brush. That wasn't fair, and Hobey was determined not to let that happen.

Finally, Renee said, "I can start, Chief, if you want."

"Saw a Sherlock Holmes movie once." Hobey overlooked Ren's comment. "He was talkin' to his friend Watson and said, 'Some evidence's like a stick on the ground. Looks like it's pointin' in one direction 'til you step on the other side of it. Then it's pointin' the other way.'" Hobey stood and walked to the window, standing there a long time before he turned back to the two women. "The next day's gonna be tough. We still don't know who the Ojibwa is that Ned saw. All I'm sayin' here's we gotta be careful. Every detail's gotta be checked and double-checked." He looked straight at Renee. "And we have to share everything with each other, no goin' off..." The chief sat down behind his desk and rifled through several files. "Here's the report on the second autopsy done by the BCA on Two Thunder. This all started with her, so let's us do that too, eh?"

Renee took the report and began to read:

> Rosa Mae Two Thunder's body was exhumed pursuant to order #1317 of the court. Autopsy was performed at the Chippewa County Coroner's office by Dr. Robert Pepperhill from the Minnesota Bureau of Criminal Apprehension. Hobart Bulieau, Red Earth Tribal Police Chief was also present.

The body was examined for trauma. Both knees showed bruising consistent with falling, or being pulled down from a standing position. A blunt impact fracture to the right radius 2cm below the epiphysis is consistent with a defensive injury as though subject was fending off an attack of some kind.

Renee wiped perspiration from her forehead, then continued reading:

A gunshot, entering the occipital region of the skull, was determined to take a downward path, tumbling through and destroying the brainstem and the right carotid artery before lodging against the right neck wall. Stippling indicated the .22-caliber pistol was fired at close range, execution-style. Cause of death was destruction of vital brainstem functions and hemorrhage.

Renee looked up from the report, eyebrows arched like two new moons. "Jesus H. Christ. They shot her at point-blank range."

Hobey leaned forward. His arms rested on his knees, bearing the weight of his upper body as he wrung the tension out of his hands. "Someone murdered her all right, and from what we've gotten so far from Rosa's blue notebook, from Ned, and from the photos, I'm convinced there's a connection between her death, Joe Crocker, that fellow Neuterbide, and all this pornography stuff."

"Agreed, and I've got a feelin' Mrs. Jablonski's son Mark is the guy with the cat hair on his pants and is right in the middle of it all." She told the two of her conversation at the Bear's Den. "That certainly seems to connect Jablonski to Crocker and to Rosa."

"I've got a bad feelin' about this." Hobey returned to his earlier concern. "My stomach tells me this is the kinda thing that could rip the community apart."

Some sickies had taken root in Granite Rock and on the rez, like deadly nightshade growing in the community, and Renee agreed with the chief, it was the kind of thing that could rip Red Earth apart.

"But you can't stop the poisonous growth until you identify its fertilizer," Hobey said, as though he'd read Renee's mind.

"Fertilizer?" Renee glanced at Jesse, then back to the chief. "Fertilizer. I was thinkin' about that too, Chief. How are they getting all the kids. Are you worried tribal social service is involved?"

Hobey grimaced at the possibility, but nodded, "It's crossed my mind."

"What made you think of social service?" Jesse squinted at Renee.

"Saw Janice Walking Bear in Rice Lake and I remembered her mom, Donna White, works over there. So I jus' started wonderin' ...about the fertilizer, I mean."

"What're ya gonna do about it?" the chief queried. Listening to Renee was lifting his mood considerably. He couldn't have been prouder of her at that moment if he were her father.

Renee told them what she'd learned so far from Donna White, then said, "After we get Ned to ID Mr. X."—she held up the photos from church—"maybe our next stop should be tribal social service? We still need an Ojibwa to fill in the quartet Ned saw at the house. Maybe he's there."

"We can't forget the sheriff's office, either, and them burying Rosa without even noticing she'd been shot." Jesse shook her head.

"Speaking of the sheriff, I can't get Rod Johanson's snarly comment about juvenile delinquent rez kids out of my mind."

"That was pretty unprovoked," Jesse added.

"Well," Hobey interjected, "somebody once said—talking about the universe—that we're either alone in the universe or we're not, and that's how I feel about the sheriff's office. They're either covering their tracks on this or they're not. At this point it really doesn't matter. Either way we've got to follow the leads and find the murderer, eh? The person guilty over there'll become obvious as we go along. And if they're involved more deeply, it'll come out."

The two women shared a bewildered glance, but they both nodded.

"I've had a thought here, since we've been talkin'," Hobey began again. "Was Josh able to lift any prints at the porn house, Jess? Ones we might be able to place with someone—like this guy?" He tapped the picture.

"House was wiped clean. No prints anywhere, just a smudge on the ON button of the VCR."

"Damn, they had a lot a time, didn't they?" Renee's eyes snapped. "It's my fault, damnit. There goes possible evidence."

"Hold on now. Don't jump to that place too soon, Renny." The chief's expression had become introspective, and the silence extended. The women waited. Hobey'd tipped back in his chair, his eyes closed, church-steeple fingers covering his face. Finally he said, "Jess, get the fingerprint kit."

"Okay."

"Let's go see if Josh might've missed something." Hobey gave the women a smile that said he believed Josh had. The three of them rose to their feet in unison.

Half an hour later they turned down the rutted road that led to the house. The darkened windows gave off an eerie feeling, looking back at the trio with a hollowness that frightened them. Entering the side door moments later, Renee peered questioningly at Jesse, then held up crossed fingers. Hobey came in behind them and stood in the middle of the tiny living room. "Jess, you said Josh dusted everything?"

"Everything. From the telephone to the bedposts to the doorknobs. He said he did everything, Chief, and it was wiped clean." Jesse held her hands up in a *what-can-I-say* gesture.

"Not yet." Hobey ran a finger over a table by the couch. The tabletop, and every other surface Josh had checked for fingerprints, were still coated with black dusting powder. "Okay, let's think about this. What would someone do who's in here, doesn't want to be seen, and maybe hears a noise outside?" The chief grinned, looking from one to the other of the women as though he'd just sent them on a scavenger hunt. "That musta happened at least once while they were here, eh?"

Renee studied the room. There were no glass panes in the front door. She moved to the window. Turning to the others and sporting a big smile, she said, "They'd come to this window over here, to peek outside?"

"Very good, LaRoche." The chief walked over and stood behind her. "My guess is a right-hander would come to here, pull this back with his left hand"—he grasped the drape covering the right window—"but just a little so he wouldn't be seen outside. And he'd probably put his right hand about here." Hobey moved his hand to the window trim, around eye level. "Jess, dust here, okay? Maybe a little higher, 'cause we're not sure how tall little Marky, or whoever, is."

It took just a few seconds for two nicely formed fingerprints and half a palm print to show up four inches above where the chief pointed.

"Yahoo!" Renee did a few fancy dance steps, arms in the air.

"*Yahoo*? Is that a technical police term?" Hobey laughed.

"So now what, Chief?" Jesse asked, lifting the prints on transfer tape and depositing them in an evidence bag.

"What did Bobbi find out about who owns this place?"

"Belongs to the Dunlaps. They're mixed bloods. Bought the land up around here after the 1906 treaty allowing whites and mixeds to buy land. A way to try and break up the reservation." Renee finished with a long moan. "Know any Dunlaps, Hobey?"

"I do, actually. A few. And I wanna say one of 'em's married to Bouchard over at social service, but I'm not sure 'bout that." The chief frowned. "I'll ask Joyce."

The women nodded and Renee said, "Should we visit Mrs. Jablonski and see if we can cop some prints of her dear son?"

"That'd be a good idea," he nodded, "but do it by the book. No mistakes. And take the picture to show her after you get an ID from Ned." He looked at Renee, who was already at the phone. "Then head over to social service. I've gotta get home. Millie's birthday's today and Joyce has a party planned." The chief slid his sleeve up over his watch. "I've got ten minutes to get across the rez. I'm gonna talk to the Feds first, see if they'll get a search warrant for Jablonski's. Then I'll let you know where to meet 'em. I'll get back to the office soon's I can."

"How old's that little *nosijhe* of yours gonna be?" Renee asked.

"Millie's the two-year-old in the brood. Todd's five, Brad's seven, Hannah's twelve."

"What? No Hobart in the bunch for grandpa?" That got a laugh from everyone.

The chief eased himself out of the overstuffed chair. "Why in hell do they make these things so low to the ground?" he complained. "Got no respect for aging knees."

"Guess they didn't expect someone's old as you'd be comin' here, eh?" Renee loosed a humorless laugh.

She called Cal. They talked on the phone and worked out a plan for a quick ID from Ned on the photos. "Soon's I call the Mrs.

I'll be ready." Renee dialed again. Then, grinning at Jesse and Hobey, she said, "I'll jus' be a minute." She smiled self-consciously and walked into the kitchen.

"Anybody check the phone records from here?" Hobey asked over his shoulder as he headed out the door.

"No, but I will." Jesse smiled.

"Good gir...woman," Hobey grimaced. "Woman jus' doesn't always fit. Sorry," he shrugged.

"Is this the Indian girl that came to my house yesterday?"

Renee and Jesse had just walked into the station when the phone rang.

"Whose house would that be?" Ren said, taken off-guard by the *Indian girl* comment from the woman on the other end.

"Jablonski. Over on Lucille Street in Granite Rock."

"Yes, yes, Mrs. Jablonski. I'm me, I mean, I'm the one."

"Well, do you think I could see you? I'm sorry about yesterday. I was very rude." Renee wondered if *rude* meant kicking them out, or that she hadn't even offered them coffee, unlike Ojibwa who'd feed you a three-course meal if you just stopped by to deliver a package. Renee waited until the woman spoke again. "There's something I...well, I've been thinking about something, and I thought—"

Anxious to get on with the plan they'd outlined at the porn house, Renee looked helplessly at Jesse. Relieving Mark Jablonski's mother of her guilt was not high on her priority list, and she didn't want to go to her house until they had their search warrant. But she offered, "Maybe I could come by later, or we could meet somewhere tomorrow?"

The pause was so long, Renee thought she might have to repeat the suggestion, but finally Mrs. Jablonski said, "I want to see you right away. How about the Malt Shop in Elko, nobody will know me th...oh, I'm sorry, Miss, I didn't mean that like it sounded."

"No, course not," Renee said in as even a tone as she could manage. *Ah, the gloriousness of northwoods racism. Please help me, lady, but come after dark with a bag over your head, will you?* Renee resisted the temptation to ask Mrs. Jablonski if she would agree to meet in public with her if she passed the paper bag test. But she doubted the woman knew the story from the '50s. How African American people had to put their arm in a paper bag, and if their skin was lighter than the bag, they'd be allowed into the white-run establishment. Giving up the idea, she swallowed her anger and the meanness it prompted. "Well, it's 1:00 now, how 'bout if we meet at 2:00?" She hung up and took a deep breath, stretching her arms above her head. "It's been a long day, Mukwa, and it's barely past lunch." She reached down and gave the cocker a pat. "Mrs. J. doesn't like us Injuns, Mukie, but she seems to want our help so...what the hell, eh? We're used to that."

Mukwa glared at her and growled. *You don't have to take that, and I don't like it when you do.*

Jesse was at the chief's desk. "Bad news, Renny. The chief called. He couldn't get the FBI to agree to a search warrant for Jablonski's. They said without an ID of the suspect we didn't have enough to go on and they weren't going to embarrass themselves appearing in front of a judge with less." Jesse leaned back in her boss's swivel chair, hooking her fingers together behind her head. "We have to get that picture to Ned."

Renee was already on the phone. Hanging up minutes later she said, "Beltrain told me there's no way to reach Ned today unless we're prepared to arrest Neuterbide, and—" She slammed her hand down hard on the desk. The loud crack brought Mukwa to her feet and off the couch. "I know we can't do that, not yet anyway. Cal said Neuterbide was at the college, but the resort was swarmin' with friends of his." The two stared at each other.

"How about we pay the professor a visit?"

Renee jumped to her feet. "Oh jeez, Jess, I gotta run. That was Mrs. Jablonski on the phone. Mark's mother? She wants to see me," Renee glanced at her watch, "and I better step off. Don't think she lives on Indian time."

"What's this about?"

"Not exactly sure. Maybe she'll give somethin' up. Or, if we really get lucky, maybe she'll take me to the house and give me the pants. I'll take the picture. At least we can be sure this was Mark at the church."

"Be careful, Renny."

"Will do. How 'bout I call when I'm done and meet you at the college? Shouldn't take too long with Mrs. J."

"Okay."

Before meeting Mrs. Jablonski, Renee stopped at a turnout parking area in the wetlands on County 3. She and Mukwa walked down the path and across a foot bridge. This was a beautiful spot now, thanks to the tribal DNR restoration efforts. Ren sat on a bench overlooking the four-hundred-twenty-acre wetlands, then sprinkled tobacco on the water and began to pray. Before leaving, she smudged herself and Mukwa with sweet grass. "*Kabe gwaiak,* Mukie, I'm ready for her. Let's go see what she has to say."

Just past the billboard displaying a caricature of a big-nosed Indian advertising Braves Liquors in Elko, Renee slowed and turned onto Mabel Street. A half block down Mabel, she pulled into the Malt Shop parking lot. Sitting across from Mrs. Jablonski a few minutes later, Renee waited respectfully for her to begin. The stoicism of Mark's mother was awesome. But having heard Bobbi's description of Mrs. J.'s life, she didn't wonder.

Bobbi's friend Joan, the school nurse, had worked with Lois Jablonski at the Red Earth Indian Health Service Hospital. She'd told Bobbi that Lois had been a widow of some eighteen years, making Mark only four years old when his father was decapitated in a bulldozer accident in the pit that had eventually become the Granite Rock State College sports coliseum. Mrs. J. went to work to support herself and the two boys, ages four and nine months. Starting as a nurse's aide at the hospital, she decided to attend school in a nearby town. Thirteen months later she'd moved up the pecking order at the hospital and had been there as an LPN for twelve years now, most of that time on the night shift so she could be home when the boys were awake. Joan said she hated working there, but the next closest hospital was fifty miles away in Bemidji, so Lois toughed it out, taking care of all those "timber niggers." Renee held onto those details now, sitting across from this woman who was embarrassed to be seen in public with her.

"My son's a good boy, Miss."

"Renee."

"What?"

"Renee, you can call me Renee."

"Oh yes dear, okay. Well, I was saying, Renee," Mrs. Jablonski smiled weakly, "he's never done a mean thing to nobody. He's a hard worker, both my boys are. We don't take handouts in this family." Unable to stop now that she'd made that first leap over talking about family secrets to a stranger, she forged ahead. "My son's been livin' in Minneapolis since he got outta the army over a year ago. About. I know the army changed Marky. He went to the west coast and lived around all those strange people for too long. He started coming up home from Minneapolis last year. Back and forth between here and the city." She glanced up at Renee. "Well, you understand, you people do that all the time. Anyway, I asked him how he could do that with his job and all, and he told me he's the manager."

"Where does he work?"

"I don't know. A video store I think."

Renee frowned.

"What, you don't believe him?"

This time the Ojibwa woman shrugged.

"My boys don't lie. Besides, he has a lot of money, and where would he get that if he didn't have a good job? But he's been hanging around that Indian, Joe Crocker. He's a bad influence on my son, and I told Marky to stop going out with him, to stop going over to that reservation. Just because I work there doesn't mean I approve of socializing. No ma'am, those are two different things."

The woman droned on as if she wasn't talking to an Ojibwa. How do white folks do that, Renee mused, barely hearing the woman's viewpoint on the evils of the reservation. Does she legitimize me by talking to me, by somehow absolving me from the sin of being Indian?

"...Shifty guy," Mrs. Jablonski said through pinched lips, then paused in her monologue, shaking her head as though to stop the tears that were welling up. It didn't work, and she began to cry. After a time her tears subsided. She took a deep breath and let out a sigh that sounded like it came from the center of her being.

Renee held in her instinct to comfort the older woman, choosing instead to push on. She removed the photo from her pack and lay it on the table between them. "This is Mark, isn't it?" Seeing the look of shock on her face, she added, "It's okay, this was taken at Joe Crocker's funeral. They took a lot of them."

For some reason the explanation made sense to Mrs. Jablonski and she said, "Yes, Roberta, that's Mark, but it's not a good picture of him. He's much more handsome when he smiles. He looks just like his father." With that, Mrs. J. began to cry again. And again, Renee waited. She was relieved when Mrs. Jablonski went back to her stoic face. "I'm sorry," the white woman apologized, taking a neatly folded handkerchief from the black plastic purse she sat clutching in her lap. Renee had to wonder if it was money, or the company, that prompted how tightly she held onto the purse.

"It's okay, Mrs. J. This must be very hard for you," Renee offered. "I was curious if you knew how your son and Joe Crocker became friends?"

The woman shook her head. "Why do you think Marky is involved in pornography?" she blurted out. "I know he's not. It's right in the paper."

"Paper?"

Mrs. Jablonski opened her plastic purse and pulled out a neatly folded article, handing it to Renee. The *Granite Rock Gazette* article claimed that unidentified sources were investigating a pornography ring on the Red Earth reservation involving a recently deceased tribal member. It offered no names and, it seemed to Renee, little concrete evidence, but the *Gazette* wasn't known for its Pulitzer prize reporting.

"And so it begins," Renee muttered.

"It certainly doesn't say anything about someone from Granite Rock, does it, Rochelle? If there's something goin' on on that reservation, then they're trying to blame it on my son and get out of trouble themselves." Mrs. Jablonski folded her arms across her chest defiantly and glared at Renee. "You betcha they are."

Adrenaline hit Renee's nerves like a shot of the espresso coffee she'd left at Ole and Lena's. "Well, I guess it won't be Joe Crocker now, will it?" she shot back, tired of being so nice.

Mrs. Jablonski looked startled. "Nevertheless," the woman harrumpfed the word, "nevertheless, Roxanne, the paper doesn't accuse anyone in Granite Rock."

Minutes passed before Mrs. Jablonski unfolded her arms and appeared to relax a little.

"Do you know where I could find Mark?" Mark's mother stiffened. Renee added quickly, "If you're right about Crocker, Mark could help clear this all up and put an end to the rumors about himself."

# 10

When Renee and Jesse arrived at Professor Floyd Neuterbide's tiny cubicle office, a reporter from the college paper was interviewing him.

"Professor, you're known around Granite Rock as a backer of town- and county-supported activities for kids. How do you feel about the current affirmative action program at the college?"

"It's a giveaway program based on some liberal's misguided sense of obligation to those in society who don't have gumption enough to make something of themselves."

"You don't believe we owe certain segments of society some assistance, at least on their first step up and out?" There was such an eagerness in the boy's voice—Renee was sure he must be a freshman.

"Now listen," Neuterbide's voice had taken on an edge of exasperation, "these kids need help a lot sooner than college age. They need discipline as youngsters, a firm hand to direct them."

Renee and Jesse leaned against the wall outside the office. Renee peeked in at the two men. "Can almost smell the testosterone in there, eh Jess? Let's give 'em five more minutes, then we'll go in. Even five minutes might be too long to subject that boy to the professor's verbal garbage."

The women were winging it. They had little to accuse Neuterbide of, but Renee hoped that if they got him to talk he'd disclose valuable information. The professor droned on in the office about how he believed kids should be raised.

Renee tuned him out again. Checking her watch, she motioned with her lips to the door. The tightness in her chest and the turmoil beginning in her stomach were familiar. Danger, excitement, stress—all initiated it. Still, the reaction never failed to surprise her.

Stepping into the doorway, Jesse said, "Professor? Got a minute?" She extended her hand, but the professor ignored it. Renee knew the snub didn't have to do with who Jesse was. Neuterbide didn't like touching anyone. She'd seen him shrug the mayor's hand off his shoulder. She wondered if it had something to do with his belief that everyone traveled through life alone, safe only in their "own company." At least that was how she remembered him describing it at a county meeting.

The tininess of the office exaggerated the professor's size, momentarily catching both women off-guard. Renee took in the room. It was the kind of office where she doubted anything was ever really put away. Moved from pile to pile or shelf to shelf maybe, but never really put away. Windowless, the office was made smaller by wall-to-ceiling bookshelves crammed with books, three-ring binders, and stacks of paper, plus three four-drawer file cabinets. Walls not filled with the bookshelves and cabinets were covered with tacked-up maps of the U.S. and other parts of the world. There were no personal mementos on the walls or desk, no display of framed diplomas or photographs. The gunmetal gray desk was probably college-issue.

The professor dismissed the student and stood regarding the women with a weighty frown, his eyebrows seeming to cover the top half of his face.

"Afternoon, Professor Neuterbide, we jus' took a chance we'd catch you here."

"You're that woman from the reservation," Neuterbide said sourly. He eyed Renee over his reading glasses.

"Yes I am. I am definitely a woman from the reservation."

"I've seen you around, at a few county meetings." Neuterbide limped noisily to his desk, fiddled with something that unlocked his braces, sat, and folded his hands carefully. Renee had never before noticed how complicated it was for him to walk.

"What can I do for you girls? Are you here to sell me raffle tickets or something? Whatever it is, you'll have to make it quick." As he talked, his hands were doing their own thing, sorting and stacking papers, putting some in his briefcase and moving others from one pile to another.

"Going somewhere?" Jesse used her official police voice.

"What? Oh, no. No. Just home to the wife and kids is all." Neuterbide seemed genuinely puzzled by their presence.

"We're not here to sell you anything, but we do have a few questions." Jesse continued with her official voice.

"I'll say it again, I don't have much time." Renee noticed a bit of an edge creeping into the professor's voice.

"This won't take long," Renee said, "do you mind?" She nodded at the chair near her and took a step toward it.

Neuterbide's irritation seemed to be growing, but he didn't object. With only space for one visitor's chair in the room, Jesse leaned against the file cabinet next to Renee's chair. The professor tapped nervously on his desk and, after a brief silence, said, "Well girls, come on. I don't have all day. Speak up, speak up. Don't be shy. I know how you reservation girls are."

Renee nudged Jesse's foot.

"Well, I'll tell you, we've run across some information that connects you to very unpleasant circumstances," Jesse began, "so we'd appreciate some honest responses from you."

"What unpleasant circumstances?" The booming voice filled the tiny room.

"Child pornography," Jesse said in a cold, even tone.

"What?" Neuterbide's response was forceful, raising both eyebrows. "I don't know what you're talking about. How dare you come in here and accuse me of such a thing. My wife and I were just foster parents of the year last year." Sweat was beginning to bead on the man's forehead, and he had turned as pale as the papers piled on his desk. Renee sat in the chair watching the exchange between Neuterbide and Jesse.

"Those aren't the honest responses we'd hoped for." Jesse leaned over the desk and stared into the professor's eyes. "Especially considering your past history with this kind of thing."

"History, what history?"

"Age thirty, Chicago? If you help us, maybe..." Jesse let the sentence hang.

"The day I waste my time on two female Indians'll be the day I've got nothing left in the world to do. Now take your ignorant, half-baked theory and get out of my office."

"How 'bout the Internet, Floyd? Done any sharing with the Orchid Club folks lately?"

"Get out of my office," Neuterbide yelled, a flush starting around his neck.

"It's your call, professor," Renee sneered. "Marky's being cooperative enough for the both of you. Jus' never figured him to be the smarter one." Out of the corner of her eye she could see that the noise was starting to draw people into the hall outside the office.

"Marky?"

"Mark Jablonski. You know him?"

Neuterbide's eyes acknowledged the question. He seemed to give it a disinterested sort of consideration before saying, "Never heard of him." The answer was without emotion and, Ren believed, given with the detachment of a trained liar.

"Never?"

A flush that had stalled at Neuterbide's jaw line seemed to take off as though being pulled by some invisible force, spreading over his face and blotching at his forehead. He glared, first at Jesse, then at Renee, before hissing, "You two girls are not going to get away with this harassment. Now leave my office or I will call security and have you removed."

"Will you be using the same phone we have the incoming log on, the one showing Mark Jablonski's and Joe Crocker's phone numbers?"

Renee flashed a smile at Jesse, proud of her friend's quick thinking, then said, "Okay, we'll leave, professor."

"But a little advice?" Jesse added. "Don't *you* leave town. We'll be back to talk with you soon." Both women walked out of the office and had to make their way through a growing throng of people in the hall. Halfway through the crowd of all white people, Renee said, "Jeez, Jesse, just looking at the man, it's hard to believe he's involved in child pornography, isn't it?" Her words echoed off the wall, and the audible gasp from the people gathered assured Ren they'd heard her comment.

"All hell's gonna break loose now, eh?" Renee said as they walked to the car. "I'll alert Caroline and tell her to be ready for a call from Ned."

"Good idea. Hobey thought he could get the FBI to help with

stakeouts at the Lone Loon. Lawton's feeling a little guilty about that search warrant. What's your plan now?"

"Think we should try and track down Donna White?" Renee glanced at her watch, adding, "Guess I'll go home and get somethin' to eat first, if that's all right. Sam's needin' a lot of reassurance these days." The remark went without comment from Jesse and Renee continued, "Glad I don't have to teach on Fridays."

"How about we meet at the office and go over to tribal social service after that?"

"Take a look at Crocker's phone records." Jesse handed Renee a computer printout.

Renee pulled up a chair next to the chief's desk where Jesse sat.

"You'll see five numbers regularly called. One's the school. One turns out to be a sister in South Dakota; I guess his parents don't have a phone. One's listed as the Granite Rock State College general number, and one is a private line to Neuterbide's office. Sure glad I knew this before we visited him."

"That was great, Jess." Renee was feeling a growing excitement— they were definitely closing in on the professor. "How 'bout the last number?"

"Your friend," Jesse smiled.

"My *friend?* Mrs. J.'s?"

"The one and only."

"Oh, by the way, she ID'd the guy in the picture as her little Marky. I don't like that woman much, but I hope she never finds out she helped finger her son as a player in a pornography ring. She told me that Mark's in the city, due back tonight. She also told me he hangs out at the Bear's Den a lot, so it figures he'd ask Rosa to meet him there. I'm gonna check the place out later. See if I can track him down."

"The chief called in while you were gone, Renny. Wants to hear from us with anything we get."

"How 'bout we make one visit before we call him?" Renee leaned back, stretching out her arms and legs.

"Social Service?"

"Social Service."

"Let's go. Oh, by the way, the chief said Joyce says a Dunlap is married to Sam Bouchard."

"Director of tribal social service?"

"That's the one."

"Oh my God, they own the porn house."

"Sick, eh?"

The social service director for Chippewa County, Peter Armstrong, was known in the reservation social service office as IBS: Indian Baby Stealer. He often bragged he'd taken over five hundred Indian children and relocated them "in loving homes." Renee knew the only way Armstrong could have had such access to Indian kids was to have help on the reservation side of placement. Something he apparently had had for years. Clearly somebody didn't consider him an IBS. Renee figured that Jed Morriseau had been the conduit up until a year ago. After his murder, someone else had to have taken over. Renee hoped their visit to the tribal social service office would discover who that was.

"Is Donna White in, Nan?" Jesse asked the young woman at the front desk.

"I'll check." Moments later, Nan returned. "Sorry, Officer Johnson, she's out on a call."

"Sam Bouchard?"

"At a county meeting in Thunder Lake."

Jesse explained the reason for their visit. If Nan could give them permission to check the social service files they wouldn't have to bother with an order from tribal court. They were in luck. Nan was new at the office and couldn't think of any reason the Red Earth tribal police shouldn't be allowed to see their files. After all, they weren't the enemy. So, with no one else available to ask, and Jesse assuring her they'd be just a minute, Nan led them back to Donna White's cubicle.

"*Megwetch*, Nan. I'll come get you if we need anything." The young woman nodded and left Jesse and Renee alone.

For the next thirty minutes, the two women tried to cull relevant information from the files. It appeared Peter Armstrong not only had had a friendly relationship with Jed Morriseau, as Renee suspected, but he now worked closely with the director of Red Earth social service, Sam Bouchard. One file after another had notations to the effect that Red Earth parents were lacking in one or more vital characteristics, and that foster placement was therefore necessary. Little was said about placement into Native families, and judging from the addresses of the foster homes, most were off reservation.

"Jess, I'm finding a lot of files where Bouchard recommends placement and Donna White provides the facts to back it up," Renee said, looking up from the stack in front of her.

Jesse nodded. "I'd like to check up on a few of these decisions."

"Gotcha."

Ten minutes later the women were ready to go, leaving behind a message for Donna White to come to the police station when she returned. "Nan, tell her we're just checking up on a few things, eh? No big deal," Jesse added, not wanting to get Nan in trouble or alarm White before she even arrived at the station.

Renee went with Jesse to call Hobey and check in with him, and then headed over to the Bear's Den to see if she could catch up with Mark Jablonski. Pulling into the parking lot behind the bar, Renee killed the lights and leaned back, absently rubbing Mukwa's head. Taking a deep breath she said, "*Niji*, why are two-leggeds so evil? You guys don't act like this, deliberately murdering one of your own kind for greed or some other ridiculous reason." Her long sigh was interrupted by Mukwa licking her face. "*Megwetch*, my girl."

Renee studied the picture of Mark one last time, said a little prayer, and gave Mukwa another pat on the head. "Wish me luck, girl. I won't be long."

Inside the Bear's Den, lights were dimmed, so Renee took a spot at the end of the bar to wait for her eyes to adjust. Surveying the still relatively empty room, she noticed someone sitting at the far end of the bar, nursing a beer. It was Mark Jablonski. *Okay, LaRoche, easy does it. You just wanna check this guy out. Go slow, be cool.*

The news had just ended on the TV mounted above the bar. The crawl along the bottom of the screen warned of another threat of severe weather, this time in the form of sleet with possibly up to an inch of rain. Renee groaned. She sat watching the man at the other end of the bar. He appeared deep in thought, folding and unfolding a napkin, his black leather jacket collar tucked up around his neck, his lanky, six-foot-plus frame hunched over the bar. *He's not an unhandsome fellow*, Ren thought, *for a white boy.* Mark fiddled with the napkin. When he ordered another beer, she made her move. Renee didn't mind him a little loose-tongued, but she didn't want him drunk.

"Didn't I see you at Joe's funeral?" Renee slid onto the stool next to Jablonski. "You were with a friend, I think." The guy took a long pull on his fresh Budweiser and slowly set it down in front of him. Renee watched his hands with fascination. They were so small it looked like a ten-year-old grasping the bottle.

Jablonski stared at her blankly. "Did you? I don't remember." He brushed a shock of thick, curly, blond hair off his forehead.

"Yeah, I think I bumped into you on the way out." Renee paused. "Too bad, eh? About Joe, I mean."

"Yeah, too bad." Mark nodded and began playing with his napkin again.

"Can't imagine why he did it," she said. "Doesn't seem like Joe, does it? Were you a friend of his?"

"Sort of."

"Name's Renee."

"Mark."

"Hi, Mark. How did you and Joe know each other?"

Another blank stare. "I don't remember. Around. Softball, maybe."

This was going too slowly. Renee fussed. Sitting very still, lips pursed, eyebrows together, she thought furiously, then leaned over, and in a hushed tone said, "Rumor goin' around the rez that it wasn't suicide."

Jablonski was just taking a drink of his beer, and her words must have clamped down on his swallow. He began coughing violently. Clapping him on the back she inquired, "You okay? Sorry about that. Didn't mean to freak you out."

"No, no problem, I'm okay," Jablonksi lied between coughing bursts. Renee waited. *Chimooks* and silence were like vacuums—always seeking to be filled. They couldn't help it. Jablonski would ask her why people thought it wasn't suicide. And sure enough, as soon as he had his breath back, he said, "Why, what's goin' on? I mean, what's makin' 'em think that?"

"They found somethin' at Joe's apartment, I guess."

It was a bait Renee prayed he'd take. She could see the wheels turning behind Mark Jablonski's eyes, as though he was scanning a checklist of the scene. At first she thought he might not say anything.

The beginnings of a large struggle were taking place behind his vacant green eyes. When he finally spoke it was haltingly, as though he was running his answers through a censor before letting them out.

"What could they have found," he muttered, more to himself than to Renee.

Renee shrugged, then leaned in again and whispered, "I've got a friend at tribal police who told me they're looking for something around the apartment."

"Around the apartment? What?"

"Wouldn't say, but I think they're lookin' for something somebody dropped, or a footprint outside. Somethin'." Renee almost chuckled when Mark glanced down at his shoes. He scribbled on the napkin.

"Somebody from over there's been buggin' my mother."

For a split second Renee panicked, remembering she'd told him her name. Then she recalled that Mark's mother'd forgotten her name the minute Renee told her. To Mark she said, "Oh, you're the one."

Jablonski swung his head around and stared at Renee. "Whadda ya mean by that?"

"Oh, nothing, nothing. I'd jus' heard they were gonna talk to someone, that's all." Renee hoped she'd planted enough alarm in Jablonski to move him to action, and possibly to a mistake.

Mark Jablonski stared off into space for several minutes. Then he jumped up, grabbed his jacket, and without a word hurried out of the Bear's Den, leaving a ten-dollar bill on the bar. Renee counted to ten, grabbed his glass, wrapped the napkin he'd written on around it, and followed him out.

A few minutes into tailing Mark Jablonski, Renee put a call into Jesse. "Any word from Donna White?"

"She called, should be here any minute," Jesse replied, then added, "Renny, it's dark and it looks like it's getting slippery. Don't go taking unnecessary chances following this guy."

"Promise. Think he's headin' to Crocker's place. Oh, got a glass with his fingerprints on it. Gotta go. I'll keep in touch."

Renee followed Jablonski out of Granite Rock onto Highway 7. At that point he picked up speed, passing cars and driving erratically. Fear began to well up in Renee's throat. "This guy's drivin' like a madman," she said to Mukwa. "Wonder how long he'd been drinkin' before I got there."

The evidence against Mark Jablonski was mounting. The picture at the church was him. She'd bet the lint on his pants was hair and dander from Joe Crocker's cat. There was evidence someone from his house made calls to the pornography house, and Ren was sure it wasn't his mother. Somebody named Mark called for Rosa at the Bear's Den and then she left, never to be seen alive again. Blond hair had been found caught on Rosa's ring. There was a matchbook in Rosa's car with his phone number on it. Neuterbide had definitely twitched when Jablonski's name was mentioned a few hours ago. That was at least some proof—if only circumstantial—that he was involved in one, maybe both, of the murders. Where was his reason, though, she wondered? Would—could—he murder twice just for money? He'd been in the army, so Ren guessed he'd been trained to kill. Following him now as he frantically drove, she had to admit he was acting a little like a guilty man. But still, she wasn't convinced. Means and opportunity, apparently. Motive, she didn't know.

His turn off Highway 7 onto County 3 almost landed him in the wetlands, but he recovered and sped toward the reservation. He slowed after his right onto Mosquito Creek Road, so Renee dropped back, afraid he might have spotted her. But then he tore off again into the darkened countryside, apparently unaware of Ren behind him. She watched with growing apprehension as the car in front of her slid and careened off Mosquito Creek Road onto Cliff Road. *He better slow the fuck down.* It was obvious Jablonski had not driven this stretch of reservation road often. She made the turn onto Cliff Road at just a barely safe speed in time to see Jablonski's Toyota 4Runner disappear around the first curve. Reaching the curve herself, she heard the spewing of gravel and dirt as Jablonski braked to correct his speed entering the next curve. Renee saw the 4Runner fishtail at the curve entrance, saw Jablonski's brake light go off, then on again. He was pumping the brakes. A no-no she knew, with ABS brakes, and she could see the result when the brakes locked and catapulted the Toyota off the road like a rock hurled by a slingshot.

As though watching the event in slow motion, Renee saw all four wheels leave the ground in graceful unison. The car stayed aloft twenty feet, the front end soaring over the cliff's edge. But its rear tires caught the rim, flipping the back end up and over the front in ballet-like motion. Unfortunately for the occupant, the graceful flight ended abruptly when the front end dug into the incline and the rear end sprang up and over the vehicle with frightening speed.

Pulling up to where the Toyota had left the road, Renee killed the jeep's engine. An eerie silence overwhelmed the spot. Reaching Jesse on the cell phone, she yelled, "Jablonski's gone over the cliff. Send an ambulance and tow truck to the second curve on Cliff Road off Mosquito Creek. We'll probably need the whole goddamned National Guard to get him up outta there. Gotta go. Tell 'em to hurry." She jumped out of the jeep and headed for the cliff's edge, Mukwa at her heels.

"Stay here, Mukie. Wait for the EMTs."

Jablonski's vehicle had gone over the edge just before the cliff began its more precipitous drop to the Journey River. But even here the incline was a good twenty degrees, and full of sumac and thimbleberry bushes, aspen and tamarack trees. The soil was rocky, slippery from the rain and sleet. Renee slid on her butt and hands, digging her heels in every fifteen to twenty feet.

Once over the rim, the 4Runner had skidded on its roof about a hundred feet down the embankment and come to a stop butting against two subcompact-size boulders at the spot where the incline began a more deadly drop down to the valley. The new black Toyota 4Runner looked like a giant turtle, tires spinning in a futile attempt to right itself.

Renee pressed her heels into the slick embankment to slow her slide, using the hand not holding the first-aid pack to try and direct herself. Rocks tore into the palm of her left hand, but she barely felt the pain she knew would keep her awake in a less crisis-oriented moment. *Damn.* She glanced at the rapidly growing bruise, wiping the blood on her jeans and continuing her almost-out-of-control descent to the Toyota. Slowing just above the vehicle, she inched her way down, unsure what was preventing the Runner from continuing off the cliff's edge into the darkness below. She moved past underbrush along the driver's side to the door. The top had held up surprisingly well. It definitely was not the advertised "adequate head space, even for the tall man" anymore, but, Ren figured, even someone as tall as Mark could come out of this alive. After considerable tugging the door opened about three feet and Ren shone her flashlight into the front seat.

Mark Jablonski's head was awash in blood, no doubt from damage done on impact with the passenger-side windshield. His right foot was pinned up under the dash in the leg well, which had been reduced to a narrow slit. The leg was twisted so severely that his knee faced backward. Obviously Jablonski had not been wearing his seat belt. "Mark, Mark. Can you hear me?" Renee called to the man as she leaned in and slipped two fingers under his collar, searching for a pulse in his neck while giving thanks to Creator for the medical training she'd gotten in the Movement. She wondered what Jablonski and his friends would think if they knew where the skill she was using to try and save his life came from. She doubted any would be pleased, especially Neuterbide.

Reassured when the Toyota seemed to hold her weight, she eased her way in and, after some searching, found the pulse, weak and thready, but there. "Hold on, help's coming," Renee whispered in his ear. Pulling a gauze roll and ace wrap from the first-aid kit, Renee located the laceration on Mark's head causing most of the bleeding. "These damn head wounds bleed like the proverbial stuffed pig," she muttered, applying a pressure dressing on the wound. Satisfied she'd stopped the main obvious ebb of life for now, she began checking the rest of him. A siren in the distance reassured Renee that help was on the way, and she knew they couldn't get there soon enough to suit her: there was a dangerous mushiness to Jablonski's chest. He released a deep sigh as she lifted her hand, and she watched anxiously until his chest rose again in a shallow breath. "Don't you dare die on us now, you asshole," Renee muttered, regretting immediately having said it. Believing a person reaches a plateau between life and death where you can choose which way you want to go, Renee didn't want to push him over the edge.

Ren released Jablonski's foot from under the dash and discovered it was badly mangled. Finding the posterial tibial pulse behind Mark's ankle was difficult from her angle, but finally her index and middle fingers slid onto the pulsing artery. It was strong, and Jablonski's skin was warm to the touch. She reached down under the injured leg and secured a plastic splint at the ankle, knee, and thigh, then inflated it. "Good job, LaRoche. At least maybe you'll save his leg." She mumbled encouragement to herself, then offered a quick prayer for his survival. "You're in bad shape here, Mark, but help's comin', so hang in there." Renee sat back on her haunches and listened to Mukwa barking to reinforcements arriving up top. "We're here," she said, standing and waving her flashlight, "down here. Bring a back board, oxygen, and the mini Jaws. He's not pinned, but we gotta get the door open wider."

"Comin' down, LaRoche," the chief called, and disappeared back over the top.

"Be careful, Chief, this rain's made the bank pretty slippery." Then she heard a groan behind her. Taking off her jacket she laid it over Jablonski. "They're comin', Mark. Don't move, we need to get a back board under you."

"Come here," the injured man rasped, trying to grab Renee's hand. "Have to tell you—"

A cough brought bubbling blood to his lips.

"Ssh, Mark. Don't talk. I think you've got a punctured lung. You can tell me later."

"No, no, no time. Have to tell." Mark struggled to take a breath. "Helped Neut…helped Neuterbide—" He fell back onto the seat.

"Slow breaths, Mark, and don't talk." She took the injured man's hand, wishing her conscience could let the guy talk more.

"Floyd's the one that organized…" He took in a shallow breath. "We killed the wo—" was all he got out before losing consciousness again. A check of his pulse reassured Renee that was all he'd lost, for now. She filed the conversation away. Hobey and the paramedics had arrived. It was time to get busy.

After immobilizing his neck and head, they widened the driver's-side door with the Jaws of Life, then slid a back board in under him. Once strapped to the board, Jablonski was lifted out and strapped into the rescue basket. An IV was started and, attached to a come-along at the head of the basket, the young man began his slow ascent to the top. Renee breathed a sigh of relief.

Once Mark Jablonski was settled in the rescue vehicle, Renee headed for her jeep. For the first time since her slide down to the Toyota, she felt a searing pain in her left hand.

"Can I catch a lift into the hospital with you two?" Hobey called.

"Hop in, sir." Once on the road, Renee said, "It was bad, Chief. I followed him from the Bear's Den thinkin' he might be goin' to

Crocker's apartment."

"Crocker's apartment?"

"It's a long story. Anyway, I was followin' him and I thought he was gonna crash and burn just by the way he was drivin'. You know nonrez folks—they take these back road curves like they're drivin' in town."

"Tell me again what he said to you down below?" Hobey shifted uncomfortably in the seat.

"Little snug?"

"Huh? Oh, yeah. I'm too old to be bumpin' around in these novelty vehicles." Hobey groaned for effect, then offered a hearty laugh.

Ren loved the chief's laugh. When he got into the heart of it, it was a sound full of richness from deep inside. It always drew one out of Renee. "Novelty vehicle? I'll have you know this is a sophisticated four-wheel-drive, all-terrain, over-the-river-and-through-the-woods-to-grandmother's—" Renee snuck a peak at her elder friend.

"Okay, okay, I give. I'm sorry I insulted your jeep. Please forgive me," Hobey said, as he patted the dashboard.

Renee let out a whoop. "God that felt good," she sighed.

"All right, Renny, let's get back to it. What did Jablonski say down below?"

"He said Neuterbide planned, or *organized* I guess is the word he used. Not sure what, but then he said we killed the wo—, and that was it, all he got out, then he coughed and lost consciousness again." Renee reached in the back seat. "Here's a glass with his prints on it for you. Got it at the Bear's Den. And," she pointed at the napkin, "he wrote somethin' on that."

Hobey pulled a couple of evidence bags out of his jacket pocket. He flattened the napkin out, slid it into one bag, and put the glass in the other. Ren switched on the map light and Hobey leaned over. "Looks like it says *key.*" He looked up at Renee.

"Key?" Renee repeated. They drove quietly for a while. Then Renee said, "Wait, remember the key I found the first time I went to the porn house? Maybe he means that one. I thought it belonged to Joe Crocker, 'cause of the J on it, but it could stand for Jablonski." Renee shrugged. "Maybe he thought he left it at Crocker's."

"I'll check the prints on it with his. That might answer that question. Drop me at the hospital will you, Renny? You better head over to the station. Jesse's talkin' to Donna White. This accident's gonna raise some nerves on Neuterbide and the Red Earther that's involved." Hobey stared out the window. "I'll bet on it."

"How so?"

"Well, sounds like you guys already got Neuterbide goin' at the college. And didn't you mention Mark?" Renee nodded. "So he hears about this and he's gonna flip. We gotta be ready." Hobey said the last very slowly. "I have a feeling Floyd's not very trusting. He'll worry about what Jablonski might have been up to and what he might say in an injured state."

"Gotcha."

"We've gotta find a weak link. I'll keep tabs on Mark Jablonski. I wanna be there when he wakes up. If you guys get anything from White, call me. I'll get Josh to check prints on this glass against the ones we found in the house."

The two drove along in a silence full of energy. Before dropping Hobey at the hospital, Renee recounted her experiences with Mark's mother.

"Shouldn't let people treat you like that, Renny."

"That's what Mukwa tells me. Guess at some level I feel sorry for her. She's not gonna like what little Marky's been up to."

# 11

"Am I too late?" Renee queried, looking around the empty office. "Where's Donna?"

"Donna," Bobbi smirked, "now there's an interesting story." Quiet descended over the tribal police office.

"And?" Renee finally took the bait, "what's the story? And where's Jesse?"

"Right behind you," Jesse said, coming in the station door.

"What's goin' on? Where's Donna?"

"Let's go into the chief's office."

Renee fell into a chair by the desk. Stretching her legs out in front of her, she groaned audibly. "Oh God, I need a vacation." She yawned, then folded herself up into the chair.

"Not now you don't." Jesse sat in the chair next to her, adjusting her shoulder holster to a more comfortable position. "Donna White found out we took some names from a few of her files. She called here furious, wanting to talk to the chief." Jesse paused.

Renee filled the silence with another big yawn. "Oops, sorry Jess. I'm awake, go on."

"When she finally got here and we started talking, she settled down a little."

"Thanks to you, no doubt."

"Maybe."

The story that unfolded was the one Renee had expected but dreaded nonetheless.

After Morriseau's murder, Peter Armstrong began fishing for another ally and landed Sam Bouchard at the tribal social service.

Unbeknownst to Armstrong, Bouchard enlisted White to supply the necessary data on cases to get the kids out of their homes. "White reported all this so innocently, like she had no concerns about the legality of it all. She believes that she, and only she, knows what's best for the kids on Red Earth. I doubt she knew anything about any child pornography. I got her to give up some details on her and Bouchard's relationship, though she claims her boss is strictly on the up and up. Hobey told me that he heard Bouchard and White were having an affair, so that probably figures into it too. White kept saying she knew what was best for the kids. Her ego, Renny, it's blinding her. She really believes she should be judge and jury on all foster cases." Jesse looked very sad. She finished her report, telling Renee that Josh was checking with a few families, hoping to prove to White she'd made mistakes in her recommendations for placement. "But I think we'll need more than just a few families before she'll admit to anything."

Jesse took in a long slow breath before continuing. "Caroline came by and picked up pictures of Jablonski and Sam Bouchard to show Ned. Bouchard fits the description of the other Indian: dark, short hair, Ojibwa. Fortyish." Jesse rubbed her hands together and, closing her eyes, laid her head on the back of the chair.

"Let's go beat the hell outta ol' Sam Bouchard," Renee said through tight lips.

"Man, would I like that," Jesse agreed, sitting up in the chair. "I'm taking this case very personally. I just don't understand how anybody could do this kind of stuff to kids. My hope for a good resolution's gone."

"The spiritual leader of the Movement used to say that hope is revolutionary patience," Renee said, looking at Jesse. "Let me tell you what the chief and I figured out on the way back from the accident." Renee's retelling of the last couple of hours was difficult. "At some level I feel kinda guilty, Jess. I mean, I got the guy all worked up and he flew outta the bar like his own shadow was chasin' him."

"Renny, that's the kinda stuff cops do. It was his own guilt that shot him out of the bar, not your words."

Renee drew in a long breath, checking her watch. "We've only got a few hours to put a stop to this. What's our next step, Geronimo?"

Jesse turned. "You're right, Renee. Time's running out and so's my revolutionary patience."

The phone rang. "Chief's on the line, Jess," Bobbi called.

"Jablonski's still unconscious," Jesse relayed, hanging up the phone. "Hobey said to check with Caroline and see if Ned's ID'd Bouchard. If he has, pick him up."

"I'll call." Renee was immediately at the phone.

"Runner, I've been tryin' to call you." Cal picked up the phone on the first ring.

"Oh, damn. I left the phone in the jeep. What's up?"

"Ned says Bouchard's the other Skin, but we've gotta get to Neuterbide's." Renee's friend was talking very fast. "They're packin' up to leave over there."

"Where?"

"At the Loon."

"Everybody?"

"I'm not sure. I met Ned down by Rocky Point, jus' long enough to show him the pictures. He said they were packin' to leave. That's all he said 'cause he had to get back to Kevin. I don't know if he meant him and Kevin and Neuterbide were packin' up, or everybody, or what."

"Take a breath, Cally, slow down girl." Renee spoke firmly into the phone.

"I'm fine, Renee. Get the fuck over there and stop that asshole, or I will."

"We're on our way, Cal. I'll be in touch."

"I'll meet you there."

"No, no, Cal. Stay where you are. I'll call you." The phone was dead. Caroline Beltrain had hung up.

"Did you hear that, Jess? We gotta fly. Cal's on her way over there I think. We gotta get there before she does."

"Let's go."

Jesse made a quick call to Hobey. As Renee was getting into her jeep, Jesse came running out of the office. "The chief said to pick Neuterbide up. We'll figure out what to charge him with later. He's callin' the Feds to let them know what's up."

"What about Bouchard?"

"I told Bobbi to send Josh," Jesse replied.

Just then Bobbi came out the door. "Go and get those kids, you guys. I talked to Con. We can take four of the Indian kids temporarily, and two on a more permanent basis."

"You're the best, McMillin. Tell Conway that too, eh?" Renee yelled as she and Mukwa pulled out of the parking lot.

In the quiet of the jeep, Renee called Samantha. She'd promised to keep her—*apprised* was the word Sam used—of what she was doing on the case. "Hi, my *sagiiwewin*."

"Hi to you too. Where are you?"

"In the jeep. Only have a few minutes but wanted to let you know what was up." Renee felt her heart racing in her chest.

"How sweet. You know how much I appreciate this. Where are you?"

"On my way over to the Lone Loon to arrest Floyd Neuterbide." She hurried the last part of the sentence, then held her breath.

"What? Renny!" Renee thought she could hear Samantha swallow on the other end. Then a calmer Sam said, "Who's *we?*"

"Me and Jesse."

"Where's the chief?"

"He'll be comin'. We talked to him and got instructions before headin' out."

"Back-up?"

"Bobbi's notifying the FeeBees."

After an extended pause, Samantha said, "Do you know the story of Icarus?" Her voice was strained, and Renee appreciated how hard she was trying to stay in control.

"Icca who?"

"Icarus. He was trapped in the labyrinth. It's a Greek tragedy."

"The tragedy is their names."

"Oh, and I suppose Wa banong Ikkwe is an easy one to pronounce?"

"Okay, okay. You got me."

"Anyway. Now I've lost my point. Oh...I was going to say, Icarus was trapped in the labyrinth. Couldn't find a way to walk out, so they made wings of wood and wax to fly over the maze. Icarus was warned by his father not to fly too high, too close to the sun, because it would melt his wings."

"Did Icchy listen to ol' dad?"

"No. He didn't listen, flew too high and fell to his death."

The silence extended through Renee's turn off Highway 7 onto College Drive in Granite Rock.

"Renny?"

"I'm here, *saiagi iwed*, I'm here. I think it's so sweet that this time you're the one tellin' the story. I get your point. I'll do whatever Hobey says, and I'll be careful, I promise. No flying too close to the sun for me."

"Thank you," came the hushed response. "I love you."

"I love you too, Sammy. Gotta go now though. I'll call when we're back at the station." Samantha's response was so soft it was lost in the sounds of the road.

Following Jesse through Granite Rock and out to Eelpout Point on Sturgeon Lake, Renee was in a state she couldn't remember being in before. Lights blossomed out from their center like ever-changing flowers. Nighttime returned the woods to the ancestors. Spirits, long gone to the Spirit World, left footprints of their memory in the forests. Renee felt it more powerfully tonight than ever before. It comforted her, and knowing they were only a veil of time away renewed Renee's commitment to the traditions they had worked so hard to preserve. "This would break their hearts," she mused. "They lived for the *abinodji*. All those damaged children."

Making the turn into the drive of the Lone Loon, Renee shook her head back and forth quickly and rolled down the window. The stress and length of the day was taking its toll. "Too bad I'm not a moose, Mukie," she yawned. "They take short naps all day and night so they'll be ready for any danger. That's what I need right now."

The Lone Loon stood foursquare to its dock, extending into Sturgeon Lake. Weather-beaten, it was a picture postcard of northern Minnesota lakeside resorts. The fish-cleaning house, where those lucky or skilled enough to catch fish on their outings could clean their catch of the day, perched at the water's edge. Just beyond the trimmed grass of the resort, Beaver Creek flowed out of the lake. The water sheeted over a granite flat at Rocky Point, narrowed and picked up speed as it snaked through the sawgrass. Then, making a sharp turn, it disappeared into the woods. It was easy for Ren to imagine the intricate harmonies alive in and around the creek. What was harder to imagine were the human goings-on here at the resort.

Renee saw Jesse approaching Neuterbide from the east side of the resort office, so she followed her lead. "Good evening," Neuterbide said, slowly looking Renee up and down. This move, done no doubt to unnerve her, made Renee sick to her stomach. Mukwa fixed Neuterbide with a menacing stare, and the man took an involuntary step backwards.

"That give you a warm feeling, professor?" Renee looked at the man like he was an escapee from a petri dish.

His smile frayed, but he said, "Make you nervous?"

"Actually, it makes me sick." Renee flung the words out like knives, missing the intended blasé sound she was reaching for.

The grin frozen on Neuterbide's face elicited a feeling similar to the one caused by the cold, violent eyes glaring at her.

Grandmother Neebagesis shone through a rent in the clouds, brightening the night, and sparkling the icy edges of Beaver Creek. Right next to the moon, Venus winked in the chilly evening air.

Renee couldn't help staring at Neuterbide, wondering what the inside of the man's soul must look like. She pictured a dimly lit barn full of musty, fermenting hay, old tools and farm machines, all oily and rusted shut, a place where the sun never shone. His eyes were shrouded by black, bushy eyebrows, and the sag of his jowls reminded Renee of an old English bulldog.

Suddenly, Ren realized she had missed Jesse's question to him. Why did she do that, let her mind wander off? But the guy fascinated her. "He's the kinda guy," Renee could hear Lydia say, "that if someone was havin' a shake-'n-bake fit in the bathtub, he'd throw in his laundry."

In the woods past where they stood, Renee noticed the green eyes of a deer caught in someone's flashlight. A momentary illumination froze the deer, who then sprinted off deeper into the woods, jolting Renee back to the moment. The bitter taste of fear filled her mouth as she listened to Neuterbide demand to know why they were back. "Has this become your hobby?" he snarled. "Harrassing me? I'm going to have to insist that you leave." He spit the words out through clenched teeth.

"This time, professor, we're here on official business," Jesse said, emphasizing the point by speaking slowly.

"What kind of official business?"

"We'd like you to come to the station with us to answer a few questions," Renee heard Jesse reply as she eyed the man intently.

"Do you have a warrant?"

Just then brush rustled near where the deer had been standing, the flashlight blinked again, and an almost imperceptible muscle twitched close to the professor's mouth. By the time Renee recognized it and thought to take action, it was too late. Neuterbide had pulled out a revolver and begun to back up.

"Don't move or I'll shoot you both," he growled, "and that little black dog."

"Hold up now, professor," Jesse said evenly. "There's no need for this. We just want your help in clearing up a few things."

"Right, and if I believe that, you've got some prime lakefront property to sell me for a string of beads, right?"

A long-striding figure sprinted to the parking lot in the shadows near the creek. Out of the corner of her eye Renee could see the figure jump into a utility vehicle, back up, and, with tires squealing, roar up to a spot in the parking lot near them. The familiar clicking of his brace followed Neuterbide to the vehicle. With only minor difficulty for a man with his disability, he climbed into the high-riding GMC. "No one will get hurt if you just stay where you are." The professor spoke in a strained, quiet voice. As the unidentified person backed the vehicle up, Neuterbide shot twice at the Ojibwa and they hit the grass. "And don't come after us," a voice called as they sped out of the lot. Jesse ran to her police jeep to send out a call to Hobey, the Granite Rock Police Department, the county sheriff, and the Minnesota Highway Patrol.

"I'm gonna check on the kids, Jess," Renee yelled, taking the bunkhouse steps two at a time. Reaching the top step, Renee saw Caroline pull in and waved to her, then opened the door and disappeared inside. She found Ned and Kevin and the rest of the kids in the far corner of the room. Ned was reading a story. The older ones were holding the little ones, and everyone sat huddled together. Generic colored drinks painted Kool-Aid smiles on the kids' faces as they listened to Ned read the story of *Annie and the Old One*. When Renee walked over, they all looked up very frightened.

"It's okay, she's cool," Ned said to the group, and Renee thought that was probably the nicest thing anyone had said about her in a very long time.

Cal came in and stood behind Renee. "Everything okay, Ned?"

The boy nodded. "It is now." He smiled his reserved smile.

"Who was that haulin' ass, oops sorry, tearin' outta here?" Cal asked.

"Neuterbide and somebody. They're trying to escape, but Jesse's callin' in the posse. I don't think they'll get very far."

# 12

The three women drove toward the launch spot at the Boundary Waters Canoe Area where Floyd Neuterbide's GMC had been found, a few hours north of Red Earth. After the Highway Patrol's discovery of the vehicle, they'd radioed Chief Bulieau, who, in turn, had tracked down the local outfitter responsible for unsuspectingly helping the two fugitives. According to Andy Slayton, they had a map and equipment enough for several weeks in the northern Minnesota back country with them when they arrived, and she'd provided a canoe and food, putting them into the BWCA at the Shagawa Lake drop point. Slayton had assured Hobey she'd be waiting for the Ojibwa women with everything they needed for their trip in after the two men.

"I can't believe you got hit when Neuterbide shot at us." Renee gave Jesse's leg a nudge. "You didn't even flinch."

"I didn't feel it until I was running to call the chief." Jesse unconsciously flexed her right shoulder.

"Makes it tough to paddle a canoe, eh?"

"I don't want to talk about it. You don't know how bad I want to go after that guy." Jesse gazed out into the darkened countryside.

"Wish you were comin' with us." Renee glanced over at her friend. "But you and Mukwa'll be waitin' for us at the drop-off when we get back?"

"Absolutely. And the chief, and probably more than your fill of FBI agents."

"Are we sure where Neuterbide and the other guy put in?" Caroline asked.

"Highway Patrol said it's at the Shagawa Lake drop. They were on their tail, but lost 'em in Winton," Jesse reported.

"We should plan for trouble, Cal."

"Good idea. I don't wanna get separated from you somewhere in never-never land without any way to make contact. It's been years since I've been in the woods."

"You a drugstore Indian now, Cally? I'm up in these parts every summer."

"You and the Mrs.?" Cal chuckled.

"Yep, me and the Mrs."

"You're the boss out here, Runner. I'm outta my element," Cal admitted reluctantly, hating to acknowledge that Renee's *chimook* lover knew more about these woods now than she did.

"Far's getting separated goes, how 'bout you stay put if that happens. I'll do the trackin' and find my way back to you. I know this area, but two steps into the forest and you could easily get lost. Even if you do know it, you gotta leave markers if you go off trail."

"Okay, Runner, I'm all yours." Cal smiled. "I've gotten too used to the easy life. I like houses, not tents; restaurants instead of camp-fires."

"...and you can't tell one tree from the other, or a coyote from a dog, eh?"

"That's about it."

"Well, I'm the gal you wanna be with in the back country, then. Long's you're a sturdy girl, you'll be all right."

"Take me to the trail head." Caroline accentuated the comment with a straight arm pointed up the highway.

The rest of the drive was quiet, each woman going over their hurried departures from home and families. Renee had had to leave a note for Samantha and Jenny, telling them to contact Gram and Lydia and, "for God's sake, don't worry." Sam would be upset she missed the call, especially when she heard that Caroline was going with her. In her note, Renee had explained Jesse's injury, and that Hobey had okayed Caroline Beltrain's involvement. She had mixed feelings herself about heading into the wilderness alone with Cal, but they'd done well together before in rough situations, so it made sense for them to go now, even if Cal was out of practice.

Renee thought about Neuterbide and his involvement in all of this. Mark Jablonski had told Renee that the professor was the main guy. When Josh did a fingerprint check on the glass Ren retrieved from the bar, and the key ring from the porn house, he also ran a check on the prints Hobey, Jesse, and Renee had gotten off the window woodwork at the house. Those prints belonged to Floyd Neuterbide, finally putting him inside the house. Ned had told them that Neuterbide came home from the college and ordered them to pack up. Before they'd finished, all hell broke loose and the professor disappeared into the countryside. Everyone agreed the man had to be tracked into the woods; hoping to catch him on the other side was too risky. There were too many places he could come out of the BWCA, on this side of the border and in Canada. No one was immediately concerned about the young Native male who, according to the kids at the resort, drove the getaway vehicle. Other than the crime of aiding a fugitive, he wasn't wanted for anything at the moment. They'd lifted prints at the resort and were checking to find out who he was.

Pulling into the Shagawa Lake turnout, Renee had a self-satisfied smile on her face, proud of the job she'd done talking Hobey into letting her lead the search party. Her adrenaline was pumping so fast she was getting a headache, and the telltale acid burn lingered in her gut. This was going to test her to the limit. In more ways than one, she thought, glancing over at Caroline.

Wilderness outfitter Andy Slayton was waiting as promised, along with two Minnesota highway patrol officers, and a Lake County sheriff's deputy. Andy told them she thought the two men were going to the first portage site by canoe and then heading off on the Echo Trail. She'd gotten the distinct feeling, she told the Ojibwa women, that they were heading for Canada.

"That means only one thing from here then, eh?" Renee half smiled at the woman.

Andy offered a playful smirk before she and Renee said in unison, "The gorge!"

Renee placed a final call to Chief Bulieau before push-off. "Tell Jess I'll be up there in about three hours with the McMillins' Winnebago. Had to promise Bobbi an extra day off to get it," Hobey laughed. "We'll keep contact with you from that."

"Any word from Samantha yet?" Renee asked carefully, not sure she wanted to know.

"Actually, Renny, she called."

"She did?"

"Yeah."

"And?" Sometimes Hobey's sparsity of words was frustrating.

"Well, she's worried about your safety. Talked about the night you target-practiced outside the cabin." Hobey paused.

"That was scary, all right. For me, too."

"She'll be okay, Renny. You can't be worryin' about anything in there. If anyone can find 'em, you can. Jus' go in there and bring 'em out."

The lake was calm but freezing cold; there still was ice in some of the coves. The women had several hours of darkness to navigate. Renee wasn't worried about being on the water at night, although capsizing in this water meant they'd have less than three minutes to get out before their muscles lost their ability to function. But there were plenty of landmarks on a moonlit night to use in traversing the lake.

A gentle breeze carried the canoe high in the water and easily out of the drop-off cove, blowing away the stresses that had been piling on Ren throughout the day. And despite her reason for being there, she felt a peace descend on the canoe. The same peace she'd come to expect whenever she set out into the wilderness.

Halfway across the narrows of Shagawa Lake, they heard from Hobey. If anyone knew who the person was Neuterbide escaped with, they weren't saying, and there was no word on his prints yet. The wilderness outfitter had described him as a quiet Indian male, a teenager. Sylvia Neuterbide had been taken to the county jail for questioning but was refusing to talk, the chief told the women. Forensic study of the hairs and dander on the pants they'd finally gotten from Jablonski determined, as suspected, that they matched Crocker's new kitten. Which meant, the chief reminded them, that he was probably there at the time of Crocker's murder with the Indian kid Melvin saw. "Unfortunately, Jablonski died without regaining consciousness. He never finished tellin' us what he started with you, Renny," Hobey added.

Then, amidst the static of his voice breaking up, the women heard Hobey plead, "Bring Neuterbide back, ladies, so we can get on with putting him away. And don't—" The rest was garbled.

"Did you get that last part, Cal?" Renee called to Caroline, who was paddling at the front of the canoe.

"Something about not getting hurt, I think."

"Okay, Chief," Renee yelled her words into the wind, "we'll bring both of 'em back home hogtied, eh Cally?"

"You got it."

They paddled in silence for most of the next two hours. Renee wished Samantha was there. A wilderness lake was a good place to practice the stillness she'd newly discovered, and Ren missed her presence. As they paddled in the moonlight, she pointed out the granite cliffs archeologists had found Indian rock paintings on near the water level. And down the shoreline, caves that could be canoed into, with rock paintings on the walls. With the moon directly above the lake, it was a near-perfect night for enjoying the beauty of the Boundary Waters.

As Andy had figured and Renee had prayed, the Neuterbide duo was on the same course the Ojibwa women had taken. In a small bay identified as the head of Echo Trail, they found the fugitives' canoe tossed carelessly onto the icy shoreline. The way it was left convinced Renee that the men were not planning to come back. The women secured the loose canoe along with their own and then set off up Echo Trail in pursuit of the suspects. Renee handed Cal two flares from the police wilderness pack. "Only use these if we get separated and if you really have to, Cal, and remember, use them in an open area. If you saw the woodlands to the north, you'd have no doubt about the consequences of shooting one off in the forest. A running crown fire 'bout fifty years ago took off the tops of trees for five miles."

Renee reminded her old friend to pace herself. Because the trail followed both a frequently used animal track and a cross-country ski route, it was fairly well packed. The latest storm had dumped six inches of new snow, however, so that in some parts the women expected they'd need the snowshoes they'd brought along. "We've got the advantage on land, Cally, with those braces Neuterbide wears on both legs. He seems to move pretty good, but the weight alone will start to wear on him before we get tired. I figure they have about two hours plus on us, and we probably didn't make up any of that on the water. If we pace, we should be able to catch up to 'em before they hit Canada."

"How long?"

"By the end of the day." Renee adjusted the fifty-pound pack on her back. "Hopefully. If we can't surprise 'em before dark tonight, we'll wait 'til tomorrow morning when we have just enough light to see what we're doin' but enough darkness to work to our advantage. One thing we don't have that Neuterbide might is night-vision goggles, so we've gotta be careful. I don't wanna go up against them."

Cal grunted, hitching the Duluth pack's waist belt.

They walked 'til sunrise, using their headlamps sparingly. The sky was clear and the moon lit their way in open areas. Near the tree tops the wind's whistle was sharp and shrill, without the pine needles to quiet its voice. In the denser part of the forest, the trees' voice took on the tone of a sighing grandfather.

Echo Trail followed the low spots at this point in the Chippewa National Forest. "Thank Creator we're ahead of the black flies and B-52-sized mosquitoes, eh Cally?" The stubby Juneberry bushes caught at their clothes; come summer, they'd crowd the trail and sometimes make passage difficult. The women occasionally walked through the sweet smell of ginseng along this stretch, a smell Ren rarely noticed anymore except in remote forests. Overcollecting in populated areas had made wild ginseng almost extinct, reminding Ren of the Ojibwa teaching to always leave some plants unpicked so they can repopulate.

At the edge of the clearing of the first state-maintained cabin, Renee stopped and Cal came up alongside her. Ren pointed to the east. At first the light just creased the horizon, a tease of what was to come. The soft light haloed the distant trees that struggled to hold onto the darkness molding them into a single image. Motioning in their direction, Renee whispered, "That where they get that can't-see-the-forest-for-the-trees thing?"

"Pay attention," Cal scolded her friend playfully, "you're s'posed to be prayin'."

When the trees could no longer hold back the powerful rays of Grandfather Sun, he peeked his head over their tops, teasing the rest of forest life, and the two women, with the promise of a new day. Then the cabin clearing on Echo Trail was filled to the tree tops with light pushing its way through the fog. Each ray was contained in its own path, straining to brighten its section of foggy air and Mother

Earth. Renee handed Caroline some of her gramps' tobacco, and the friends drifted off to say morning prayers.

After reassuring themselves that the fugitives were not holed up in the cabin, the women entered the clearing. Spring mud in protected areas showed fresh footprints. The men had been walking normally, unhurried. "This is good," Renee pointed at the tracks. "They don't seem to be worried about being followed. That gives us a big advantage, but one thing I don't see yet is Neuterbide showing any obvious signs of tiring. His limp doesn't seem any worse. Yet." The inside of the men's prints revealed some drying, telling Renee they'd been made less than two hours before. "We're gainin' on 'em, Cal. Made up 'bout a half hour so far. How ya doin'?"

"Not too bad, a little tired. Guess I'm limping more'n the professor is."

Renee and Caroline took their hiking boots off to air their feet out. They'd gotten damp at the lakeshore, and Renee didn't want any fungus problems if it turned out their tracking went on longer than a day or two. Caution was rule number one in the wilderness. Cal had the beginning of a blister on the ball of her left foot. Powdering both feet and repairing the blister with moleskin, Renee commented, "Left-handers always get blisters on their left foot first. Did you know that?"

Her friend shook her head. "You're just full of little wilderness tidbits, aren't you? Seems to me I remember that about you."

"Here's another one. Remember the sign near the drop-off point at the lake that said, *Private. No Cross Country Skiing Allowed?*"

"Uh-huh."

"Whenever Mollie and I'd see one of those we'd change it to *Private? No. Cross-Country Skiing Allowed.* Or fishing allowed, or whatever. Opened up a lotta options for us."

"Clever girls, you two." Cal grinned, and then looked wistful.

The two Ojibwa women set off again, crossing what a wooden sign identified as Little Manitou Creek on a series of stepping stones. The water gurgled and sparkled brilliantly under ice shards along the rocky shore. Approaching the western edge of a marsh around the next curve, Renee, who was leading, stopped suddenly and held up her hand, signaling Caroline to quiet. Along the northern edge, a newly born moose next to its mother, his ungainliness comical, staggered out of the woods. He looked like he couldn't take another step without running into a tree or falling over, but as they watched, a peculiar gracefulness emerged.

"Cally," Renee whispered, "do you know Mons Kitchigami?"

"In the southeast corner of the rez?"

"I remember Gram tellin' me the lake wasn't named because it was shaped like a moose head, the way *chimooks* thought when they first came. It was actually the lake moose swam across in their migration. All you could see of their big ol' clumsy-lookin' body was their head. Herds of moose heads gliding across that big lake. So they named it Moose Lake. The first time I saw that I was about six, I think. Benny took me to watch it. I got so excited and screamed so loud the last moose actually turned around and stared at us."

"My grandmother used to tell me about how the moose'd always come out of the woods on our rez for a couple weeks in early summer 'cause the black flies were so bad. Drove 'em right out," Caroline said. "Granny said that folks on the rez shared the space gladly with their four-legged cousins, and the little ones squealed as they watched the moose amble through the school parking lot or across the softball field. The moose's adolescent-looking body makes it seem a lot more nonthreatening than it is, though." Renee nodded in agreement. Most people found it hard to feel threatened by something 80 percent legs, with a face like a camel and oversized ears. Every year Red Earthers were reminded in the paper and on the radio to keep their distance from cousin moose. Even this far north, some natural migratory paths of the moose had been disrupted as small towns and communities were built, making contact between two-leggeds and moose inevitable. One of the saddest sights Renee could remember seeing was a moose on its knees, licking salt from the road because it couldn't be found in natural settings anymore.

The moose turned upwind from the women, and they continued on their way.

The pair crossed a meadow near mid-day, and Renee found a spot on the edge of the forest where they could rest. The Boundary Waters Canoe Area was evergreen country. Except for aspen, willows, and birch, the great deciduous forests of the north country fell off just to the south. Original, large stands of virgin pine throughout the area had been felled by 1930, but regrowth was now at a respectable height. Jack and white pine, balsam fir, tamarack, Norway, black, and white spruce grew in stands of their own and mixed together. The kind of growths Gram used in her stories as examples to two-leggeds of how different kinds of the same species live side by side in harmony. The thickly needled evergreens held a deep, dark green this time of year. Only each branch's tip told of the approaching spring with the light green of new growth.

The brilliance of the light green seemed to cheer the women on, presenting an encouraging face, affirming life. Renee felt happy and serene, totally at odds with the reason she'd come to this beautiful spot. "Awesome forest, eh Cal? I remember last year, Walter Leaper tellin' me used to be a squirrel could climb a tree on the east coast and not come down again 'til it hit the prairies on the western edge of Minnesota." They gazed at the trees and let that thought sink in.

"That must of been some sight, Runner. Just imagine..."

Ren watched Caroline adjust the leather scabbard holding the antler-handled skinning knife on her left hip. "Remember, Cally, when Delores told us the story about Minnesota becoming an 'Indian-free' state in, what was it, 1862? Our scalps goin' for a hundred dollars a head the next year?"

"I remember."

"S'pose they used the kind a skinning knives we use now?" She nodded at Cal's knife.

Her friend unconsciously made another adjustment of the knife on her hip. "Hope not."

After repacking their food, the women moved through the finger of forest and entered another small marshland. "What the heck's that smell?"

"Skunk cabbage." Renee turned around to see her friend wrinkling her nose. "Grows in marshy areas. I'd bet those two stepped on some of it comin' through here. Makes it give off that smell. Yeah, see, here's some." Renee pointed to a large brownish-purple plant. New green leaves had just begun to open and unfold, giving the plant its cabbage-like appearance. "Guess we're gainin' on 'em, Cal. From the cabbage smell, I'd say they were here little over an hour ago. How you doin', anyway?"

"Little tired. Think I'm still limping more than the professor is," she said, holding up her blistered foot.

Renee checked Caroline's foot again and found that the blister had worsened slightly, but the moleskin was doing its job. "Try and walk lightly on that foot."

"Walk lightly?"

"Yeah, you know, when you step with your left foot, think light, airy thoughts." Renee grinned at her friend.

"I'll give it a try," Caroline answered, a note of skepticism in her voice. "How much longer we gonna hike?" she added, pulling her boot back on.

"'Til we get there, I guess."

"Get where?"

"To wherever it is we're goin'." Ren laughed.

Spring warmth came packaged in icy wind, the warmth caressing and enticing skin between breezes that raised goose bumps. Renee took her jacket and wool sweater off to better enjoy the seduction. "Spring—ain't it great, Cally? Livens every pore and cell in your body." Ren stretched her bare arms skyward.

The women set off again, engrossed in their own thoughts. They walked until late afternoon. "I was jus' thinkin' about how much longer to go," Renee said. She had stopped to wait for Caroline. "I can't imagine they'll continue a lot longer. They were up all night, too, and Neuterbide is older than either one of us. From the looks of the trail, he's startin' to drag his right leg a little. See?" Renee pointed to a scrape on the trail. "How 'bout we go another two hours, 'til sundown. Unless we come upon them before, of course," she laughed.

"I'll give it a try," Cal said. "My blister's gettin' a little sore, though."

"Don't be macho, Cally. You can say it hurts like hell."

They had to scrabble up a turtle shell-like rocky rise, which told Renee it wasn't far to the gorge. Windblown and worn free of vegetation, the smooth, dark granite was slippery, and it took both women a few tries to make it up top with the fifty-pound packs strapped to their backs. The now-rocky trail continued for sixty yards or so, then cut sharply left, dipping into a small ravine. The stones were cold and unwelcoming today, but in another month, lying on these rocks in late afternoon would be like getting a dry heat muscle treatment. Today they sent a chill through the women.

Up to this point the trail had seemed relatively flat, but after a while they became aware of a slight yet steady incline. Renee thought she remembered it was about twenty-two feet a mile. Soon the incline was more apparent, and the women realized just how high they'd climbed in the last seven or eight hours.

They stood at the edge of a two-hundred-foot gorge. A gorge too steep to walk down and through, and too long to be hiked around, at least not quickly. Following the tracks of their suspects along Echo Trail had brought them to the edge of the Pike River gorge, and the only means of getting across it: a pull-trolley spanning the expanse. A cable sloped to the middle of the gorge, allowing the basket a gravity slide to the halfway point of the three-hundred-foot span. Halfway across, and two hundred feet up from springtime's wild-running Pike River, a rope was secured to the cable. The trolley basket could then be pulled, hand over hand using this rope, to traverse the remaining one hundred fifty feet. After reaching the other side, the basket slid back to the middle of the gorge to await the next hiker. No matter which direction you crossed Pike River gorge, the first hundred-fifty feet was a charm.

Renee dropped her pack on the trolley platform and walked to the cable pole to check its attachment. A clutch of fear—or excitement—tightened her chest and rocked her onto the balls of her feet. She touched the medicine bag hanging around her neck on a leather thong, visualizing the contents, contents she alone knew, except for the hair she'd gotten from Sam, J.J., and Mukwa. "Whadda ya think, Cal?"

"Jeez, I don't know. What do *you* think?"

"I guess I'd worry if we'd seen signs they were trying to hide their tracks, or were hurryin' or somethin'. 'Course they could've deliberately not done any of that, knowing they were comin' here. You know, wanting us to think they didn't believe anyone was following them. Lull us to sleep, then drop us into the gorge? Not a bad plan, eh?" Renee grinned, trying to be light and flip.

The women peered into the gorge. Even in the growing darkness, it looked ominous and threatening. "Oh my God, look at that," Caroline gasped, grabbing Renee's arm. "Let's go home, Mom."

Renee's laugh was forced. "My sentiments exactly."

From this far up the women could barely appreciate the root beer color of the Pike River water. The iron content of spring run-off was so high, bathing in it changed the color of your skin for a few hours. They could hear the river thundering below as massive snow-melt tried to flow through a too-narrow passageway Pike made as it came off the upper falls, rounded the northeast corner of the lava rock gorge, and bore down, picking up speed for its last eighty miles to Lake Superior. The bubbling, churning, frothy brown water cas-caded over house-size boulders and blasted rooster tails between closely placed ridges in the rocky river bottom. Upstream, in a back-water area, fertile sediment nurtured ostrich ferns and meadow rue, spindly flowers that grew up to seven feet tall, giving the area a jungle-like feeling. If the women took the trail behind the gorge trolley pole, they would follow the lower rim along the river, then catch a spur going up and over a birch-lined ridge. Staying on the trail, the hikers could make the eighty-mile trek to a rock cliff holding a two hun-dred-year-old stand of cedar trees overlooking Lake Superior and, a hundred feet below, Agate Beach.

"Boy, if this view doesn't make a believer out of you." Cal sucked in her breath. They sat on the rocky edge, legs hanging over, eating apples and handfuls of gorp, and taking long pulls from their water bottles. "Can you imagine our ancestors when they came on this the first time?"

"Awesome."

"This was one of the routes Ojibwa showed the French voya-geurs to get to Lake Superior. A super highway back then."

"How far's Lake Superior from here?"

"Oh, pro'bly seventy-five miles or so."

Minutes passed. The vegetation-rich land put forth a myriad of smells that, especially in spring after months of snow covering, assaulted the senses. The moisture-laden southerly winds of sum-mer were not yet here to wring themselves out over the northern forest, but when they did, you could almost see the flora and fauna grow. Layers and layers of rich forest loam supported thousands of plants growing and flourishing under the canopy of trees, for centu-ries nourished by yearly layers of new compost and the spring rains. Finally Renee said, "Well, my friend, what's your pleasure?"

"You're the lead, Renny. You say go, I go. I just won't look down." Cal laughed nervously. "You know how I feel about heights."

"Yeah, pathological." Ren giggled. "Let's call the chief, run it by him."

Cal made the call and handed the phone to Renee. Hobey's voice cracked the solitude, the static sounding out of place in the middle of the forest. "Where will they come out if we let 'em go and try to pick 'em up on the other side?" The chief's voice sounded thin.

"Well," Renee closed her eyes, visualizing the northern section of Echo Trail, "they could cross over a lot of different spots on land. Echo Trail branches off in three or four directions near the border. Plus, if they had transportation they could get back on the water and go across on Basswood Lake, or even Crooked Lake if they headed west. Lotta water along the border, Chief. It's hard tellin' what Neuterbide was doin' out of town the last few days, or who he mighta contacted to plan this trip. You might wanna call our friends at Lac laCroix, Chief. The rez could be right in their path, depending on which way they go."

There was an extended pause before Chief Bulieau said, "Your best guess is they're not expecting a tail?"

"That's my guess. And the basket doesn't look like it's been tampered with. Near's we can tell, anyway." Ren and Cal nodded at each other. "Cable looks fine."

"You say go, LaRoche?" Hobey's voice was hushed.

Again Renee looked at Caroline and nodded. When she returned the nod, Renee said, "We say go, Chief."

"Then go it is, but for God's sake be careful."

Moments later the women were standing on the platform retrieving the basket from the middle of the Pike River gorge.

"Don't look down. I always recommend that," Renee said, turning and walking to her pack. She loaded the basket, and Cal followed suit. In less than five minutes, after Ren had offered tobacco and a prayer to the Great Spirit, they were heading off over the darkening gorge. The slide to the middle was easy, but the stop was jolting, and the basket began swinging wildly. "Grab the basket support ropes, Cally, and pull them toward each other," Renee called, as she reached to untie the pull rope. "We hit the damn pull rope, that's why we stopped so quick. They either didn't know what they were doing, or deliberately tied it too far up the cable." Renee watched the basket's attachment to the cable nervously. Though the S-hook had a deep curl over the cable, she'd heard stories of people trying to cross in a high wind and swinging the S-hook right off the cable. It took both of their muscle but, after several scary minutes, they brought the basket under control.

"I hate to push you, Cally, but we gotta get movin'. This is not a good spot to be hanging out. Wind sheers come down the gorge unexpectedly, plus we're sitting ducks for anyone wanting to stop us. With the weight we've got in the basket, sitting here puts stress on the cable. You're not supposed to stress the cable more'n the few minutes it usually takes to start using the pull rope—we're already about three minutes beyond that." Renee heard Caroline's nervous gulp of air.

"Cal, you okay?" Ren said, struggling to get a firm grip on the pull rope. When she heard no response she glanced over at her friend, who was frozen in mid-action staring into the rushing water below. A chill shivered down Renee's spine. "Cally," Renee began, her voice a mere thread of sound, barely rippling the silence. "Cally, look at me," she said, more firmly this time. She lightly touched her friend's shoulder. "Cally, look at me."

A guttural sound escaped from Caroline's throat. "Runner, I can't, I wanna go back." Her sudden turn set the basket swaying again.

Renee grabbed her shoulders. "Caroline Beltrain, get a grip," she said through clenched teeth. "Get a grip or sit down on the pack and put your head between your knees." Renee forced her friend to look her in the eye.

Caroline blinked, then swallowed hard.

"I told you not to look down," Ren growled.

After another hard swallow Cal said, "I know, I know. I—" She grabbed the rope in front of Renee's hands and began pulling. Renee breathed a long sigh of relief and added her hands to the effort. It was hard to tell whether it was nervous energy pumping extra adrenaline into them or what, but they traveled the remaining one-hundred-fifty feet quickly.

At the platform on the north side of the gorge, Renee let the basket go and watched it slide effortlessly back to the middle of the gorge. "See you soon, I hope," she whispered, then to Caroline, "way to go, ace. We made it." Renee embraced her friend, deciding to downplay Cal's fear. They still had to come back this way.

"There's another state-maintained cabin about a half mile from here, Cal. I think we should go for it. We may get lucky and find them camped there, or if it's empty, we may get luckier and actually catch some sleep."

"Boy, you sure know how to push a gal," Caroline gasped, but added, "I'm not complaining, understand, just making an observation."

Before moving on, they radioed back to Hobey to let him know they'd made it across the gorge. The only new news he had to report was a storm coming into the BWCA with possibly up to a foot of springtime snow—wet and heavy. "How long do we have?" Caroline called into the radio.

"Three, possibly four hours." Static filled the airwaves until they heard the chief's voice again, "I wish I could give you guys some hope that the storm's not comin', but we checked and double-checked. I want you to bust your...well, you know, try hard to wrap this up. Special Agent Lawton is here. He wants me to tell you you're out of your jurisdiction. You have no authority out there."

"Do you think the two suspects know that?" Renee barked into the radio.

"Doubt they'll think of that," an unidentifiable voice responded.

"Okay then," the women said in unison, "we're off. Ten-four. See you in a few." Cal was about to turn the radio off when it squawked again.

"Hold up, Beltrain. Put LaRoche on."

"Yo," Ren said into the phone.

"Hi, sweetie," a faraway voice said.

"Sam? Sammy? Is that you?"

"Oh God," Cal groaned.

"It's me, my love. How are you? Where are you?"

"Just crossed the Pike River gorge. Remember the trolley ride we took last summer?"

"I remember," Ren's partner replied. "Scary."

"No kiddin'."

"I'm wearing your buffalo-plaid wool shirt. Helps me feel close to you," Sam cooed into the phone. But it was difficult being romantic when you had to yell to be heard.

To Renee's relief, the call confirmed her hope that Samantha wasn't mad about her leaving, or about Caroline being along. At least that's what she said. After a short visit with Jenny, Ren had to hang up to conserve battery time.

"White girl had to follow you all the way up here?" Cal said through clenched teeth.

"Caroline Beltrain! I swear, you lay your tongue on some nasty words, girl." Renee poked her friend for emphasis and received a grunt in response.

Light was draining from the sky, east to west, taking the little heat it'd supplied for the day with it. Caroline tugged her jacket around herself and hugged her knees. A soft orange sunset flowed along the western horizon, the last rays useless now against the coming night.

"Get your butt up and let's get goin'," Ren said finally. Without comment, the two women set off.

"How're we doin' on batteries for the radio, Cal?" Renee asked after they'd walked for several minutes.

"The one in it's good for about two, three more calls, and the other one I put in your pack. That should give us six more calls, easy." That relaxed Renee some. The coming storm could present a problem for travel and, if they had to hole up for a few days, it'd be nice to have a working radio.

"Leave it to a FeeBee to think about that jurisdiction crap, eh Cal?"

"He's a piece a work."

"Spoken in true, understated Ojibwa style, Beltrain." Renee laughed, jabbing her friend and trying to clear the air after their earlier tiff.

Fifty yards down trail a sudden, high-pitched scream stopped both women dead in their tracks. Renee recovered quickly. "Cal, jus' keep walkin'. It's a mama fox and she's not happy. We must be too close to her kits." The women moved quickly up the trail and the screaming stopped.

"Boy, that'll get your fight-or-flight urge going, eh?" Caroline let out a long sigh.

Bluebead lilies and red columbine lined the trail. Ren caught the bluebeads' yellowish-green bell flowers in her flashlight. They were in full bloom, but the blueberries wouldn't appear for another few months. "Cally, check the lilies," Renee flashed a light on them again. "Did you know they're bisexual?" She glanced back at Cal, catching her friend's face in the light. "I knew that'd make you blush," she laughed. "It's true, though, they are. I don't know 'bout the columbine there. Prob'ly are, they're so handsome," Ren teased. "I do know they like long tongues..."

"Renee LaRoche!"

"I mean on insects, long-tongued insects. They need long ones to reach the nectar way up in the flower." Renee paused. "Okay, think I'll stop now...while I'm ahead."

Cal came up close and peeked at Renee's face. "Now look who's blushing," she grinned.

Darkness had finally completed its entrance, so enveloping that the two women couldn't see their hands in front of their faces. Clouds had covered Nikomis Moon. Using flashlights, they made their way slowly, turning them on only for brief moments to gauge their progress. The going on this side of the gorge was tedious. The cross-country trail had doubled-backed at the other side of the gorge, and this side hadn't been cleared yet for summer traffic. A few of the fallen limbs and branches had been thrown off trail, probably by the two who'd gone before them, but they'd come through when there was still light. Stepping over debris in light meant stumbling or tripping over it in darkness. It took the two Ojibwa over an hour to walk a half mile. Then, from two hundred yards off, Renee saw a light shining through the trees. As she had hoped, the fugitives had stopped for the night at the state cabin.

Renee waited until Caroline caught up. "They're here," she whispered, pointing to the light. "Even if they aren't expecting company," Ren cautioned, "they'll hear snapping twigs or any noise we make. Out here, a noise a hundred yards away sounds like it's right next to you. We've got to move like moccasin Indians, Cally."

"Right behind you, Hiawatha."

The two women talked for several minutes before getting closer, planning how to take the cabin. Both knew that waiting until morning was no longer a luxury they could afford. Waiting could mean being buried in a foot of snow.

"We've got the advantage here, Cal. Our third person is surprise, so it's three to two, our favor." Caroline squeezed her friend's hand tightly. "This cabin will be just like the last one we were at. One door, a window on the wall facing the door, a small one just left of the door, and a small wood stove in the southwest corner. Both windows are bear-proofed so they're not escape routes. There's no place to hide in the cabin. If you remember, the bunks are attached to the wall and too low to get under. The cabinet's attached and so small, Mukwa couldn't hide in it. They can't barricade the door because there's nothing in there to do it with. It doesn't lock, and just like the last one, it opens out, another bear-proof precaution." Renee paused.

"Runner, how about we check the window, see where the two of them are before we charge the door?"

"I'll bet the back window's got underbrush all around it, like the last one. The front one's prob'ly up too high. You know how they set the cabins up on those bricks. We'd prob'ly make too much noise trying to see into it." Cal agreed and Renee added, "But I think we can charge the door without too much worry 'cause they got no place to go. How 'bout we take the high-low approach?"

"Let's do it."

Fear was slamming into Renee's gut. She swallowed hard, coaxing the gorp she'd eaten earlier back down. Tracking the fugitives had been easy for her; she'd felt at home and in control. But this, this was an altogether different matter. Taking down criminals was something she'd never done before, nothing she'd ever dreamed of doing. She made another tobacco offering next to a newly sprouting cedar tree, asking Creator to keep not only her and Cal safe, but also those inside the cabin. "I know one of them's a murderer, Gitchi Manitou, but I don't wanna have to shoot anyone," Caroline overheard Renee whisper.

Approaching the cabin seemed like slow motion. Ren visualized Samantha and Jenny to try and control the rising panic she felt holding the .38 Smith and Wesson. Hobey, you finally get your way, Renee thought, though she was sure he'd rather this wasn't happening. On the final two hundred feet, Renee lifted and set each foot down with concentrated deliberation. Caroline followed suit. One snap of a twig could bring one or both men out, and their advantage of surprise would dissolve.

They made it to the door without a sound. Communicating with some people was easy. Even without words, the relaying of messages between the two women was effortless. Ren tapped Cal on the shoulder, circled thumb and forefinger, and pointed into the cabin. Cal nodded, doing the same. Renee blew her friend a kiss. They were ready. Grasping the door handle, Renee prayed she was right about it opening easily. Caroline reached up from her crouched position and gave Ren's hand on the door handle a squeeze. Touching Auntie's yellow bundle of sage and cedar around her neck, Renee returned the squeeze. The two Ojibwa women burst into the cabin.

# 13

The men were already fast asleep on the beds. Neuterbide must have drifted off examining the map lying across his chest; his companion stretched out still wearing his jacket and boots on the top bunk.

Neuterbide awoke and let go a yell so animal-like Renee scanned the room to see if there actually was a four-legged in the cabin. She pulled the professor to a sitting position. "Evenin', Neutie, aren't ya even gonna say hello?"

Caroline rolled the mystery man off the top bunk and onto his stomach, cuffing his hands behind his back before he was totally awake. Letting him stand and regain his bearings, she warned him against any sudden or threatening moves. "What's your name, son?" Caroline Beltrain said in her most serious voice. The young man looked dazed, snatching peeks around the cabin like a sleepy bear cub.

Neuterbide began to struggle and Renee noticed he'd taken one of his braces off. She allowed herself be distracted, pitying him for his handicap, and he took that opportunity to stand and swing the brace at her. She caught the movement out of the corner of her eye. A fifteen-pound piece of fire-hardened steel came straight for her. Raising her arm, she bore the brunt of the blow on her right forearm, and her pistol skittered across the floor. "Cal, Cal," Renee yelled, but Cal's prisoner had come awake and was resisting her attempts to secure him to the bunk bedpost. Grabbing Neuterbide's arm, Renee tried pulling him down, but he was too strong. He wrapped his huge hand into the collar of her parka and, leaning against the bunk beds, lifted her straight up off the floor. Renee did the only thing left for her to do in that position—she swung her leg back and brought it full force into the crotch of the man now trying to choke the life out of her. Neuterbide doubled up and fell to the floor, dragging Renee down on top of him as he twisted the collar tighter around her neck.

With his voice abandoning him, he rumbled ferociously, "I'm gonna kill you, you goddamn squaw. I'm gonna kill you."

Renee could barely hear Neuterbide's voice over the roaring in her ears. The room was spinning, going black around the edges. She knew if she couldn't take a breath soon she'd pass out. Neuterbide was raging like a wounded animal, the pain in his groin seeming to incite him and compound his strength. He tried to roll over onto Renee but she resisted, raising the lower part of her body up like she was doing push-ups and coming down hard again into his groin, this time with both knees. Everything seemed fuzzy now. She knew it was happening to her, but it felt like she was watching it from far away. The rim of blackness was growing, as if she was looking through the lens of a camera with the shutter at 40 percent and closing. She was losing the feeling in her arms, making them heavy to move.

Meantime Neuterbide was trying to recoil from Renee's attack, to wall off the pain, but Renee was still on top of him. Finally he released his grip on her collar and pushed her off.

She rolled over clutching at her throat, taking in huge gulps of air, oblivious for a moment to anything but the air right in front of her mouth. "Caroline, Cal," Renee croaked. "Give it up, professor," she gasped, "it's over."

"Killin' you's gonna be easy compared to that other bitch. Goddamn sneaky Indian."

"Stop!" Caroline screamed and was at Renee's side holding the retrieved .38 Smith and Wesson on Neuterbide. Renee leaned against the north wall of the cabin, supporting her right arm. Tears were streaming down her cheeks as she continued struggling to fill her air-starved lungs. After handcuffing Neuterbide, Caroline turned her attention again to his traveling companion: a young Indian man, seventeen, eighteen at the most, his shoulder-length raven hair covered with a red bandana. He looked over at Cal, staring blankly, and she saw a row of surprisingly straight white teeth. Someone had been taking care of this boy, down to the brand new Columbia parka and pants, Sorrel boots, and gear that looked like it just came off the shelf at L.L. Bean or REI. Who had footed the bill for all that expensive equipment wasn't too hard to figure out.

"Did you hear Officer Beltrain?" Ren coughed out, taking liberty with the word *officer*. "What's your name?"

"Chris Antler," was the mumbled response.

Renee took in the name before gasping in disbelief. The conversations she'd had with Donna White and Jenny came flooding back. This was Jenny's classmate's cousin, the boy White had told her about. The young man, Josh later discovered, who had fled to Minneapolis at the age of fifteen, away from his "perfect" foster family, the Neuterbides. Staring at Chris Antler, Renee wondered if Neuterbide's sudden reappearance in the boy's life, his apparent generosity, hadn't been his way of grooming Chris to take care of the kind of problems the professor'd run into recently. But there was no time for philosophizing about it all now, they had to get going. "Pack up you two, it's time to go." Renee grimaced. Moving her right arm was going to be painful. "Cally, how ya holdin' up?" she queried as they hurriedly packed up the handcuffed prisoners.

"Little tired," she whispered. "You?"

"Same. We gotta be careful. Let me know if you start to fade."

"Will do. Who is this kid, Antler, anyway?"

"I'll tell ya about him after we get to the gorge," Renee whispered. "Heard about him first from Donna White, then from Jenny. He was one of the foster cases Josh checked into. He followed his paper trail to Neuterbide. We gotta call Hobey and see if he can trace Antler's moves back there. I wonder if maybe he's the Indian boy Melvin saw. How 'bout you take off with those two. I'll try and get Hobey."

Caroline nodded, retrieving the radio for her friend.

"Cal, they haven't given up just because we've got them in handcuffs. Remember how we used to feel after they cuffed us. We'll have to be on full throttle, at least until the helicopter brings us help at the trail head."

"If they bring us help, you mean?"

"If," Ren said wistfully, "if they do."

"At least we can use our flashlights on the way back," Caroline chuckled. "My shins are gonna be black and blue for weeks."

"By the way, how's the blister?"

"Forgot all about it. Come you two, let's go."

Renee caught up to the trio about halfway to the pull trolley, giving Cal a thumbs-up on the call to Chief Bulieau. Nearing the pulley platform, the women discussed the trip over the gorge.

"I'm not goin' over that gorge with either one a you guys," Chris said petulantly, crossing his arms over his chest like the defiant child he still was.

"You either cross with one of us," Renee said firmly, glancing over the edge into the blackness, "or drop alone," she added peevishly. "Now get up there with your buddy." Chris's sullen look changed quickly from defiance to shock to fear, as he apparently envisioned taking a nose dive into the black hole on his left. Scrutinizing him, Renee pondered why the young man's life had taken the turns it did. Maybe they weren't choices he'd made at all, just Chris failing to say no to each seemingly easy way to make a little—or a lot—of money, until finally it was too late and he thought there was no turning back.

"Put the gear up on the platform," Caroline instructed, taking one cuff off first from Neuterbide and then Antler.

"Do it yourself, squaw," Neuterbide sneered.

Renee drew the Smith and Wesson out of her shoulder holster without a word, aiming it at the two men. After a staring standoff, they did what they were told.

A gust of wind whistled down the canyon. It came on with such force, taking over every molecule of air, that it wasn't hard at all to believe in its having its own will and spirit. The wind, together with the roar from the river, made Renee grateful for the darkness. She just wanted to get everyone to the other side. Caroline was going over first with the professor. He was exhausted after the hike back to the trolley and was limping badly, and Caroline's fear and unfamiliarity with the trolley made her a logical match with the exhausted professor.

By the time the two were set to go, it had started to snow. The flakes were small and infrequent, but they increased Renee's anxiety. She kept the most powerful flashlight so she could track the basket's progress and coach Cal.

"Don't get any funny ideas, professor." Renee grabbed the man's jacket collar. "If you value your measly goddamned life, and that spot between your legs, you'll cross the gorge cooperatively." Neuterbide's piercing glare sent a chill through Renee, but he limped to the platform without comment. Renee pulled her friend aside. "Watch him, Cally. This guy's sly like Coyote. If he tries anything and you have to knock him out or anything, can you get across without his help?"

"I can do it, Runner." Caroline flexed her biceps. "Don't rock the basket, and don't hang out in one place too long."

"Right."

"Don't worry about me, you just watch your own back. And you gotta promise me that if it comes down to a choice between you and Antler, you'll pull the trigger."

Renee frowned.

"I mean it, Renee—LaRoche, as the chief would say—you just think about what he'd do."

Renee grimaced, but said, "Okay, I'll do that."

The light snow had left a fine mist on Renee's hair. As Cal swung her flashlight, the beam captured the gray at Ren's widow's peek in a silver, shimmering wave, and her breath caught in her throat. "If I need to find you, I'll just wave my flashlight and catch this shine here," she grinned, tussling the front of Ren's hair.

"Hey now, you're messin' up my do," Ren laughed.

"That isn't all I'd like to mess up," Cal whispered into her hiking partner's ear.

"Cal," Ren grumbled, eyeing her disapprovingly.

"Okay, okay."

Subtle, intermittent tremors began chasing each other up and down Renee's spine. One long, then one short. She stopped and inhaled a purposefully long and deep breath, raising her arms as high above her head as her backpack would allow.

Once the basket was on its way and Neuterbide was out of earshot, Renee turned to Chris. "Chris, what in hell is going on with you? How are you involved with this guy? You bein' a street hustler was more honest than this crap." The air stretched around the comment until Renee thought it might shoot them both off to tumble amidst the stars.

Finally Chris snarled, "You don't know anything about me."

"I know you ran from Neuterbide's three years ago. I know your good looks got you tricks in Loring Park and a job in the kiddie porn business. I know that old fool has somethin' over you to get you to kill for him."

"Whadda you talkin' about? He's got nothin' over me." Antler's retort was sullen, and he turned his back.

Renee had noticed an unusual scar on Antler's arm back at the cabin, and she'd been dredging up every memory she could about seeing and repairing trauma on Indian people in the Movement, hoping to trigger where she'd seen a scar like that before. Finally it came to her. Nick Standing Deer had had one on his thigh. It was from a fireplace poker laid flat on the skin, leaving a burn that looked like a calligrapher's *L*. It was not an accidental injury. Renee tapped Antler's right forearm. "Neuterbide did that to you, didn't he?"

"What?"

"The scar you've got there, on your arm. It's from a fireplace poker. Did he do that to you right before you ran away to Minneapolis?" Renee took a stab at the circumstances and came up a winner.

"So what? What's it to you? I deserved it, I know that now." Chris added the last statement with less conviction, and in the voice of a small boy, he said, "He helped sober me up. I owe him."

"You owe him for what? Teaching you how to spread your legs and lay on your stomach? Or grab your crotch and say cheese?" Renee knew she was taking a chance pushing, but she hoped this boy's abuse by Neuterbide made his loyalty thin. "Staying sober is something *you* do," she said. "You deserve the credit, Chris. He owes you. He owes you for all the abuse you suffered when you lived with him."

As she watched the young man his mouth opened slightly, the lower lip began to tremble, and his eyes filled with a fear and pain that spilled out on his cheeks as tears. Then, just as quickly, a curtain was drawn and Chris's face went blank. "How'd you hear about that? Who the fuck told you that?" Antler seemed startled by the declaration but continued. "It's not true," he yelled angrily. Renee stared into Chris Antler's eyes. They had the same look she'd seen in Ned's, who'd apparently taken Chris's place at Neuterbide's.

"You can put an end to it," Renee pleaded, adding grimly, "he's already got boys taking your place." The hoped-for response was not forthcoming, and the look on Antler's face disturbed her. She observed him for a long time before conceding, "But you knew that, didn't you?" Ren asked the question, but her tone of voice sounded like she had the answer. "Of course, you already knew."

"Fuck you," Antler snarled. "You can't make me feel guilty because some little sniveler can't take care of himself."

"No, I can see that, Chris. Been a while since you've seen your soul?"

"And it's not true. Nobody touches me I don't want touchin' me. And they pay big time for it. Hustlin' pays a six-figure income in some places."

"It is true, Chris, and you know it. Why did you kill Joe Crocker for him?" Renee hoped the surprise change in topic would catch Antler off-guard.

"I...I didn't. Whoever said that is lyin' too." He kicked a branch and turned away from Renee.

"Goddamnit, Chris, don't turn away from me. Don't try and deny it. We have evidence and a witness."

"That mental Melvin, you mean? Who'd believe him?" As the words escaped from his lips, Chris realized he'd just put himself at the scene of the crime.

Renee didn't say anything for a long time. She was studying the movements over the gorge and couldn't figure out what they were doing. For the time being, Chris's unintended admission had to wait.

"Cal? How's it goin', girl? Makin' time out there?" She tried to cover the anxiety broiling in her gut about all the things that could go wrong. The beam from the flashlight dissipated just past the middle of the gorge, blurring any movement beyond.

For what seemed like an eternity she heard no response from the basket swaying high above Pike River in the cold darkness, then finally Caroline called, "Making progress. Slowly but surely, Runner. Had to catch my breath. We'll be sending the basket back momentarily."

"Way to go, girlfriend," Renee called cheerily as she turned back to Chris Antler.

"Okay, tough guy. Now that you've confessed to one murder, how 'bout the other one. Rosa Mae Two Thunder?" Somewhere between her mind and her voice was the memory of what it was like to be scared, out of control, desperate. Could you blame this boy for choosing the path of least resistance? The one that kept him in food, with a roof over his head? Renee agreed with Caroline, Chris was one of the kids they fought the system on behalf of, but he was also involved in Joe Crocker's and—probably—Rosa's murders. No doubt he was a victim; his life had been one trauma after another. But he was also a punk. And now she was sure—a murderer. Underneath his tough guy veneer, she could feel his pain, even see some of herself. How could anyone who had grown up in foster homes sexually and emotionally abused, then sent to the streets to prostitute for a living, how could anyone turn out normally? But many had. The elders said that these were interruptions in your journey. Times for learning. What you did with them was up to you.

"Listen, Chris, it isn't just a witness to the murder. We also have physical evidence to place you at the scene," Renee lied. "But there are a lot of extenuating circumstances about your involvement. Chief Bulieau might be willing to help you, if you help us. Come on, Chris," Ren prodded.

"Help you guys? I don't think so," Antler said contemptuously.

"You're Anishanabe, Chris. First and last."

"Yeah, right, and what's it got me? Poverty, a drunk for a parent, racists for neighbors."

"You can turn it around. A lot of us have." Renee took a step toward him, but Antler withdrew.

"Step off. Not interested."

"Chris, don't you see," Renee's tone had become soft, "you remind me of the elder's story about the musk deer who's always looking for that fabulous odor of musk up ahead, everywhere, anywhere, not realizing that the wonderful scent comes from within themselves."

Antler turned around, and for a second Renee saw the look in his eyes she'd been praying for. But it was gone quicker than she could take a breath. "I said, step off with that crap. Get outta my life. I don't want your help."

"It's your call." Renee shrugged, abandoning all pretense of being nice. "If you wanna spend the rest of your life in prison, being someone's dolly and prostitute, while Neuterbide goes merrily on his way, destroying other boys' lives, it's your call."

"You're breakin' my heart."

"Folks like the professor love suckers like you, Antler. He used you as his boy-toy, then threw you to the wolves, doping you to make you malleable and submissive; then when he needed someone to do some dirty work for him, he pushed your buttons again. Yup, suckers like you come in real handy," she repeated.

"Shut the fuck up," Antler said, lunging at her. Renee stepped aside and Antler went down in a heap, but he was back on his feet quickly. Not, however, before Renee could get her revolver out.

"Take it easy, Antler, take it easy. Truth hurts, doesn't it?" Renee was angry now. "Hard to admit to bein' someone's *namebin*, especially a *chimook*, but they see a sucker like you comin', my friend." Renee drew in a breath. "Now, go over and pull in the basket. I just heard them release it."

"Pull it the hell in yourself," he challenged.

Stepping closer and cocking the .38 Smith and Wesson, Renee said, "I'm tired and I'm in no mood for a smart-ass two-bit punk." Raising the gun shoulder high, she continued, "Now do it before you snap what's left of my last nerve."

Antler kicked another tree limb, swearing under his breath. His face took on a surreal look in the artificial glow of the flashlight. He was all eyes and mouth. It was a look so wild and animalistic that Renee was frozen in mid-movement. She followed him to the cable, released one handcuff, and stood a few feet off to the side while Antler pulled the basket in.

"Cally, everything okay over there?"

"No problem, Runner. What's goin' on? You yellin'?"

"We'll be over in a minute." Renee dodged the question. "How was the wind on the way over?"

"Not too bad, but it's picking up, so hurry, will ya?"

Hunger put an edge on everything now. As she slogged to the gorge, Ren's legs had felt like she was lifting lead boots every time she took a step. "Will do. Start supper, eh?"

Renee handed the gear up to Chris, then hopped onto the platform, keeping her pistol leveled on the prisoner. Once they were out over the gorge she'd relax a little. It might take both of them to get across if it was windy, and she doubted Antler wanted to die plunging two hundred feet into freezing water. At least, she didn't think he did, judging from his reaction earlier at the edge of the gorge.

Once they were in the basket, the slide down to the halfway point went easily, and the stop was gentle. Caroline had remembered to tie the pull rope in a good spot. "Who tied the rope up when you guys came over earlier?"

"He did." Antler clipped his answer.

"Figures. Leave it to him to tie it too far up just for spite." Antler untied the rope without comment.

The basket had begun to sway a little in the wind. Renee turned to her companion. "Let's move it, Chris. I don't like the strength of this wind."

"You don't like the wind?" Antler mocked, and began rocking the basket, "How 'bout this?"

"Cut it out, Antler. That's dangerous."

"Dangerous? You don't know dangerous." The young man was becoming agitated. "Dangerous is fallin' asleep in a box in an alley in Minneapolis and not knowin' if you're gonna wake up the next morning or not. Dangerous is going home with some old geezer to blow him off just for a warm place to sleep and some food and not knowin' if he's the one that's gonna go off on you and cut you up with his razor blade." He was starting to shout. "Dangerous is hangin' in the park, never knowin' if the next car to cruise you has a bunch of gay bashers in it." The louder Antler yelled, the more he rocked the basket. "And dangerous is smokin' one pipe of crack after another, not knowin', and not carin', if this is the time you're gonna OD and instead of gettin' high, get dead."

Renee heard Chris suck in a huge breath of air. She was unnerved by the turn of events, and fought off her growing fear. She hadn't read him right, Renee realized. Pushing him had not been a good idea: he didn't care if he went over the edge, and he didn't intend to give Neuterbide up.

"Remember the snuff films a few years ago?"

"Story I heard was they were fake."

"My best friend Adam was snuffed in one of those things. After that, every time one of us signed on to a movie, that was in the back of our minds."

"What happened to Adam's murderer?"

"You're kidding, right? A black faggot prostitute. Who'd spend time lookin' for his murderer?" Renee could see Chris's rage at the memory of his friend take over his body.

"Way to go, LaRoche," she muttered. Instead of scaring Chris into helping, she'd backed him into a corner and he'd reverted to familiar behavior. And survival behavior now meant intimidating her by swinging a basket two hundred feet above a raging river gorge. She smiled at Chris, a smile lacking any emotion, not an easy accomplishment given the state of her nerves. "Don't do this, Chris. You don't want to die. We can help you." Renee's words sounded hollow even to her.

The boy was perched, immobilized, at the edge of the basket, seemingly unconcerned with what the woman in the basket with him was saying. Grabbing at the young man's arm, Renee reeled in her thoughts. She could feel the hairs raise on the back of her neck like a cornered animal. Chris pushed her away with such force the gun flew out of her hand and into the bottom of the wildly swaying basket. She grabbed the flashlight and shined it up at the S hook, the only tangible thing between them and the canyon floor. *If I don't do something soon, I'll be over the edge and all this discussion I'm havin' with myself will be academic.*

Chris wasn't a big man, five-feet-ten and probably one-hundred-sixty pounds soaking wet. Renee was counting on him being weakened from his druggy lifestyle, and for her own adrenaline to be pumping fast enough to give her an advantage. He was still ranting about the dangers he'd confronted in his life. Then Renee heard him mumble, "They had to die. He said they'd mess everything up. They had to." She stooped to retrieve the .38. Catching Chris off-guard, she grabbed the unhooked handcuff hanging from his left wrist and, at the same time, smashed the butt of the gun into his shin. As he went down, she snapped the cuff around his right ankle and gave him a quick karate chop to the back of his neck.

Renee straddled Antler. Arms extended, her fingers numb and stiff from the cold and the mist from the river, she clutched recklessly at the trolley ropes. Her face scraped against the rough support ropes and something wet and warm slid down her cheek. At the moment she couldn't care less what it was. She had to get a hold of herself, and quickly, before it was too late. The wind was rocking the basket without Antler's help now, and Renee could see the S-hook slip to its very tip before the cable dropped with a jolt back into the top curve of the S. "*Kinawa*, Creator, please," she pleaded above the howling from the young man laying over the packs in the bottom of the basket.

Her back screamed with pain, and the right scapular muscle

spasmed and cramped. She had to let go of one of the three support ropes she was trying to stop from swinging erratically. Cursing with increasing ferocity, she tried to shake out the cramp without letting go of the other two ropes. Finally, she was able to bring the basket under control. Renee released the support ropes and grabbed the pull rope. They'd far outstayed their welcome here in the middle of the gorge. Just as the thought passed through her mind, Renee heard Cal. "Renny, the cable's startin' to slip down the pole here. Your weight's too much, you gotta get out of the middle. Quick."

"I'm comin'. Can you shinny up the pole and jam somethin' into it to stop it slipping?" Renee assumed the silence that followed meant Caroline was working on the suggestion. She couldn't concern herself. Pulling with all the strength she could gather, she began moving them across the gorge. The basket was heavy and her muscles burned with anger at being called on to do the work of two. Each pull sent flames shooting across her shoulders.

She had just reached out as far as she could to grab the pull rope when she heard herself shriek and felt a searing pain in her left side. Looking down, she saw Chris Antler coming at her again, with what looked to be a small pen knife they'd apparently missed in their search. His first attempt had cut through her jacket and into her side. Fear stirred as she felt the warmth of her own blood ooze down her body and begin to pool around her waist. Antler was mumbling that Renee wouldn't leave the basket on her feet as he flailed wildly with the knife.

She grabbed ineffectively at his wrist. He was striking dangerously close to the basket support ropes with the knife, and, in her rising panic, Renee was not using her head or her strength. She forced herself to stop, to take a slow, careful breath, and called on all the spirits to calm her. As she closed her eyes to fight a wave of dizziness, Renee heard the wings of an eagle just before she felt them brush across her face. Then the bobcat, all but extinct in northern Minnesota except in the dreams of the Ojibwa, flashed before her. Its eyes fixed on Ren from their perfect triangle of nose and ears. The ears, dramatically oversized to reveal the importance of the sense, were turned in her direction. As she watched, the cat pushed off from the edge of the darkness with its powerful hind legs and disappeared from view. "Balance," she whispered. "Power, thought, intent." With her next breath she felt a veil drop softly over her. Renee caught Antler's forearm with hers, pushing it down into the basket. As she grabbed for the knife, he twisted away, slicing a bracelet into her left wrist. She wrested the knife away from him, screaming, and flung it over the basket into the night. Retrieving her gun from the floor she swung the butt at Antler's head, catching him just above the left ear. He moaned, sliding down the side of the basket onto the packs.

Renee tried to take a deep breath, but pain was consuming her now. She was determined that it, and the rage it engendered toward this boy, were not going to end her life in a swan dive over the basket, not if she could help it. Random thoughts and scenes crowded her brain, but the throbbing pushed them out. The stabbing pain left her momentarily breathless and a little disoriented. "Focus," Renee grunted. She drew her world into the edges of the basket. "You and me, my friend, you and me, and bobcat and *migizi*," she said, patting the metal and wooden structure. The basket swaying in the darkness was having an hypnotic effect on her. She had to concentrate on the task at hand, and the young man with her who was trying to kill at least her, if not both of them.

Ren could feel the S-hook nearly slip off the cable each time the basket made a half-loop out and back. She wasn't sure what was keeping it on. Her prayers, maybe. Gulping air, she braced herself on the sides of the basket to get a higher grasp of the support ropes, willing the basket to slow its swaying. *Come on, LaRoche. This is gonna take all you got, girl. You can do this because Bear says you can do it. And so does Gram.* She shook her head, trying to clear extraneous energies, then grabbed for the pull rope.

But the damage had been done: they'd lost ground. How much, Renee wasn't sure, but with her side shooting pain every time she pulled on the rope, any was too much. She leaned on one of the ropes holding the basket in place and took several slow breaths, pressing her arm into her side. Random thoughts continued to distract her and drain energy. Blood loss, free falling into the river, Jenny growing up, Samantha alone, death.

Caroline's voice came out of the blackness. "Runner, come on girl, you gotta keep movin'. I've stopped it from slipping for now. I hammered two crampons into the pole, but that cable's pressin' on them pretty hard, they won't hold for long. Come on, Runner, you can do it." Cal paused, then in her sternest voice, she said, "Get your sorry butt in gear out there, LaRoche. I'm not haulin' ass all the way back from here by myself."

Cal's tone had the desired effect—Renee snapped out of her downward spiral. She leaned into the pull rope one hand over the other. With Caroline cheering from the platform, the basket inched forward. But it was heavy and the incline increased the closer they got to the other side of the gorge. Cal shined her flashlight on the basket, encouraging her friend. She kept up a nonstop patter. "Come on, Runner, keep movin'. Think about who's waiting for you back home. Your girlfriend'll kill you if you give up and drop two hundred feet into this gorge. And Jenny. What about her? And your gram and auntie, and that little dog of yours."

That cheer gave Renee a shot of adrenaline, and she got two good pulls in before she had to stop and take a breath.

"Just a few more, Runner. Remember when you told me to think lightly when I stepped on my left foot? I want you to think strong when you grab the rope. All the strength you need is in your hands and arms. I know you're hurt, but you can rest in just a few feet, girlfriend. Let's go. Pull, pull." Caroline's voice was getting closer and clearer. Renee peered into the night toward the sound. She thought she could make out Cal's silhouette on the platform.

A hand clamped around Renee's left ankle. Antler. Groaning, she said, "Goddamnit, Antler, let go."

"Runner, what's the matter? What's goin' on?" Cal called from the southern edge of Pike River gorge. Struggling to free herself of Antler's grasp, Renee started the basket swaying wildly again. "Antler," she gasped, "let go of me." Grabbing at the Indian boy's head, she got a handful of the red bandana and tossed it angrily over the side. Then, holding a fistful of his beautiful raven hair, she snapped his head from side to side and caught him under the chin with her knee. One last groan and Antler again slumped to the bottom of the basket.

With the basket rotating wildly now, Ren let out another piercing scream as she grappled with the tangle of ropes. The level of violence was becoming more than she could handle. As it swung high up to Ren's back, the basket stalled, as though hitting a wall, then rolled over on itself. This is it, she thought, the S-hook's popped off and I'm gonna die with this punk brother and his wasted, no-good life.

"Renee." Caroline's voice came out of the darkness. "The first crampon came loose. You gotta pull, girl."

Renee sucked in air and grabbed for the rope, breathing a *megwetch* to Creator for a chance to change her last thought. Dying with hatred on her lips was not how she'd been raised. She reached as far up as she could, trying to bring the ropes together and stop their rolling in every direction. Then, and she didn't know how it happened, the basket stabilized and the swaying slowed. The thought that she could already be dead, lying shattered on the rocks below, kept her going.

Caroline was leaning over the edge of the platform. "I can see ya, Cally, I can see ya," Renee yelled. As she pulled with everything she had left, the basket crawled forward. About ten feet from the platform it stalled again. She'd gone as far as she could. The incline was too steep, the basket too heavy, her muscles too tired, and the pain had sapped her resolve. Holding onto the pull rope for dear life, she leaned over the edge of the basket. "Oh God, I can't, I can't, I've got nothin' left," she moaned. The searing pain in her side, and now the stinging throb every time her jacket rubbed on the open wound on her right wrist, had worn her down. Muscles she didn't know she had burned like she was standing in the middle of a raging fire.

On the platform, Caroline was starting to panic. She could hear Renee gasping for breath. Speaking in a calm and even voice, Cal said, "Renee, listen to me. You've got less than ten feet to go. A couple of pulls and you're home free. I can almost reach the basket now." Then she added, "A few more pulls and I can help you the rest of the way." Renee looked up. Cal was shining her flashlight into her own face so Renee could see her. "Ten feet, Runner. You can do it. You-can-do-it, girl," Cal said, emphasizing each word.

Renee pushed herself away from the basket's side and gripped the rope tightly in both hands. "I can do it, I can do it," she whispered. Hauling the rope toward her, hand over hand, Renee let out a wail of exertion and the basket moved a foot. She leaned out again, tugging the pull rope, and again they moved a foot closer to the platform. A couple more, she told herself, reaching out as far as she could and pulling.

Then she heard it. A popping sound. The last crampon came

off the pole with such force it flew fifty feet straight out and over the cliff. The sound of it hitting bottom seconds later was missed by everyone up top. All they heard was the whipping of the cable as it slid down the pole and slapped the platform. That, and the shriek from Renee as she clutched the rope and pulled with every muscle in her body. The basket dropped like it was falling through a trap door. But Creator was there. And Cal. Close enough to clamp her hand around Renee's flailing arm just as the cable smacked limply onto the platform. For what seemed like an eternity, Renee hung, suspended over the Pike River gorge. And then, with one mighty pull, Caroline catapulted Renee onto the platform, face first. Ren's right boot caught on one of the basket's support ropes. For an instant, it threatened to pull her into the darkness. But Cal kicked the boot free as the basket disappeared over the edge of the platform. Cal saw it bounce once on the lip of the cliff, six feet down, then drop off the edge. The women heard the cable stretch to its new limit and, in slingshot fashion, hurl the basket back up level with the platform.

Caroline's flashlight caught the basket as it flipped and then disappeared out of the light's beam. The scream that came next was so primal, so agonizing, that in the blackness it could have come from the cliffs themselves. Pain and abandonment given voice. If the young man's sorrow had taken form it would have filled the gorge. Then through the flashlight's beam, the contents passed, one following the other like lemmings to the sea: Renee's pack, Chris's pack, and Chris himself plunged to the river below. After, all was silent.

Caroline dropped to her knees. "Runner, Runner, you okay?" At that moment, Renee couldn't manage to put two thoughts together. She thought light was shining in her eyes. Where it was from, she couldn't tell. "Renee—" a voice far away filled her consciousness. *Was it Samantha? Had Sammy come?* "Renee, it's okay girlfriend, stop struggling, you're safe."

"Sam? Sammy?" And with that, enveloped in someone's strong arms—she wasn't quite sure whose—the Ojibwa woman let go.

# 14

When she finally opened her eyes it was snowing harder. It felt to Renee like time had crawled inside itself. The wet flakes on her face felt like Mukwa's kisses. Turning her head carefully for fear it'd roll off her shoulders, she forced her eyes open and looked around. Her body was leaden, and when she raised an arm to sit up, it was as if she was pushing through heavy snow.

"Hi, sunshine," Cal smiled, "good to have you back."

Renee groaned, responding with a ghost of a laugh. "Yeah," she said, laying her head back down.

"You're gonna be all right," Cal promised her friend.

The steady, firm hand offered by Caroline reassured Renee and calmed the cells in her body, which still felt like they were being tossed and drop-kicked into the gorge. The realization that she'd survived, and all her pieces were intact, brought a sob to her lips. Huge tears spilled over and down her cheeks. She wasn't exactly sure why she was crying, but it didn't matter; it was making her feel better. She pressed herself against the platform, hugging its sturdiness, its safety. After several minutes of feeling the solidness, her body began to release the swaying motion it had absorbed. Then the pain in her left side intruded into her consciousness. Renee rolled over and threw up.

"Better?" Cal's voice came from someplace far away.

"Not sure."

"You're safe now," Caroline repeated. "It's all over." She took her mitten off and laid her hand on Renee's cheek.

The warmth brought Renee back to the moment. "Antler?"

"He's gone, Runner, over the edge. He didn't make it. The basket flipped and everything went over. He did a full gainer out of the basket."

"We gotta check, Cal, he might be alive." Renee struggled to get up.

Placing her hands on Renee's shoulders, Cal gently urged her back down on the platform. "Renee, listen to me," her friend said slowly. "Chris's body accelerated down the gorge at close to fifty feet a second at the start of his fall, more at the end. At that rate he would've been going fifty miles an hour, maybe even faster, when he hit the water, or the rocks. There's no chance he survived the fall."

Renee laid her head on Caroline Beltrain's leg, releasing a long, agonizing sigh. "Are you sure, Cally? Maybe he landed feet first in the water. It's higher this time of year."

"Think of it like this, Renny. People who fall three stories rarely survive. Chris Antler fell about fourteen. And hitting the water from that height's like slammin' into concrete. But I'll check in a minute."

"What's going on? What did you do to Chris?" a voice called out of the night.

"Oh, Jesus. Neuterbide," Cal whispered. With all that had been happening, Caroline had all but forgotten about Floyd Neuterbide, handcuffed to a metal bracing of the cable pole. "Calm down, professor, calm down," she yelled back at him. "Runner, I'll be right back." She laid Renee's head on her mittens and walked over to their remaining prisoner.

"What happened?" Neuterbide demanded. "Did you say Chris went over the ledge? Is he dead?"

"Yes, he is. Now get on your feet, we're going to be leaving shortly," Beltrain added in an official voice.

Caroline found a way to climb to the ledge six feet down the side of the canyon wall where Chris's pack had wedged itself. Rather than try and haul the fifty pounds back up, she flipped open the top of the royal blue rip-stop nylon bag. The inside of the flap had a net pocket. Cal unzipped it and pulled out a map along with some papers, stuffing them inside her jacket. Nothing in the body of the pack held much interest until she reached the bottom. There, crammed in a stuff sack, Cal found packets of money. A lot of packets. An awful lot of money.

Caroline's flashlight beam located Chris's body at the bottom

of the gorge. He was lodged between two boulders, visible only because Cal's light caught the reflector tape circling the bottom of his
gaiters. Icy river water moved Antler's beautiful raven hair in its last
dance. She offered a silent prayer that his spirit's journey would be
less painful than the one he just left.

The storm hit quickly. It had been toying with them for over
two hours, but now it came with a vengeance. After returning up top
with the papers—poems written by Chris—and the money, Cal put
in a call to Hobey reporting what happened, and what she'd found
on the ledge. The chief promised to send someone as soon as the
weather cleared to recover Chris's body. Cal told him they'd lost the
other radio battery and would have to limit their calls, then signed
off and turned her attention to Renee. Antler's swipe had cut clean
through both layers of Ren's parka, her wool sweater, long underwear, and the fatty layer of her left side just under the rib cage. Thank-
fully, the muscle seemed uninjured, but under different circumstances
the laceration would have needed thirty stitches or more to repair
the damage. If it wasn't stitched within twenty-four hours, it could
be too late because of the danger of closing infection into the wound.
Caroline devised makeshift butterfly closures, per Renee's instructions, doing her best to draw the sides of the wound together as tightly
as possible, then covered the site and bound it with a pressure dressing. There was some worry about infection, but Renee's underwear
and sweater were soaked with blood, so Cal's first concern was blood
loss.
By the time the trio set off they were walking through ankle-
deep snow in open areas—deeper where it was drifting—and it was
snowing harder. Visibility was only about five feet. After three hours
of making increasingly slower time in the storm, Renee pulled
Caroline back. Daylight was on the way, but they had eight hours or
more of slow going just to reach the first cabin they'd passed coming
in. Whether it was post-traumatic shock, lack-of-sleep paranoia, the
storm, or her body being sapped of strength from the pain, something had stolen Renee's resolve. "You guys go on. Leave me here and
send someone back for me," she said. "I can't go any further."
"I don't know how you made it this far."
"I can hole up here, dig a snow cave. You keep going on with

Neuterbide. When you reach help, send someone back for me."

"No deal, Renee. I'm not leavin' you here. You told me the most important thing out here is to not get separated."

"I know, Cal, but that was before—"

"Before nothin', LaRoche. You stop, we all stop."

"I'll be okay, Cal. It's just like winter camping. I've done it a hundred times." Renee shifted uncomfortably.

"Right, then we'll all be okay doin' it." Caroline looked into Renee's eyes. "We can all use the rest. Tell me what to do." Renee could hear in Caroline's voice the same quality she'd heard when her friend talked her in over the gorge. There'd be no changing the woman's mind, so Renee gave in and leaned back against a nearby tree. She closed her eyes and felt herself begin to doze off. When Cal returned with Neuterbide, Ren started awake, amazed at how quickly she'd drifted off.

The professor's pale, pink-rimmed eyes followed Renee menacingly. She was sure he'd like nothing better than to leave her on the trail to die. Her gore-tex rainpants had ripped in the near-fatal second crossing, and with her undergear wet and soggy, a chill had settled over her now that her muscles had stopped generating heat. Renee remembered Gram's story about people wandering through a snowstorm and, at the moment when hypothermia wound the body's thermometer so tight the body began to feel hot, they would tear off their clothes and be found days later, frozen stiff and buck naked. She needed to get her muscles moving again to warm up.

Once she stood, it didn't take Renee long to find a spot in a nearby gully with trees protecting the east side. New snow had drifted and piled onto an already high mound in the low-lying area.

Renee showed them how to dig out for a snow cave. It was cold and slow going. They only had metal dishes to dig with, but she urged them on with promised comfort once the cave was ready. With one digging and the other two packing snow around the sides, they made a six-by-six-by-four-foot-high snow cave. Renee spread the remaining one-person mountain mummy tent on the floor, along with a tarp Neuterbide had been carrying. Caroline lit a small camp light and, in spite of the cold, Renee made everyone strip to their underwear, to get some of the dampness away from their bodies and to try and dry out their clothes. With only two sleeping bags left, they would have to share. Renee and Cal decided on two-hour intervals, Cal insisting Renee take the first sleep. They removed Neuterbide's braces—he could barely walk without them—and agreed that whoever was sleeping would lie with their arms wrapped around the metal supports. Coupled with his bone-crunching fatigue, they hoped it would be enough to make him stay put. The professor was asleep almost before they were settled in. Renee and Caroline gave each other a satisfied nod as his snoring filled the cave. Before Renee closed her eyes, she reminded Cal how to keep herself awake and helped her bundle up with clothes from the packs.

Renee tumbled into a dream almost immediately.

*"Gram, I think it's my fault Chris Antler's dead." Renee and her grandmother were standing on the cliff overlooking the Journey River. "I pushed him, taunted him about his life."*

*"Nosijhe. Can you know a person's journey they walk to the end?" Renee shook her head. "Then how do you think you changed someone's path? The carver begins his task not knowing what shape it will take, believing within each stone, or piece of wood, is the knowledge of what it's to become. The spirit of the piece comes out as the carver works. So, within each piece lies a* mukwa, *a* migizi, *an* amik—*waiting. That is how, my girl, we must shape our youth. With the belief, the faith, that within each one is the knowledge of what they'll become. I'm afraid young Chris didn't have that. He didn't have parents, uncles, aunties, grandparents who could be his carver to help him chip away at all that isn't important to his spirit. Like the fly before the spider, he was lured away from the things that feed his soul. He was a partially formed person looking for someone to connect with to make him whole, and that's always hopeless. But he was surrounded by enough touches of humanity to glimpse the possibilities. It was his choice not to see them, nosijhe."*

*Renee stopped pacing. She came and sat next to her grandmother on the spirit rock. She'd barely noticed the sun's warmth before. Now she leaned back and let it wash over her face and arms. "Feels good, Gram. I've been so cold lately." Renee shivered. She took Gram's willowy hand in her own, noticing the darker chestnut of the elder's skin, translucent now in her ninety-fourth year on Mother Earth. "You always know what to say to me, don't you, Gram?"*

*"Well, my girl, maybe it's that you know the right things to hear."*

The dream dissolved into a deep sleep.

"Runner, hey girl, it's time to wake up and stop dreamin' about your girlfriend." Renee opened one eye to Cal's touch, looking at her friend like she couldn't quite place her, then groaned and tried to sit up. "I'm not sure, but I think that little rest helped. Am I lookin' any better?"

Caroline glanced at her friend in the light from the flashlight. "My great-granny died at a hundred and one. I saw her at the funeral home, and Runner, she looked a whole sight better four days dead than you do right now."

"Thanks a lot, my friend. Jesus H. Christ," she groaned, "I'm so stiff you could break my legs off like icicles." They struggled to switch places, and Cal snuggled down into the sleeping bag. Renee shifted her position slightly so Cal could stretch her legs full out. Actually, she was amazed at how much two hours of sleep had done for her body and brain. Renee felt surprisingly alert and ready to move on despite, apparently, how she looked.

There is complete silence in the wilderness only in the winter. There is too much life happening at other times, with its rustlings, crunchings, squeakings, snappings, and chirpings. Renee closed her eyes for a minute and took in the silence, then settled down to review the life of the man before her. A pedophile, she guessed, might be the technical name for someone like him. The fact that Chris Antler had fallen to his death was upsetting; what added to her anger was that he'd done it before giving up Floyd Neuterbide. In the quiet of the snow cave, she began to formulate a plan.

Ren didn't know how long she'd been lying there scrutinizing him, but as if he'd been drawn out of his sleep by her glaring energy, Neuterbide stirred and opened his eyes. Glancing first at Caroline, then at Renee, he tried to roll over and sit up. The quarters were cramped, and he was too big a man to balance himself on his wasted legs. Renee stared at him without moving or offering assistance. "Well, well, missy, you're awake I see," Neuterbide muttered, finally bringing himself up by leaning on one elbow.

"Visualizing more pleasant things to look at," Renee said. She watched the workings of Neuterbide's facial muscles in fascination. Each one seemed to have its own plan as waves and twitches changed his cheeks into something Ren thought looked like a rageful Lake

Superior, his bushy eyebrows stand-ins for the tree-lined cliffs. She wondered if the twitches were his nerves or the result of years of alcohol abuse. His florid skin color seemed to indicate the latter.

Noticing Renee was not simply looking at him, but examining him like an ant under a magnifying glass, the large man grunted, "What are you staring at, lezzie."

"I'm trying to figure you out. First you plan summer youth programs, help the kids go to college, then you turn around and abuse them."

"You people don't know how to raise children."

"Oh, and you do?" Renee hunkered down, leaning into her left side.

"What's the matter, honey? Not feeling too good?"

"I feel just fine. Finer every time I picture you helpless in the slammer," Renee sneered. "You're goin' down, Neutie."

"And you and what army are going to do that, my dear? You don't have a thing on me." The self-confidence of the man irritated Renee.

"No army needed, Mr. Egotistical Professor. I've got all I need here." She pointed at her head. "And here," she said, tapping the pocket on the inside of her parka.

"What's that?"

Renee could see she'd generated some nervousness, so she extended her pause far beyond what she normally would have. Finally, she leaned over and whispered, "Nah, I think I'll wait. That's for me to know and you to wonder until you hear me testify at your trial."

Neuterbide's face flushed and a neck vein began to pulsate. She could almost see his blood pressure rise. After fifteen or twenty minutes of trying to rest more, Neuterbide gave up. "I want to get out of here," he yelled. "I want to get out of this place, it's too crowded." A sudden claustrophobia started him tossing gear around the cave.

Caroline stirred and sat up as she always woke, alert and totally aware of her surroundings. "What's the matter here?" she said, looking from Neuterbide to Renee, and then checking her watch.

"Tried to think of a novel way to wake you up, Cally, and our prisoner yelling seemed pretty creative." Renee jabbed her friend playfully. "Don't you think?"

Caroline rubbed her eyes. "If you say so. Time to head out?"

Everyone dressed, then the trio each ate a handful of gorp and shared two oranges, saving an equal amount for later. The realization that Ren had to pee so bad she was afraid to breathe told her she was alive. The fact that she ached everywhere, and had serious pain in several places, meant she wished she wasn't. Twenty minutes later they had packed and were trudging through a foot of new snow. The storm had dissipated, leaving a Hallmark card countryside. Echo Trail wound through forest, meadow, bog, marsh, over Manitou Creek and Pike River gorge on its way into the Canadian section of the BWCA, Quetico Park. Even trudging through a foot of snow in intense pain did not stop Renee from being awed by the beauty of this back country. Other parts of North America had oceans and mountains; the southwest had its own special beauty. But for an Ojibwa, this was the beauty that stirred the soul—the awesome abundance of Mother Earth's living things. The northwoods had laid an imprint on Renee, and out from its center came a passion for how so many different living things survived in unity. It was one of the facts that made her believe two-leggeds could do the same. Even now, slogging through snow with a brutal killer.

As the daytime temperature climbed into the low forties, the light snowfall turned to a fine mist. The water-logged snow on the ground made it slow going for the two women and near impossible for Neuterbide. His swing gait was difficult to do under these conditions. Caroline and Renee were taking turns bulldozing the trail with the one remaining pair of snowshoes. It was late afternoon when Cal called back to Renee, "How far are we from the cabin?"

"'Bout two more curves before we cross the creek, then one more bend should do it." Renee shivered. Her chill hadn't totally left, despite the exercise. Approaching the meadow, she visualized it two months from now—the sun out, ablaze in the multi-colors of summer; she looked out under the snowfall to yellow Indian blanket, purple joe-pye weed, blue wild iris, and red Indian paint brush blanketing the ground. The image warmed her a little and she promised herself to bring Samantha up here on a backpacking trip this summer when the flowers really had bloomed.

Creeping up behind Neuterbide, Renee picked up their conversation from the snow cave. "Ya know, professor, you're not as smart as you think you are," she said matter-of-factly.

The professor's jaw set hard. Between gulps of air he said, "You don't know what you're talking about. You know squaw, you don't scare me."

Renee gave a short, humorless laugh. "Professor, you're a fox hidin' behind a locoweed. And soon everyone will know, they'll know you abused Chris Antler," she whispered in the man's ear.

Neuterbide's eyes were intent, narrowing to slits.

"Oh." His reply had such a sound of relief to it, it surprised Renee. Why did that accusation relieve him? Was he expecting another question, or accusation? What? Then it dawned on her. The statute of limitation was probably up on what he'd done to Chris. Should she mention Ned? Did she dare chance it? If they got back and for some freak reason he wasn't arrested, social service wouldn't give Ned back to him, would they? Even the outside chance scared her. She'd better wait.

"I know you killed Rosa Mae Two Thunder and ordered Joe Crocker's murder." Renee jabbed a finger at him.

"You're bluffing." Sullen hostility was displayed on his face.

"You have no idea what Antler and I talked about waiting for you and Caroline to cross the gorge."

"Oh, and what was that?"

"About how you abused him when he lived with you. About how you sobered him up, Chris thinking it was because you cared about him, you because you had plans for him to do your dirty work." Renee held her breath. She was glad she'd learned some things about Chris from Donna White and Josh. It made her bluffing more credible.

Neuterbide stumbled and fell in the snow off the left side of the trail. Renee ambled over to the flailing man. Heaving an exaggerated sigh, she said, "My, my, professor, lookit the mess you've gotten yourself into." She clucked her tongue to show how seriously she was taking his problem. An unintelligible growl came from somewhere amidst the tangle of arms and legs and pack. After watching him struggle like a bug on its back, Renee leaned over and gave him a hand up as Neuterbide said, "You don't know what you're talking about. I didn't abuse anybody."

"Well, like I said, we'll see at your trial. I've got a whole tape full of facts and names of people to talk to." Renee patted her chest pocket.

"Never mind what we already had, like your fingerprints at the pornography house."

After catching his breath, the prisoner turned hate-filled eyes to Renee. "Did you know the Los Angeles police were looking for Chris to talk to him about the murder of a street hustler he used to run with out there? I saved the little bastard's life."

He's good, Renee thought. The best defense is an aggressive offense. He's done this before. But lies like this were told for a reason. So what was this lie about?

She patted her pocket again. "Guess you didn't know Chris as well as you thought you did," Renee said sourly, thinking just the opposite. The Ojibwa gave her one remaining prisoner a slight push. "Come on, we're falling behind, get movin'." The ensuing silence lay between them like a string of dead fish.

A pod of river otters peeked up from the swirling water, tumbling and diving playfully in the full Little Manitou Creek. Heading out to find slippery banks and whirling rapids, the otters noticed the trio but seemed uninterested in their passing, even when Neuterbide nearly fell headlong into the creek and Renee and Caroline had to grab him. The crossing stones were slippery, so the women took up positions to the front and back, steadying and pushing him along the rocks to get him safely across the freezing water.

When they reached the cabin, exhausted and hungry, Caroline's first action was to call Chief Bulieau and let him know their position. Moving away from Renee and Neuterbide, she told the chief she was worried about her friend. Caroline reported they were having to change Ren's pressure dressing about every three hours, that she was still oozing blood after already losing a fair amount. "She should've been in the hospital hours ago, Chief."

Hobey agreed. He'd checked on sending a helicopter in to them at the lakeshore, but it wasn't possible. The storm had cut a swath several hundred miles wide through northern Minnesota, and all available rescue vehicles of the highway patrol and county sheriffs' departments were in use, helping people stranded on their farms and in their cars throughout the area. "Keep a watch on her, Cal. If need be you could stay at the cabin a day or two, and by then we could fly someone in." Cal caught the note of concern in Hobey's voice. "Meantime, we've found out a few things I want to pass on."

"Runner, Hobey on line," Caroline called, moving next to her friend. Neuterbide was sitting on the cabin step.

"The blond hair found in Two Thunder's ring is Jablonski's. I'm guessing that's what he started to tell Renee at the accident before he passed out. Prob'ly gonna say he helped Neuterbide kill her. You already know the prints in the porn house are Neuterbide's and—" Cal held the radio near both of their ears. They could hear the chief talking to someone before he said, "Remember the video we found in the VCR?"

"Yes," they answered in unison.

"Got a search warrant for the professor's office and found two tapes that are the same lot number as that one. They sell 'em in packs of three a lot of times, and we matched the set, which means they were bought as a unit. The chief cleared his throat. "Actually, Lawton here matched the lot number." Caroline adjusted the radio by their ears.

There was the sound of movement. Then, "Hello, ladies."

"Afternoon, Agent Lawton," Renee said. Cal held her nose.

"And the FBI secured the audio tapes from the sheriff's department. They're reviewing them now for the call you talked about, Caroline. Renny?"

"Here, Chief."

"You listening?"

"Yes sir."

"Agent Lawton cleared Caroline's name of any suspicion on that nuclear plant bombing."

"That's great, Chief." Renee clapped Cal on the back, then grimaced, grabbing her side.

"*Megwetch*, Chief." Caroline added gratefully, "'Preciate that."

"Glad it's cleared up, Beltrain."

"Better go, Chief. Gotta save the battery. We'll be home sometime soon. Ten-four." Cal stuffed the radio in her pocket. Ren felt an arm over her shoulders, light but with a comforting firmness. She leaned in. The pain in her left side was excruciating and the loving touch was a welcome distraction.

Shagawa Lake was abroil by the time they reached it. A northerly wind pushed the water up into deep waves, creating white caps out in the middle. Renee sat on one of the overturned canoes, favoring her right side. The pain from the laceration was intense. It felt like a hot knife had been left in, twisting with every breath and step she took. But this was it, the final leg. They'd lost half their supplies. One of their prisoners and their radio were dead. What food wasn't lost was gone. Renee couldn't remember ever being so beat up or in so much pain.

The three of them, thrown together by circumstance, sat quietly contemplating the remainder of their trip. Silence blanketed the moment, something the two Ojibwa found warm and familiar. Renee noticed a large nest atop a dead Eastern pine. Just as she called to Caroline, its occupant soared down the shoreline with what looked to be lunch for the impatient brood waiting in the nest.

The beauty of the bald eagle took Renee's breath away. She sat speechless, watching the three eaglets straining eagerly in the nest, mouths open to the universe, trusting that what they were about to receive was nourishment.

Neuterbide's gravelly voice intruded. "This is as far as I go. You squaws are gonna have to make it on your own. You can't force me to get in the canoe because I know you won't kill me."

Renee marveled at the arrogance. Arching her eyebrows like two new moons, she said, "Ugh, *awema*, he such big help, how we sisters make it? Need big, strong, *chimook* man to show way."

"Ugh, *awema*. We in bad trouble. How we get back across *kitchi nibi*? No, no way without help from *chimook* man."

"I sure as hell don't need the help of you two to get myself across," he shot back.

The laughter burst out of both women simultaneously. "Better be careful, Neutie," Renee snarled, "your ego's making promises your body can't keep."

"Sarcasm is the response of fools."

"And humor is a survival tool of the wise," Renee shot back. "Give up your arrogance, Neutie. It's unbecoming on someone in as helpless a position as yourself."

The professor cursed and turned his head away.

"You seem to be having some trouble grasping the reality of the situation here. I'd advise you to cooperate when we get to the other side of the lake," Ren drew the sentence out, "in case someone's inclined to take pity on you."

"I'm not going down for anyone else, that's for damn sure," Neuterbide mumbled under his breath.

"Nobody, meaning Bouchard and Peter Armstrong?" Caroline queried.

"Peter Armstrong? What in hell do you think—" Neuterbide stopped in mid-sentence. "Nobody means nobody. Call your chief up and tell him that."

"It'll keep. I think we should take off," Cal suggested. "It's early afternoon—we'll be paddling in the dark some as it is. Lucky for us the wind out there's blowin' our way."

"Let's go, Neutie." Renee snarled her words for effect. The professor glared from one to the other woman as though weighing his odds, then stood and stumble-danced his way to the canoe. "And he thought he could make it alone," Ren said, loud enough for Neuterbide to hear. Eyes snapping she added, "Sit in the front, Neutie. We don't trust you to drive."

In the duffer's seat, Renee's eyes bored through Neuterbide's back. When he stopped paddling, she said, "Thought you could do this yourself, big guy," and the professor resumed paddling furiously. Ren turned around and gave Cal the high sign.

Cal whispered, leaning forward, "You keep that up and we'll be across in an hour."

Paddling past Bear Island, Renee could hear the sighing pines. "Samantha told me once that the trees' *sisi gwaad* sounded like the ocean to her," she said to no one in particular. "I like that image. Gram always said your mind could transport you anywhere, it's external forces that stop us." Ren sighed deeply. "I guess when you realize that there are more cells in your brain than stars in the whole universe, you can appreciate the possibilities."

Neuterbide's voice startled her. She hadn't realized he'd been listening. "That's a quaint turn of phrase, but there should be an addendum: timber niggers excluded."

The silence that followed was heavy, and the wordless lake began to feel lonely and dangerous. Renee didn't even notice when Neuterbide laid his paddle across the gunwale. As much tension as there was between Red Earth Ojibwa and non-Indians in surrounding towns, the one thing most held in common was their love of

Minnesota's north country. Beautiful crimson sunsets, the dancing aurora borealis, crisp renewing winters, summer thunderheads that simultaneously thrilled and terrified, and one of the most brilliant, dazzling autumns in North America. To hear Neuterbide utter one of his racist epithets in connection with a conversation about the wilderness was not only shocking to the women, it felt bone-chillingly evil.

Finally Renee regained her voice. "You're lucky, Neuterbide. If Cal or I were more hateful people, you'd be in the lake right now for saying that, with no one the wiser." Turning to Cal, she said, "Lydia told me that the day of the human being was over: the white man was here. She got that right, eh?"

Caroline nodded.

Neuterbide retorted. "See what I mean? That makes no damn sense whatsoever."

The night call of a lonely loon echoed across the lake. The unusual *teacher, teacher, teacher* of the ovenbird followed. The rest of nature was going on without them.

# 15

Renee opened her eyes to find Hobey sitting alone at her bedside. "*Boozho.*"

"Hey girl, you're awake."

"Well, not really sure about that." Renee shifted uncomfortably, then said into the silence, "Heard any good jokes lately?"

"What do you call an Indian who owns five rabbits in South Dakota?"

"I give up."

"A rancher."

Renee managed a short laugh before wincing from the pain. "Been deserted, Chief?"

"Samantha and Jenny went downstairs to rescue the hospital guard from your auntie. She used the hedge at the end of the parking lot to stop her car and the guard, an off-reservation white fellow, doesn't know your auntie."

"Enough said," Renee chuckled.

"Only thing that saved him at first was your gram." Hobey's smile built up to a belly laugh. "When the desk called up here, Auntie had the guy pinned between the hedge and her car." This image brought a laugh from both Hobey and Renee.

"How ya doin', kid?" The chief leaned forward, resting his arms on his knees.

It was the kind of Hobey question that didn't require an answer. Renee responded nonetheless. "I'm fine."

"Right, and my favorite person is Agent Lawton," Hobey observed somewhat sourly. "Speaking of Lawton, poor guy—no matter what he does he can't get a transfer to someplace warm." The chief grunted, unable to hold back a smile at that thought. "I wanted to tell ya, Renny, I'm proud of you. You two did a good job out there."

"Neuterbide didn't think so."

"He turned whiter than he already is when we confronted him with what he said to you on the hike back. He started screamin' and yellin' about how stupid us Injuns all are. Then, as your auntie'd say, 'the mustard's off the hot dog,' 'cause he screamed that if he had his way he'd do away with more than jus' that snoopy b-i-t-c-h Two Thunder and that weak-livered Crocker. Took a while to calm him down. Wouldn't admit to us he killed Rosa, but he gave it up to Lawton— his social and intellectual class, don'tcha know. Jablonski helped dump the body. That's why his hair was caught in the ring."

"I didn't think Jablonski did it. Jus' didn't make sense." Renee sighed.

"He lured her over to the Lone Loon though, Renny, so don't give him too much credit." The chief leaned forward again, regarding his friend closely. "Melvin ID'd Chris Antler from a school picture of his as the guy who killed Crocker. Turns out Melvin actually helped Antler and Jablonski string Crocker up after Antler strangled him."

"Is he in trouble?"

"Doubt it. Crocker was already dead and sounds like they forced Melvin to help. Might even prompt gettin' him some psychiatric help."

"That'd be good."

"Yeah, that'd be good. The tape at the sheriff's office had been recorded over, no doubt to hide the call about Rosa Mae. But Jesse was right, Lawton sent it to the FBI lab and the end result was that Deputy Rod Johanson took the call. It was his voice on the tape."

"No kidding. Jess wondered about that guy."

"Yup. He claimed not to remember the call, which made me and Lawton more suspicious, so we showed his and the county social service guy, Peter Armstrong's, pictures to Ned and Kevin and, sure 'nuff, Johanson was the other white guy, not Peter Armstrong. 'Course we'd already grilled Armstrong, so it was embarrassing to have to apologize to him." Hobey gave Renee a big grin. "Left that to Lawton."

"Armstrong's no saint, Chief. He's been stealin' kids off the rez for years."

"That's our next task, Renny. Cleanin' up social service here."

"Not to change the subject, Chief, but how's Samantha?"

"Well...you scared the heck outta her, but she's glad you're back." Hobey patted Renee's arm.

"You think?" Renee let a smile flicker across her face. Sometimes she wished she believed in a religion like Hinduism. Thirty-six hundred gates to heaven were better odds than one Red Road. A road she was on even if she often found herself heading straight for the ditch. "Oh well," she sighed, "Creator loves me despite the ass I make of myself. Samantha will too." She'd remind Sam that forgiveness was good for the soul. Or was that, confession was good...? "Damn, growing up with that Catholic influence sure scrambled my brain," she muttered.

"Say somethin', Renny?"

"No, no. Jus' thinkin' 'bout Sammy."

"Gotta make a phone call," Hobey said, standing. "Check up on Lawton. Make sure he's doin' his job. You know those FeeBees, Renny, soon's we do the grunt work, they're descendin' on the case like Canadian honkers on a cornfield."

After Hobey left, Ren lifted her hospital gown to examine the gash in her side. Hearing Samantha and Jenny gasp was the first she realized her family had come into the room. Renee turned away. It was an automatic response. She didn't take sympathy well. Up to then, anger and fear had kept her from wallowing in anything resembling self-pity. A joke would be Lydia's recommendation. "Hey girls, don't look so glum. It was nothin', really. Remember the movie *Alien*? That bugger jumped right outta there," Renee said, patting her side. "We sent the friendly little fella on its way and Cal taped me right back up."

Only Lydia and Jenny laughed as the four most important women in Ren's life surrounded the bed. Jenny came round to the foot and set her jacket down on the sheets. Renee felt a pressure against her leg, then a cold, wet nose nuzzled into her hand. Mukwa looked up at her with coal black eyes that said how glad she was to have her two-legged back. She crawled up into Renee's arms, licking her face and whining excitedly. "Whoa, Mukie, slow up a little my girl," Renee said, hugging Mukwa and everyone else she could get her arms around. "It's so good to see you all." Tears came spilling out and down Renee's checks onto the top of Mukwa's head.

They released Renee from the hospital the next afternoon. The laceration on her left side had been debrided and closed. Her right arm required a cast, Ren having cracked a bone in the fight with Neuterbide. All in all, she was amazed at what a warm night's sleep, food, and the attention of her loved ones had done for her. She actually felt pretty good. Renee, Samantha, and Mukwa left with Chief Bulieau and Jesse, who'd stopped by to tell Renee that all parties— Rod Johanson, Sam Bouchard, and Floyd Neuterbide—had now been charged and were in jail in Thunder Lake. Ned and his brother, along with two girls from the foster home, were at Bobbi's, and the rest of the kids had also been placed. Mrs. Neuterbide and Donna White had not been charged.

"You go home and get some rest, Renny. We'll be in touch." Hobey gave Renee an uncharacteristically long hug.

"Any word from Caroline?" Samantha broke the silence as they walked to the car.

Renee shook her head. "She called the nurses' station and left a message she was on her way to the northwest. Washington, I think. Folks need help with some salmon fishing rights. Dragonfly," she nodded, "jus' like the dragonfly. Auntie's right again."

"Mmm, I guess you'll tell me what that means sometime?"

"Yes, my love."

The lower level of the LaRoche cabin, holding the kitchen, living room—which doubled as Ren and Sam's bedroom—and bathroom, was a good fifty-by-fifty feet. Jenny's bedroom was in the loft, tucked back under the rear half of the cabin's steep roof. Over the winter Ren and Sam had sanded the log walls, which gave the rooms a scrubbed baby's butt shine. It had been Samantha's idea, and Renee hadn't liked it then. Resting in bed, staring at it now, she still didn't like it. But Samantha did; it fulfilled some of her neat needs that had been lying dormant since her move to the country.

Renee pulled back from Samantha and studied her flushed face. "God, I love you," she murmured, clutching at her partner again. With a tenderness born of gratitude for this woman in her life, she brushed her lips up her lover's arm and neck to her favorite spot behind her ear, in pain with every movement but not wanting to stop.

"Oh, Renny." Samantha squirmed a little beneath Renee's touch.

Ren nuzzled Sam's ear, using gentle bites around it to raise a moan from her lover's throat.

"Renny," Sam managed again before Renee's mouth closed over hers.

Just then, Jenny grasped the ladder and slid down from the loft, letting her feet grab the side just firmly enough to control her descent. Hitting the bottom she made a half-turn jump and headed for the kitchen. Renee and Samantha hurriedly arranged themselves. Then Sam got out of bed and followed Jenny.

Once she'd browned the venison roast, Samantha put it in the pan along with the diced onions and cubed potatoes she'd retrieved from the root cellar, four whole carrots, two cloves of diced garlic, and enough water to give her New England pot roast dinner some moisture to bake with. She covered it and set it in the oven. The freezer was getting dangerously close to empty of last season's berry crop, much to Samantha's disappointment. The taste of the fresh berries on pancakes, waffles, and ice cream wasn't hard to get used to. "When can we start picking berries again, Renny?" Sam inquired plaintively from the open freezer.

"My sweet, this is the third season you've asked me that question."

"I know, it's just so long in between, I forget."

"Well, it'll be several months yet. We bloom about a month later than the southern part of the state."

"Oh no, we're going to run out!"

"Oh no, we'll have to pick more flats this year."

"Promise?"

"Promise," Renee grinned, thrilled with her lover's growing assimilation to rez life.

Sam had three hours before supper to work on her article about the effects of the hard winter on the plowing and planting dates for north country farmers. A northern Minnesota stringer for the Minneapolis paper wasn't her idea of challenging writing, but it helped with her share of the bills. She'd just laid out her notes and graphs from the weather bureau and local farmers' coop and turned on the computer, when she heard someone pull up outside.

"I remember it used to be the only action we'd see around here in a week is someone's car pulling up to our cabin," Ren called from the living room. "The good ol' days! Where'd they go?"

"You're asking me? Don't get me started." Sam shot Ren a keen look. "Sorry," she added, not at all sounding like it. Outside, the golden-crowned sparrow let loose its three-descending-note warble announcing *spring is here* at the same time someone knocked on their door.

"What's causing that frown on your beautiful face?" Renee watched her partner turn away from the door and come toward the bed. The New England pot roast sizzled in the oven, the aroma of garlic and meat filling the cabin. "What do you have to frown about with these wonderful smells filling our home sweet home, all of us together? Come on over here." Renee patted the bed next to her. Jenny moaned as she retreated back up to her loft.

Samantha sat on the bed, leaned over, and gave Ren a peck on the cheek. Then she laid a letter in her lap. Closing her eyes, she sighed. If she could, she'd stay in this moment forever.

"What's this?" Ren wiggled the letter out from under Sam.

"Registered letter for you." Into the silence she added, "From Caroline."

Renee handed it back to her lover. "Will you read it to me? I'm tired."

Samantha's eyes acknowledged the question, but she couldn't get her voice to respond. She seemed to give it a sort of detached consideration. In a whisper she said, "Are you sure you want me to read this?"

"Yes, *saiagi iwed*, I'm sure." Renee lay back and closed her eyes, resting a hand on Samantha's leg. She could hear Sam open the letter and clear her throat.

"Looks like she sent it from Seattle," Sam began. "She says, 'Dear Runner, Sorry I had to leave so quick. Never have been good at good-byes, but then you probably remember that, eh? You're an amazing woman, Runner. Those two and a half days in the woods blew me away. Felt good to be together again, you and me against the world.'" Renee peeked at Samantha and saw tears welling up in her eyes. She rubbed her partner's leg lovingly. "'But it also made me realize that that's what feeds our relationship and you can't always live on the edge just to get the emotion and passion you need to make it work. You and'—here it looks like she erased *white girl* and put in *your partner, Samantha*—'have something we never had. I see it in your eyes when you talk about her. It's a connection I gotta respect because I can see it comes from the spirits. Who'da believed it? You and a *chimook*. Not me! The docs told me you were gonna survive, *washkobisid'*—washko...what?"

"*Bisid.* Sweetcakes."

"Cute," Samantha grumbled, then wished with everything in her she could take it back. "I'm sorry, Renny, I didn't mean that. Okay, she goes on, 'so I took them at their word and left. But I'll keep in touch and you better do the same—butthead! You know that I love you. Always have always will. Be well, Runner, and keep up the good work for the People.'" There was a long pause before Sam said, "She signed it, *Cally.*"

Samantha touched Renee's arm as they stepped out onto the porch after supper. "Look at the stars, Renny. Aren't they beautiful? See the big dipper?"

Renee nodded, then pointed out Orion opposite the big dipper. "Us Injuns call the big dipper the celestial bear."

Samantha drew Renee to the bench on the cabin's porch and they sat huddled in the chilly air. "Feel like telling me more?"

"More?"

"You know I love your stories," Sam cooed, tweaking Ren's lips.

"No more Icchy-whatever stories for me?"

"Not tonight."

"Well, let's see. Okay. Bear. This time of year Bear's climbing out of her den. By the middle of summer you'll see her running along the northern horizon being chased by seven hunters. Come fall, Bear stands on her hind legs, ready to defend herself against the three hunters you can still see in the sky. Then, in winter, Bear looks like she's falling over on her back, all fat and ready for hibernation. Next spring the cycle starts all over."

"Thank you, my love. *Megwetch,*" Samantha added. Grinning, she slid her arm through Renee's, sticking her hand in her lover's jacket pocket.

"Look, Sammy, the lights." Blanketing the northern sky, lights of green, red, and blue moved like a giant fan in a soft breeze. "Somethin' about the northern lights," Ren whispered. "They always put me in a romantic mood."

"Romantic?"

"Yeah, wanna take a walk down to the cliff? *Neeba gesis* is bright enough tonight, don't even need a flashlight."

"Are you sure? Shouldn't you rest?"

"I already rested. Besides, this is resting," Renee said, allowing Sam to help her up from the bench.

"It's kind of cold, Renny. You cold?"

"Naw. Used to call this crunchy air when I was a kid. I love it." Renee grabbed Samantha's hand and leaned into her. They walked in silence on Renee's running trail to the cliff overlooking the Journey River. Mukwa danced and jumped beside them. "It's amazing, Sammy, how much more snow they have up near the border."

"I'm glad it's almost gone here. I'm more than ready for spring. Don't you love walking outside like this, just the two of us, without having to worry about being mugged or raped?"

"Mmm," Renee mumbled, fighting off the apprehension that peace like this seemed to be fast disappearing.

The night grew old, the two lovers stood leaning into each other. "These woods have seen their share of stories, haven't they?" Samantha said sleepily. They moved together to Renee's spirit rock. Mukwa lay down over her two-legged's feet, resting her chin on her paws. Eyes following the activity, she was ever alert for movement from her friend. Content for the first time in several days, the cocker was happy to have Renee back safe from her trip into the forest. She didn't approve when her *niji* thought she could do that kind of thing without her.

"I've been thinkin', *saiagi iwed,* how'd you like to have a ceremony? For the two of us." Renee slid her arm tighter around Samantha. Taking her hand, she played absently with Sam's fingers.

One thing Renee was learning about her lover: Samantha's relationship with change was not friendly. She resisted change in their relationship and pretty much rejected it in her own life—at least at first. Ren didn't dare spring a change on her partner. Any change had to be suggested, left to sit, discussed, left to sit, discussed again, then maybe, just maybe, a decision could be made. This style didn't blend well with Renee's machete approach to life, but the most Ren could say about the situation was, they were both aware of it.

After a long pause, Samantha responded, "Ceremony? You

mean…like a wedding?"

"Well, a traditional ceremony, an exchange of promises, it's called."

"I don't know, Renny, I'm not much for that kinda thing. What else can you tell me about it?"

"Basically, they wrap us in a quilt, symbolizing our joining together, our partnership. We'd ask Gram to do that. The folks we invite to witness the ceremony make a promise to always be there for us to help us remember our promises. Then we not only promise each other, but we promise from then on to be there to share our wisdom with the young ones of the tribe." Renee paused, gazing off at the aurora borealis dancing its exotic dance in the sky. She was filled with a sense of gratitude to the ancestors, for the suffering they went through in order to pass on all the Ojibwa traditions.

"The kids?" Sam's voice penetrated Ren's dreaming.

"The kids." Renee smiled. "You're not up to bein' a momma to a couple hundred kids?" Feeling Samantha lay her head on her shoulder, Ren tipped hers over to meet it. Closing her eyes, she whispered, "*Nin sagiiwe kimi nibiwa nin sagiiwewin nin,* Sam. I love you so much, my love." It was a long time before either moved.

# ACKNOWLEDGMENTS

*Megwetch* to family and friends for their continued support of my efforts—I love you all. To Linda Nelson for the time and energy she gave to reviewing the manuscript. And to Nancy Bereano: I now know the meaning of having a sensitive and experienced editor. She's the best!

A special *megwetch* to Sharon Day for her beadwork on the original cover. She's a wonderful Ojibwa artist, and a friend.

I also want to acknowledge the thousands of Native American kids torn from their cultural circles and placed in non-Native foster homes. It's from their experiences that the soul of this story springs.

# AFTERWORD

*Theresa Lafavor*

It has been twenty years since my mother's novel *Along the Journey River* was first published. After finishing its sequel, *Evil Dead Center,* she toured the country reading from her books and dreamt many other stories that unfortunately did not find their way to print. Carole laFavor died in 2011. While I would have been pleased to write this piece for her republished stories regardless, given her death I am more motivated, dedicated, and inspired to help bring her ideas to life once again.

My mother was an avid reader, conversationalist, and storyteller. She often became teary during television dramas, comedies, and even commercials, and it was her genuine and deeply rooted compassion for all living creatures that inspired her waterworks and her stories. I remember as a child watching with mixed embarrassment and awe as she cried. I couldn't imagine being so moved by a greeting card advertisement or an after school special. I did know that she truly felt the joy, pain, frustration, and confusion of characters and countless animals that paraded across the screen or came to life in the pages of a magazine or newspaper. At some point in my teen years, I stopped going to movies with her: I was too concerned about what other people thought of her frequent guffaws, gulps, and gasps to enjoy the films. I was impressed and relieved when she formed a middle-age women's matinee movie club with two of her closest friends, and I imagined them sitting front and center, oblivious to the other filmgoers. Luckily for me, I got over myself after my teens, and my mother warmly welcomed me to join her again at the movies. Experiencing the world through my mother's eyes was remarkable—and often emotionally exhausting.

My mother was an eternal optimist, which seemed counterintuitive to me when I was young, given her willingness to fight for her beliefs. As I matured, I understood that her optimism was the inspiration for her activism. She believed social change was possible and that we owed it *to* each other to work our hardest *for* each other. I learned early that it was not enough to think positively about each other; you had to stand up and take part.

The same compassion, interest in others, optimism, commitment to address challenge, injustice, and adversity, and wholehearted acceptance of our individuality drew my mother to write stories like *Along the Journey River* and *Evil Dead Center*. Before she wrote about protecting the rights of others, she fought for them. She stood on the front lines of countless marches, protests, and picket lines. Her voice was strong and her convictions were unbending. She vehemently opposed war and the destruction of our planet. She believed in the equality of all living things. She spoke out for the elderly, disabled, abused, disenfranchised, and oppressed. She was confident that writing, even fiction, could be big-hearted activist work, that it could bring people together and illuminate ideas. And she was overjoyed to find out that people believed that *her* writing did just that. She rated publishing her two novels high on her list of accomplishments, but maybe more importantly these books gave her hope that people were still interested in learning about each other.

My mother's novels were unique when they were first published in the 1990s, and they continue to be their own unique genre twenty years later. She skillfully and artistically wove together two mysteries about a Native American lesbian mother living on a rural reservation in an interracial partnership. She brought to life crime and abuse that are all too common in our society but rarely discussed. She gave a voice to people largely underrepresented in published literature: women, lesbians, Native Americans. My mother chose a feminist publisher, Firebrand Books, to publish her novels because she wanted to support female entrepreneurs and small businesses. She would be honored that the University of Minnesota Press is republishing her novels today and would be excited that her writing will reach a new and expanded audience.

My mother was introverted and deeply private. How then did she convince herself to travel the country, visiting feminist bookstores from coast to coast, reading her personal thoughts, ideas, and creative musings in front of rooms full of people she didn't know? She questioned her choices on many occasions, choices that left her feeling fatigued and exposed. But each time she peeked around a corner and saw a room of many eager and excited people she mustered the courage to put one foot in front of the other and take the stage. Although she collapsed exhausted after every reading, she was equal parts exhilarated, inspired, and grateful to share her stories.

*Along the Journey River* and *Evil Dead Center* are works of fiction, but that does not mean they do not reflect real struggles, personalities and characters, and complex landscapes. There are many parallels throughout both stories to my mother's life, my family, the communities where I grew up, and our people's history. I have no doubt that Renee LaRoche personified the values and ideals my mother held dear. Renee's voice is so familiar to me, and I recognize my mother in her love for her daughter, her unending energy for her animal companions, her shy and slightly reserved nature, her passion for conversation and communication, and her curiosity for knowledge, connection, and belonging.

The lessons imparted by Renee LaRoche's adventures are more relevant now than ever before. We are at another important crossroads in history, where we have the choice to burrow back into our comfort zones or stand up and fight for each other's rights, like my mother did. We have the opportunity to use our voices for good, to unite people. I am comforted knowing my mother believed there was hope in the world and that words can bring people together. I look forward to a new generation of readers discovering her calm way with words and the deep sentiments that *Along the Journey River* and *Evil Dead Center* express.

**Carole laFavor** (1948–2011), a Two-Spirit Ojibwa from Minnesota, was a novelist, a nurse, and an activist. She was a founding member of Positively Native, an organization committed to helping Native Americans with HIV and AIDS, and was appointed to the first Presidential Advisory Council on HIV/AIDS in 1995. She also wrote *Along the Journey River* (Minnesota, 2017).

**Lisa Tatonetti** is professor of English at Kansas State University. She is the author of *The Queerness of Native American Literature* (Minnesota, 2014) and coeditor of *Sovereign Erotics: A Collection of Contemporary Two-Spirit Literature*.

**Theresa Lafavor** is a professor of psychology at Pacific University in Oregon. She is the daughter of Carole laFavor.